# THE TRUTHSPOKEN HEIR

THE STARS AND GREEN MAGICS
BOOK 1

NOVAE CAELUM

Robot Dinosaur Press

https://robotdinosaurpress.com

Robot Dinosaur Press is an imprint of Chipped Cup Collective.

The Truthspoken Heir: The Stars and Green Magics Season One



ISBN 978-1-958696-01-9

Ebook ISBN 978-1-958696-00-2

Proofreading by Maya Evan MacGregor

Cover art and book design by Novae Caelum

Author photo credit Novae Caelum

https://novaecaelum.com

# AUTHOR'S NOTE

*The Truthspoken Heir* was originally published as season one of the ongoing serial *The Stars and Green Magics*, covering episodes 1-36, as well as three prelude episodes (chapters 1-3 here).

I made some minor editing changes from the original serial version, most notably that Rhys's last name is now Delor.

This book features several characters who use gender neutral pronouns (they/them/their, fae/faer/faerself, e/em/eir, or other neopronouns).

This book, barring the occasional and inspired burst of strong language, is a solid PG-13.

For detailed content notes, please see:
https://novaecaelum.com/content-notes

and persona in the public eye. She didn't want to spend a significant portion of her time entertaining her future wife.

There were very few people she actually liked in the universe, and she was sure that this Lesander Javieri would not be one of them. Hardly anyone was on a level enough to be interesting to her.

"I will, of course, meet with her if that's what you wish," she said.

"Arianna, I've already made the formal overtures to the Javieris. Lesander is on her way. That's a two-week trip from the Javieri homeworld near the Dynasty border. We'll convert one of the upcoming balls into an engagement ball in your honor. That popular band, the Rings of Vietor, will be in the city then—your sister would swoon to line them up for the ball. It will be an excellent opportunity to build your popular image, make your engagement a cultural event."

"Father," Arianna said carefully, smoothing out the edges of her green silk tunic, "is there something I should know, that you're rushing this engagement?"

He'd already made the plans. Adeius, then it was done. She'd have no choice.

Not that she ever had a choice. Her life was her kingdom's. Her life would never be her own.

She met his eyes and saw something there, just a flash of unease, that set her senses on alert.

"The political climate is volatile," he said. "Perhaps more than you know."

She knew a lot. She knew the politics of the Kingdom of Valoris with its one hundred and eighty-seven vassal worlds. She knew the ongoing schemes of the high houses to gain power and potentially overthrow the Truthspoken who ruled the kingdom. She knew the internal tensions around the Green Magicker sect and their need for more power, and the intensely alien Kidaa on the anti-spin border. She knew all of this, and she couldn't see where that added up to her needing to secure an engagement to the Javieri prince in the next two weeks.

"How? How is it more volatile than I know? I've been sitting Reception for the last month, listening to the courtiers' woes. The situation with the Javieris isn't any less stable now than it was a month ago. I've been judging, I've been ruling—"

"While I gather information. While I deal with the Navy and the Army. While I deal with the diplomats and ongoing treaty negotiations. Yes, Daughter, you have been ruling over much this last month, but don't forget, you are not the Seritarchus. You're not the ruler of this kingdom—I am. Power needs to be rebalanced, and this alliance with the Javieris will do that. Can you set aside your dislike for people of all kinds—"

"I don't dislike people."

Arianna stilled as she watched the disapproval on her father's face. She was losing control of her temper. Adeius, she'd been talking over him. She never got rattled enough to do that. She had to stay in control. The Truthspoken Heir must always be in control.

"I don't dislike people," she said again, her tone more moderate this time. "But I truly don't see how an engagement now will benefit the kingdom. It will only take me away from my duties, and you need me—"

"Arianna, I need you to do your duty as the Heir, and at this moment, that is to marry into the house that is most advantageous for the kingdom. You must marry, and you must have your own heirs."

She caught something in his tone, and her focus sharpened. "Is your life in danger? Have you been threatened more than usual—"

He laughed, a jarring, bitter sound. The red nova hearts in his earrings sparked in the light.

He so seldom laughed it gave her pause.

"Truthspoken are always in danger of assassination. The

sooner you are married and your heirs are started in their incubators, the better for all of us. If I'm killed, you'll be the ruler. If you're killed—well, your sister isn't ready to rule a kingdom. I'm giving you every chance I can to give you a strong and stable rule when that time comes. May it be many, many long years off."

But she didn't like the edge in his voice. If she was always in control, he—well. He was the Seritarchus. He was control itself.

He stood, tugged down the cuffs of his midnight coat. "Do your duty, Arianna. Marry the prince. If you have to craft another persona for yourself to make it work—do that. Just make it work. The engagement will be in two weeks. Now, if you will excuse me, I have work to do, and so do you."

## 2

# MEETING LESANDER

> *My dear prince, you stole my heart by just walking in.*
>
> — OLUN SHIRALL IN THE VID DRAMA *NOVA HEARTS*, SEASON 8, EPISODE 12, "ORBITAL DANCE"

Dressa Rhialden, second Truthspoken heir to the Kingdom of Valoris, caught her breath as Prince Lesander Javieri entered the reception room. Lesander was grace itself, tall, with pale pink skin, her flame-red hair bound up and cascading around bare shoulders, deep blue shirt and tan trousers cut at just the right angles to show off her curves without flaunting them. Diamond earrings that caught the light. Lips slightly parted as she held out her hands to greet . . . Dressa's sister.

Dressa was trained to never let any emotion show that she didn't want to. She kept her smile open and genuine, if not overly wide. Delighted to meet the prince who would marry her older sister, but not so delighted as to cause an interstellar incident.

Her chest constricted as her sister, Arianna, *the* Truthspoken Heir, took Lesander's hands, exchanging chaste kisses. Arianna was perfectly poised herself, not one of her hairs out of place in her elegant knot, minimal makeup on her flawless, copper-brown skin.

Dressa could be flawless, too. She could be whoever she wanted—but flawless wasn't the persona she portrayed to the court. And anyhow, flawless wouldn't matter here in a political marriage.

And this woman, this prince who almost outshone the Truthspoken Heir herself, was forever out of Dressa's reach.

Adeius, she had no wish at all to be the Heir, but the thought of having Lesander as her wife was so tempting. But she had no wish to rule the kingdom someday. She was perfectly happy to leave that chore to her sister.

"Prince Lesander, it is good to see you well." Dressa's father, the Truthspoken Ruler of the Kingdom of Valoris, stood on the other side of Arianna, hands clasped loosely in front of him. He was wearing his own body today—or what body he publicly showed as himself to the court. Athletic build, long black hair bound in a tight braid down his back. Wearing a ring on every finger and a purple high-collared coat that matched his purple color-shifting lipstick.

Lesander broke from Arianna to clasp his hands as well, though she didn't go so far as to kiss his cheeks, and he didn't offer.

"Seritarchus. I am honored to join your family."

"You haven't joined it yet," the Seritarchus said dryly, and Dressa watched Lesander stiffen the slightest degree.

The marriage, of course, was all politics. Lesander's family was one of a number of high house families actively clawing their way to the highest seat of power in the kingdom—which was right here, in this palace, in this ornate reception room.

Lesander wasn't *quite* the enemy. But she wasn't coming from an allied family, either.

"Of course," her father went on, "after the ball tomorrow evening, the engagement will be formally signed, and we will start the process of acclimating you into our household. Until then, please enjoy your rooms in the guest suites, and make use of every amenity you wish to. The palace staff is at your command—within reason, of course."

The problem with a political marriage, Dressa knew, was no one knew just how the marriage would work out. If Arianna wasn't attracted to Lesander—well, a marriage could succeed without physical love, they did all the time.

Dressa knew her sister, though. Arianna's true wife would be the good of the kingdom, and where would that leave Lesander? Their marriage contract required mandatory exclusivity until they'd pulled their second child from the synthetic womb, whether they themselves consummated their marriage or not.

When Dressa was right there, feeling warmth she absolutely should not feel. This was going to be an excruciating next few years for everyone, wasn't it? An excruciating lifetime for Dressa.

And what was she thinking? There were plenty of courtiers for her to have flings with. Her father would negotiate her own marriage in a year or two, and then she'd have her own spouse to deal with. Lesander was beautiful, yes, but she was one of many, many beautiful people in the Rhialden Court.

Dressa shifted, the slightest betrayal of her agitation, and caught her father's eye—not good. She didn't see her father often these days, and that was by choice. Probably mutual.

"Of course, Seritarchus," Lesander said with a slight bow. "I will only and ever treat the palace staff with respect."

She glanced at Dressa, and the Seritarchus stepped back, waving at his second daughter.

"By all means, greet your future sister."

The words grated, but Dressa didn't let it show. This couldn't work out any other way—she wasn't the Heir, only the second. And High House Javieri wouldn't settle for the second.

Lesander's hands when they took hers were warm and soft. Lesander's smile quirked sardonically at the corners. Her blue eyes flashed with more personality than she was letting show through, too. As a high house prince, whether she was trained in the Truthspoken social arts or not, she certainly wouldn't lack control.

"Sister," Lesander said. "It is good to see you again. You were"—she bent to hold a hand less than a meter off the floor—"this tall when I last saw you."

"You weren't much taller," Dressa shot back, and Lesander flashed bright teeth before tamping her grin back again and returning to Arianna's side.

As she left, her perfume, like ocean juniper, lingered.

She couldn't stare, Dressa absolutely couldn't stare. Lesander would be her *sister*.

And Lesander would be tied to Arianna, who only seemed to get stiffer and more controlled every year. Dressa couldn't think of a worse fate than being married to her sister—

All right, no, that wasn't fair. She didn't hate her sister, and Arianna was by far the more effective Truthspoken—she could shapeshift her appearance and personality with so much more ease than Dressa. She was born to rule and exuded that birthright in everything she did. It was simply who she was.

While Dressa did her absolute best to flow with the court, laughing and making friends, the opposite of what a future Truthspoken Ruler should be.

But—by Adeius, Arianna could at least *try* to be anything other than cold and calculated. Outwardly, of course, Arianna's public actions would show exactly as much romance as she calculated would help the kingdom. But it wasn't Arianna's image Dressa was worried about.

Why couldn't Dressa marry the prince and they raise the kingdom's heirs and leave Arianna to what she really wanted—ruling the kingdom? Then everyone would be happy.

Alas, alas. Happiness wasn't a thing often afforded to Truthspoken.

Arianna was looking a little wan that night, as she had been for the last few days, which was worrying. Dressa did, truly, care for her sister, petty tyrant though she could be. Arianna should never look other than vibrant—that could only mean enough stress for a lack of control.

Dressa's father stepped closer to her as Arianna led Lesander to a set of chairs. The whole point of this meeting had been for Lesander to meet their family, but also to meet her future wife.

"Lesander can hold her own with Arianna," her father said softly. "She will do well here, I think. Be welcoming, Daughter. That is your role."

Dressa pressed her lips tightly together. Nothing, with her father, meant only one thing, and seldom what it seemed. He'd seen her reaction to Lesander, she knew it. Was this a warning? An admonishment?

She turned to her father. Put on her most vacuous courtly smile. "Absolutely. Of course I'll welcome my new sister."

If he liked Lesander, if he'd chosen her for his favorite daughter the Heir, of course Lesander would do well. And Dressa would watch, every day, as Lesander lived in the royal residence, talking with her sister, attending functions with her sister, and maybe—*maybe*—sleeping with her sister, though that was by no means required and Dressa was pretty sure that would never happen. Well, and maybe that was a good thing.

She strode past her father to take a chair beside her sister, to play the dutiful sister. She always did. She always would—it was her place in the palace court. And truly, she wasn't unhappy with that.

Except for Lesander.

Dressa's eyes kept meeting Lesander's, until she finally looked away, because that could lead to nothing good. The engagement ball was tomorrow night, and they'd all be on full display. She'd better start burying her feelings now.

# 3

## THE COURTYARD

> *Palace Rhialden, established during the rule of Jisorian Rhialden, Seritarchus III, was largely designed by the Seritarchus Consort, Wang Xiu ne Fantine Rhialden. Wang Xiu was co-ruler in all but name until the assassination of the Seritarchus in the eighteenth year of his rule. Because he died from an attack by a guest staying in the residence wing, Wang Xiu ordered, as her last act as Consort, that the new guest wing be built separately from the palace itself.*
>
> — DR. AMI TIERNEY IN HER POPULAR BANNED ARTICLE, "A SHORT HISTORY OF PALACE RHIALDEN, BY ASSASSINATIONS"

Lesander Javieri, heir to a high house princedom, paused in the broad courtyard of Palace Rhialden. Flagstones spread out like a lake around her, crossed by courtiers and various palace functionaries. Behind and to her left were the administrative and residence wings of the palace; to her right was the guest wing. At the far end of the courtyard, the Adeium, the religious heart of the kingdom, sat with its vaulted steel peaks and cream stone walls, an iron fence surrounding it.

Courtiers paused when they saw her. They were watching her, she knew. A few had approached her in the palace entrance when she'd arrived, but most kept their distance, feeling the social divide outside of hours that would allow such an imposition. A high house prince wasn't that far removed from the power of the Truthspoken themselves.

This palace—this was going to be her home. All of this would be hers someday. Through her wife, sure, but hers all the same. She had no intention of being a passive consort like the current Seritarchus Consort, her future mother-in-law.

"Ser Prince?"

She turned, seeing her young servant in green and gold High House Javieri livery, weighted down under her luggage. Lesander had sent some of her luggage to be freighted from the spaceport when she'd landed, but she'd brought her most personal items with her into the palace. She hadn't been given a chance to set up her own rooms before she'd been taken straight to see the Seritarchus and his two heirs. Her servant had waited in the corridor with her guards while she'd chatted with her future wife.

She'd studied enough of Arianna's life and personality to know it would be a mistake to flirt with her. But Adeius, the second Truthspoken, Ondressarie, hadn't been as subtle as she'd thought about making eyes at Lesander herself.

Not that Lesander hadn't found her own eyes trying to stray to Dressa. Her expertly styled, loose, wavy dark hair. Her round face, full figure. Her overall air of openness that couldn't . . . just couldn't be all that there was to her. Dressa's focus had been far too sharp, and she was Truthspoken, after all.

Lesander would have to be careful there. She was here to

marry the Heir, not the Heir's sister. She could keep her eyes from straying. She had to.

"Yes, yes," she said, waving her servant toward the entrance to the palace's guest wing, which, while it connected to the palace by a covered walkway, wasn't actually part of the main building. "I'm on the second floor, I believe." She turned to one of the four guards she'd brought with her from her homeworld. "Go, get the floor attendant so we can find our rooms and settle in."

Lesander looked back to survey the courtyard once more, noting those who were still watching her and those who'd moved on. She stopped when she saw a figure far across the courtyard, just coming through the gates of the Adeium, accompanied by her own guards.

The woman had the same air of unconscious power about her as the Seritarchus. Steel-gray hair, dark brown skin, wearing a trim gray suit with amethyst and ruby stud earrings. She wasn't wearing her official red and purple robes, or the gold pendant of office, but Lesander had no doubt she was Ceorre Gatri, the Truthspeaker, religious head of the Adeium. The second most powerful person in the kingdom.

Lesander froze as the Truthspeaker spotted her and changed course to intercept.

She'd already met all three Truthspoken today; she didn't know if she had it in her to match wits with the Truthspeaker, too. But she couldn't walk away, so she braced herself and walked forward.

"Prince Lesander Javieri," Ceorre said. She held out her hands to clasp Lesander's, her posture welcoming. Was the welcome real? Lesander's family had allies at court, but also many enemies. The Truthspeaker would, of course, favor the Truthspoken, but where did Lesander now fit into that equation, if she was going to marry the Truthspoken Heir?

"Truthspeaker," Lesander said, dipping a slight bow. "I'd hoped to see you before the engagement."

One of Ceorre's impeccably groomed eyebrows shot up as she released Lesander's hands. "Oh? If you're seeking the counsel of Adeius before you're betrothed, I'm happy to make time."

"Yes, thank you."

She'd been seeking to understand her place here and how to navigate it best to her advantage, but counsel from the god was as good a reason as any.

The Truthspeaker's smile was tight and too knowing. Lesander had to fight hard to keep from stiffening, from losing sight of who she was and why she was here under that matriarchal glare. It reminded her far too much of her grandmother's stare, and the dowager prince could penetrate steel with her glare.

"Tomorrow morning, then," the Truthspeaker said. "Before the ball, before you need to get ready and dress. I'll be in my office." She waved at the Adeium. "Come into the sanctum, one of the speakers will show you to me."

Lesander held up her hands. "Thank you, but I'm sure you're busy—"

"I am. But you'll be marrying one of my charges, and that makes you my charge as well. Feel free to call on me as Arianna might. But I do have a meeting to get to now, so I will have to see you tomorrow. I'm glad to see you're well, Lesander."

And the Truthspeaker was striding toward the administrative wing of the palace, not once looking back.

Lesander was aware people were watching. More people than had been watching before. Slowly, exhaling, she turned, the guards who'd followed her to the Truthspeaker now following her back to her waiting servant with the luggage.

"All right, come on, come on. I don't want to be out in this sun."

She strode for the entrance to the guest wing, her staff following. She didn't dare look back, either.

Lesander had no thoughts at all that meeting had been an accident. She'd been at the palace all of two hours, and already she was knee-deep in palace intrigue.

Which was what she'd come here for. This was her life now. This was her new home. And she had to find her place quickly, because she had too many plans for her to screw things up now.

## 4

# A FORMAL ENGAGEMENT

> *A Truthspoken's greatest weapon isn't the ability to Change their appearance, to create or destroy or enhance their beauty. We chart everything around us so we can create the illusion of power or strength or whatever is needed in the moment. What's needed isn't always beauty.*
>
> — ARIANNA RHIALDEN, MELESORIE X IN *THE CHANGE DIALOGUES*

Arianna surveyed the cosmetics arrayed around her prep table with dismay. She'd never needed more than the barest makeup, had never spent much time learning how. The dark bruises under her eyes weren't going to go away on their own, though. No matter how much she'd tried to Change them, they'd only gotten darker.

She grimaced and smoothed on the smart foundation that was supposed to give her optimal skin texture and coloration, but it didn't help much. Neither did the violet lipstick. And neither did swarming her eyes with so much blue shadow she looked like a vid star.

Well, at least it hid the bruising. Vid star was acceptable; the Truthspoken Heir could be audacious, but never, ever exhausted.

There was a light rap on the door, and she looked up as her sister, Ondressarie, swept into her prep room. Completely ignoring the genetic lock Arianna had set on the door, as usual. She should get an actual physical dead bolt one of these days, one her sister couldn't Change the DNA in her fingertips to circumvent.

Dressa was gorgeous, of course, all round, flowing edges. She wore deep blue trousers and a matching sleeveless shirt trimmed in gold. Her makeup was impeccable, as always. Her expression open and curious, just a touch vapid—but Arianna knew better. Dressa was a wild pond; the surface was one thing, but it hid the teeth beneath.

They both had their father's silky black hair, their mother's copper-brown skin. They both had golden brown eyes, and that husky burr to their voices that people tended to find charming. Truthspoken could be anyone they wished with the Change—within limitations. They had to at least resemble the family line.

Dressa narrowed her eyes. "Stop analyzing me. And Adeius, Arianna, what did you do to your face?"

Arianna stiffened. Had Dressa seen the bruising? But no, she only meant the overabundance of makeup.

Dressa reached for Arianna's cheek, scowling at the residue of powder. "We don't have time to redo this—seriously. Where's your bloodservant? Whatever, no time to get faer. Okay, hold still."

Dressa moved like a whirlwind of fabric and makeup brushes and jewelry, finishing with a wide titanium mesh necklace that glittered with precious stones—red nova hearts and pale teal volcanic glass from Zeoman IV.

Dressa shifted her around to look back in the mirror. She'd added some rhinestones beside Arianna's garishly shadowed eyes. Vid star, at least, had been upgraded to royal rock star? Possibly. Flowing black trousers, silk coat in shifting black and red that caught the eye with its endless depths. Dressa had fixed the lipstick—it was deep red now.

"Good," Arianna pronounced, regaining some of her usual poise. She eyed the sweat gathering at the top of her brow. She tried to Change it, to reabsorb the moisture—Truthspoken weren't supposed to sweat when they didn't want to. But the effort only caused her headache to intensify.

What was wrong with her?

"Nervous?"

"Hardly." It was a lie, and Dressa knew it. Arianna waved a frustrated hand, now set with rings. "If I never married, I would be happy."

"Well, Lesander at least seems nice."

Arianna cut Dressa a sharp look. She'd seen the way Dressa got flustered around the prince when they'd all met informally the night before. They'd both known Lesander vaguely as children, her being the heir to a high house princedom and them being the Truthspoken heirs to the kingdom—but, well, Lesander had grown up. She was a tower of pale beauty and flame-red hair. Arianna could appreciate the aesthetics, could even appreciate Lesander's quick wit. But she was not interested in marrying her.

"Mm. So you marry her."

Dressa shrugged a bit helplessly. She'd know, of course, that Arianna had seen the evidence of her crush. Truthspoken saw everything.

And as far as marriage went, neither of them had a choice in this one. Engagements were made at an interstellar policy level, not on the level of two Truthspoken who'd barely passed their legal adulthood. Engagements were made by their father and were not negotiable—for them.

Dressa bit her lip. Waved at Arianna to cover her own embarrassment. "You look a little—"

"It's just stress. I'm fine. It'll be better after the engagement ball." And in truth, it might be stress. Arianna had taken over more of her father's meetings these last weeks, assuming more duties as Heir with her engagement and then wedding approaching.

She patted at her hair, braided in a rope down her back. She caught her hands trembling in her reflection and closed them into fists, locked them behind her.

At least she wouldn't have to sleep with this prince she didn't know well and had no intention of loving. That part of formal marriage contracts had been consigned to historical dramas. Sex and gender just weren't necessary factors when a lab tech could make an heir with two strands of DNA and an artificial womb.

Arianna's stomach churned. Not hungry—a half-eaten plate of pastries still sat on a nearby table, all she'd been able to force down. She was regretting that now, no matter how faint she'd felt at the time.

It had to be stress. Stress could slow or hinder a Truthspoken's ability to Change. She'd never had that problem before. But then, she'd never gotten engaged before.

Dressa touched her arm. Arianna wasn't sure if it was in sympathy, or her need for Arianna to fit into her own plans.

"It's just the ball tonight," Dressa said. "You'll all sign the papers tomorrow, and that's private. You'll be fine. You're always in control. And we're late."

She gripped Arianna's wrist and pulled her toward the door.

Arianna truly hated that flippant part of Dressa's personality, and Dressa was leaning hard into it now, using it to push her where otherwise it would be inappropriate. It *was* inappropriate for the second Truthspoken to so handle the Truthspoken Heir, even in private.

"Dressa—"

Arianna stumbled, steadying herself on her sister's shoulder, and Dressa paused. Gave her a calculating look.

She held her breath, waiting for Dressa to say something more. She could read the question, maybe a little of the worry, in the tight bow of Dressa's shoulders, in the crease between her brows.

Because Arianna was always in control. Whatever this weakness was now, this shakiness, the bruising, the ache in her bones and fog in her thoughts—in Dressa's eyes, and in her own, it would either have to be deliberate, or something she couldn't control.

If she, as Truthspoken, couldn't control the responses of her own body, and especially couldn't control them in public . . . that could be dangerous.

She met Dressa's eyes.

For three heartbeats, Dressa stared back.

In those heartbeats, Arianna felt some of the power of her position pass to Dressa. Because they both knew they wouldn't pull off a flawless night tonight without Dressa helping her. And Arianna couldn't just not show up, no matter how much she wanted to. Truthspoken were always in control. That was the foundation the kingdom stood on. And it would still stand on that, no matter how much she wanted to shove into her bedroom, collapse on the bed, and just sleep.

Dressa, as the second Truthspoken, had always made a show of how glad she was that she wasn't *the* Heir. She could afford to be whimsical, she could afford to laugh and flirt and all the other things that were so carefully controlled for Arianna. Dressa didn't want to be Heir, and Arianna had no fear her sister would try to leverage her momentary weakness in that way. But she'd owe Dressa, and Dressa, who would deny that she needed repayment at all, would collect in subtler ways.

Dressa's tone remained light. "Okay. I don't know why you're playing it clumsy tonight, but don't overdo it, okay?"

Patronizing already. Arianna's lips drew tight, and she tried to will strength back into her body, to will clarity into her mind. To not need Dressa at all.

But her limbs were not responding as they should, were they?

Arianna smoothed out her coat, drew a breath that caught in her chest.

Was this just nerves? But what else could it possibly be? Truthspoken didn't get sick, it just wasn't possible.

"This ball is in my honor. It's impossible for me to be late," she said. She could will strength into her voice, at least.

Dressa rolled her eyes and made a mocking bow, waving toward the door. "After you, then, Truthspoken."

## 5

# WEAKNESS

> *The relationship between Truthspoken and those they rule is alarmingly fragile. One misstep, one move to show the Truthspoken are not fully in control—as described in the mandates and holy books of the Adeium—and those who'd wish to replace them can make their case.*
>
> — HOMAJ RHIALDEN, SERITARCHUS IX IN A PRIVATE LETTER, NEVER SENT; PUBLISHED IN *THE CHANGE DIALOGUES*

Dressa dragged Arianna toward the door. Adeius, they were so late.

But late or not, she let go of her sister's arm before they left the sanctuary of Arianna's rooms. In private, they could be less of who they were expected to be and more of who they were—not that Arianna had ever seen much difference between the two. But in public? They must be absolutely Truthspoken, true to the personas they'd crafted into perfectly shaped tools.

In the corridor, guards peeled off from their posts on either side of the door and fell into step around them. Two of Arianna's in front, two of hers in the back.

Dressa opened her posture, graceful but not as rehearsed as Arianna, her expression open and friendly. Her job, always, was to be the foil to Arianna's rigidity. To be the friendlier sibling, the one people could approach and confess their secrets to. This suited her well enough—she had no desire whatsoever to move through life with Arianna's obsession for control.

She walked a few paces behind Arianna and to her left, as was proper. As they made the turn from the residential wing to the heart of Palace Rhialden, the walls went from patterned cream to smoky glass, a mirror in which to better study her sister.

She watched Arianna with Truthspoken-trained eyes. Her sister's gait was slower than usual, more measured. Her shoulders weren't as squared, or her posture as formally stiff, though Dressa didn't think it was for lack of trying. Arianna looked . . . small, and that was a startling thought. She'd always preferred being short, a coiled mass of power, but tonight she was unwound. She looked, for the first time Dressa could ever remember, younger than she was.

Could the engagement be affecting her that badly? All of these things—her gait, her posture, the sallowness of her skin and bruising that she hadn't quite covered under her eyes—should have been something she could take care of, either through her training or through Change.

Yes, Arianna didn't want to marry, but they'd both known the inevitability of arranged marriages since they were young. Nothing would actually happen except a shuffling of statuses—Arianna would move to a larger apartment, and Lesander would be given her own apartment at the palace. It was all very proper, very humane. They hardly had to see each other more than the occasional acknowledgement that the other existed, and their fidelity clause only lasted until their second child was born to make the next generation of Truthspoken. The public certainly wasn't expecting love, though of course the public always loved a spectacle. They'd write love into whatever Arianna and Lesander did—love wasn't the point, and everyone knew it.

So why was Arianna freaked out enough that she was having trouble with the Change?

Was it a lover? Could Arianna possibly have fallen in love without Dressa noticing? She tried to picture her sister sneaking around the gardens, grinning while some unknown suitor twirled her among the rose bushes. Yeah, no. Arianna was allergic to breaking rules. Or twirling.

Arianna made an awkward step and her breath caught. One of the nearby guards shifted, but Dressa moved closer, faster, protocol be damned. They were approaching the balcony rail, where two grand stairways curved down to the entry hall below. Where they'd be totally on display, and Arianna would be on her own. The two Truthspoken siblings—there were always two—would descend from opposite sides to show the guests below how the Truthspoken were always on every side of them, always watching.

Arianna pressed her hands tight against her pant legs, her jaw set. Not even the makeup could hide the sweat rimming her brow. Whatever was going on with her, it was more than the stress of the engagement. Whatever she thought of this night, Arianna would never purposely endanger the kingdom with her lack of control. Not unless their father had told her to, if it was some plot within a plot . . . ?

No, Dressa couldn't believe that, either. The Seritarchus maneuvered people like breathing, but he'd never been in favor of showing weakness—with good reason.

Dressa's hand hovered near Arianna's arm. She could tell how much Arianna wanted to bat it away, but she didn't.

Arianna always lorded over her, was always the better Truthspoken, the one their father praised, the picture of perfection. Dressa would have thought seeing Arianna less than in control would be satisfying in some small, petty way. Instead, Dressa was working hard to unknot her own insides.

"You can do this," she said in a low voice, so low she wasn't even sure Arianna would hear.

But Arianna swallowed, gave the smallest of nods.

The buzz of voices in the entry below grew louder as they approached the balcony rail. They were still out of sight. Five more meters, and they'd be fully on display.

Dressa stopped Arianna as respectfully as she could. She waited for Arianna to beckon her to lean closer, then said in her ear, "We can go down your stairs together. Make it look like I'm being rowdy—I'll trip and take you down with me. Act like you've broken something and need time to Change it to heal."

Arianna tilted her head, her face a puzzle within her heavy makeup. It was garish and strange to see on her usually austere face. "No. Good, but no. I must do this." She paused, looked toward the balcony rail. "Come down my stairs with me. Make a show of this being a celebration." She snorted. "I certainly look like I'm ready to celebrate."

Yeah. Dressa could do that. And that was a better plan anyway. She'd turn as much attention to herself as she could, let people be annoyed with her so they wouldn't be looking as closely at Arianna. Which was in itself risky—this engagement was a major show of Truthspoken strength, uniting the Rhialden Truthspoken to the Javieri Princedom line, one of the only high houses with whom they hadn't yet intermarried. But drawing attention from Arianna wasn't nearly as risky as letting her lack of control show in front of everyone.

Oh, Adeius. This would not be easy, would it?

Dressa ran personality aspects through herself, calculating

the results of each one, until she settled on the right keys she wanted to play.

Right, then. She looped her arm through Arianna's, who glanced at her in startlement—that looked real, bravo, Arianna—and ran toward the balcony, pulling her sister with her.

"Dressa, I didn't mean—"

"Hey!" Dressa crowed at the top of Arianna's staircase. She waved and the crowd below, a sea of nobles and diplomats, celebrities and businesspeople, turned their faces to her. "Hey, everyone! Guess who's getting engaged tomorrow? Rhialden plus Javieri, yes!"

A confused sort of cheer went up from the crowd.

Arianna lifted her chin as if this was all meant to happen and held up her hand in a regal wave.

The murmurs started, then intensified as Dressa wrapped her arm around Arianna's waist and descended the stairs with her way too quickly. Arianna did stumble, and she held onto Dressa tightly, but all of that would be minimized in the bluster of the show.

A deep chime sounded, which should have sounded when both of the Truthspoken began to sedately descend their stairs.

Well. Not tonight.

Dressa spun as they reached the tiled floor, pulling Arianna into three tight spirals of a dance move before she spun her out, grinning.

"The soon-to-be-betrothed Arianna Rhialden, Truthspoken Heir of Valoris!"

Now there were a few more cheers, some clinkings of wine glasses, people deciding to get into the enthusiasm no matter how odd it was. They were here for a party, after all. Someone Dressa pegged as a genuine rock star put their fingers to their lips and blew an obnoxious whistle, which engaged the crowd enough that Dressa had a chance to help Arianna steady.

Her sister's attention was caught on something to her left

and Dressa turned, seeing the elegant knot of red hair before she spotted Lesander cutting through the crowd like a fighter through an asteroid field. Her perfume preceded her, an exquisitely expensive-smelling scent of ocean flowers and sea breeze. Oh Adeius, could she not do anything without elegance?

Lesander bowed to Dressa first, flashing the barest bemused smile—and even that made Dressa's heart beat faster.

"Truthspoken Ondressarie. It's good to see you well." Not that she hadn't seen Dressa well the night before, too. Not that Dressa wouldn't be perfectly happy seeing a lot of her.

Adeius, no, she couldn't think like that. Lesander would be her *sister*. Never, ever to be her lover.

Dressa gave a shallow bow in return. "And you, Prince Lesander."

Her grin came back as she looked between Arianna and her sister's soon-to-be-betrothed. She didn't think about how much Lesander's smile made her insides turn to goo. She smiled right through Lesander bowing more deeply to her sister, and Arianna imperiously drawing Lesander up to kiss her lightly on the lips.

Dressa absolutely did not think about how those cherry red lips would taste.

So she cupped her hands to her mouth and howled. And the crowd, which had fully caught on to the mood of merriment now, went wild, hooting and producing more of those shrill whistles.

Arianna smiled enough to actually show teeth for once, looped her arm through Lesander's, and raised both their hands to the crowd. She was leaning fully into that rock star grace now, shaking her head to spill out a few strands of hair. Lesander might be a head taller than her, but Arianna's presence grounded everyone at her own eye level—a different sort of presence than the stiffness she usually carried. The crowd was loving it, caught up in the glamor and romance of it all.

Arianna was building an illusion so alluring that people wouldn't want to look beyond it. Arianna's acting skills were second to none. Except maybe their father's.

Was their father in this crowd? He would certainly be there, but not as the Seritarchus. He'd be among the crowd, any one of the anonymous faces. Her track record of picking him out among a crowd was maybe sixty percent at best—Arianna's was near perfect.

She could not think about her father and if he would be watching—which he would—and what he'd say about all this later. Or worse, not say, and leave her to worry over it for weeks.

Dressa continued to smile and scanned the crowd with Truthspoken-trained awareness for anyone who might have noticed they were working hard to misdirect the crowd's attention. Could anyone see the signs of bruising beneath Arianna's makeup? Could they see just how much she was leaning on Lesander now? And what would Lesander think about that?

"Truthspoken Ondressarie," Lesander said, snapping her attention back. "Will you be dancing tonight? I'd love to share a dance. I heard you picked the band? I adore The Rings of Vietor."

"Uh, yeah!" Dressa turned to the crowd, who were watching now like this was all a play staged for their amusement—which it was—and threw up her arms. "The Rings of Vietorrrrr!"

They cheered. And that was easy.

"Sure!" she said, turning back to Lesander. "I'm dancing."

"But we won't be." Arianna held Lesander's arm tighter to her own. She raised a brow at Dressa and her antics. "One of us has to be the respectable one here."

Roars of laughter from the crowd—seriously, that hadn't been funny. That crowd was good and managed.

Still, Dressa kept looking for the signs of suspicion, of

distaste. There were no other Truthspoken here—there could only ever be three, the ruler and two heirs, so the Adeium decreed. But the bloodline power to Change was in enough of the nobility, and their drive to have an advantage strong enough, that you could never be sure who'd risked everything to illegally train themselves. Some nobles with the bloodline found ways to use it in minor, unprovable ways, enhancing their natural beauty or keeping perfect health. And most nobles, bloodline abilities or not, had learned at least a watered-down version of evaku, the Truthspoken art of reading people and adapting their gestures and personality for maximum effect.

Who among this crowd knew that form of evaku? Who could spot that she was using it now, who could see through her cheerfulness, see her worry beneath?

"Well," Dressa said, swaggering a bow. "Excuse me, Truthspoken. If you are all done having fun here, I have a party to go to! Who's with me?" This last was shouted again and drowned out by the crowd.

The younger members of the crowd, and those more ambitious, followed her in a wave toward the ballroom doors. Arianna, even as this slightly more accessible version, was still too lofty a target for most.

Dressa glanced back once at Arianna and made a silly face, quickly turning back to a grin.

"Don't forget to have fun!" she shouted back over the din.

Arianna made a shooing wave, but she was still smiling. Still leaning heavily on Lesander.

Adeius, get her through the night.

Arianna was in Lesander's hands now. And Dressa had to hope their father truly hadn't made a match just on politics alone. That Lesander's own training, both political and evaku, if she had it, was up to rolling with the show tonight.

## 6

# A SEMI-ROYAL SIBLING

*We tell ourselves to dance through life*
*We never learn the straightest line*
*We always spin to cross the void*
*So life will never catch us.*

— THE RINGS OF VIETOR IN THEIR
POPULAR SONG "DANCE THROUGH LIFE"

Dressa danced. She danced because it kept the crowds around her occupied. She drew their attention, made the people focus on her from sheer force of kinetic magnetism. She danced because it was expected of her. She danced because yes, this was her favorite band, and they were amazing, and for a moment, just a moment, she could forget about everything else and flow with the movement of the music.

On the stage at one end of the ballroom, The Rings of Vietor launched into a slamming rock ballad about two icer lovers stuck on colliding asteroids signaling each other with their lights. Totally implausible, but romantic nonetheless. She sighed, ending up in the arms of a courtier she barely knew as they slow-danced with everyone else, trying to catch their breaths.

The band had been her pick; Arianna would have gone with a string and drum ensemble, but that was so last century.

When she absolutely had to step outside the throng to get a drink, she waited until a pause between songs and shouted, "Okay, everyone, I need to step out, but don't let the party stop without me!"

They carried on. The music thrummed up again, the lead guitarist shredding a chord that rattled the floor. Out of the rush of the dance, Dressa grimaced, knowing there'd be complaints—never outwardly spoken, but hinted in all the right corners—about how rowdy this ball had been. Well, let them complain. She'd only get to dance at the Truthspoken Heir's engagement ball once, wouldn't she?

Dressa fought to catch her breath—she might be Truthspoken, but she still needed oxygen. She shifted her posture to less sure, more ordinary, less *obviously* Truthspoken, and threaded through the crowds to the back of the ballroom.

Tables with drinks and finger foods were set along the long wall of curtained windows overlooking the palace courtyard. She reached one, snatching up a flute of pale blue wine and a mint pastry. Acoustic dampeners set on stands behind the tables made a bubble of diminished sound near the refreshments. The blast of music faded—if not into the background, at least becoming more conducive to conversation. People of all genders and presentations talked in groups nearby, or stood watching alone, as she did now. Several looked her way, looking as if they might approach, but she took a trick from Arianna's book and stiffened every angle of her body to project an air of a fortress not to be assailed.

As she sipped her drink, she turned to survey the ballroom, something she'd only been doing in bursts while she danced and drew the attention of the crowd. Where were Arianna and Lesander now? Had her shift of attention been enough? They'd hovered near the doors to the entry hall for a while with a crowd of older nobles, but they weren't there anymore.

She spotted them on the opposite side from the band, near the sound-dampened wall, within a group of varied courtiers. Lesander had an interested smile as one of the nobles—a person whom Dressa recognized as a lesser lord—gesticulated while they talked. Arianna still held onto Lesander's arm, but her face was attentive, her posture steady. Was she feeling better? Had it really been nerves, and had being with Lesander—getting over the anticipation of it—helped?

"Cousin," a familiar voice said behind her, and Dressa's eyes widened.

She spun, flinging herself at a wall of pale blue Navy dress uniform, enveloping her very favorite person in a hug.

"Rhys! Oh Adeius, you made it!"

She'd looked for them the night before, hoping against hope their captain would have granted them leave to attend Arianna's engagement ball. Well, and could their captain actually forbid them from attending their sister the Truthspoken Heir's engagement?

Rhys stiffened. "Dressa, everyone's watching—"

She pulled back, but she was grinning. And they were grinning. Her very favorite half-sibling—though they had to call each other "cousin" in public, Rhys being the contract child of her mother and not her father, and she being Truthspoken. "Sibling" for Truthspoken was reserved for her and Arianna alone.

She took in the junior lieutenant's pins on their lapels, which had only been cadet's pins the last time she'd seen them. Their polished black boots, the—Adeius—shock of phosphorescent white hair. That was new. It was only a budding fashion, but Rhys was usually at the forefront of those. Or maybe they'd started the damned thing. They were certainly the best example of it she'd seen, the phosphorescence making their flawless brown skin and shimmery eye makeup glow.

Rhys's grin widened, and they preened. "Like it? My captain hasn't been in favor, I don't think, but it's not against the regs, so. I got one of the other lieutenants to dye hers, too."

"Oh, Rhys." She caught their hands, swinging their arms as she took in the wonderful sight of them.

Rhys stiffened again, gently pulled their arms back.

"Cousin," they said, emphasizing the only role they could ever have in public.

"Yeah," she said, swiping stray hair out of her eyes. She was sweatier than she'd like, but she couldn't reabsorb all of it. "Yeah, I know."

The band launched into another blazing chorus, and while the acoustic dampeners were still working, the music was annoying now that she wanted to hear what Rhys had to say.

Rhys followed her gaze to the stage. "The Rings of Vietor, right? I thought I recognized some of the songs. 'Fireball, baby, oh baby, fireball!'" This said with a little shuffle that could never be called coordinated.

"Ugh, no! That's the only one of theirs I don't like! And don't dance, Rhys."

"My favorite."

"No, it isn't. No, I'll make you change it."

Rhys relaxed a little, their posture becoming more like their own, not as stiff, and wary of all the watching eyes. Wary of all the people who'd love to find fault with or curry favor from the half-sibling to a Truthspoken.

They snagged a wine glass for themself and took a long gulp.

"So yeah, I made it here. It was a near thing—the transport got delayed in Ricket system because of some trouble they've been having with pirates. Really stupid civilian procedures they've put in place and such, they don't want to let us help police their system better, blah blah blah. But yeah, I'm here. I've missed you. You look good, you look—"

They glanced over to where Arianna and Lesander were still talking. Arianna looking well enough. But—

But Rhys, though not explicitly Truthspoken-trained themself, had spent all of their teen years around their Truthspoken sisters. It would have been a miracle if they hadn't picked up evaku by proxy, and not the watered-down version, either. Rhys, among anyone here, would know something was off.

"Arianna looks well," Rhys said with absolute confidence in their voice.

Dressa smiled, because people were watching and listening. "She's happy, I think. Really, truly happy."

Rhys smiled, too. Oh, they were good at this. They were aware something was off, and wanted her to know they'd support her and Arianna if needed, even if they didn't know exactly what was wrong. Message conveyed.

And oh, how she'd missed them. She'd had eight glorious years with them in the palace growing up. Truthspoken weren't supposed to socialize with other children outside of controlled conditions, but Rhys's general father had deposited them with their royal mother when he'd shifted from his Academy teaching position to a field command. Their mother was not . . . a hands-on parent. Twelve-year-old Rhys had wandered into nine-year-old Arianna and eight-year-old Dressa, who were both desperate for new faces that weren't twice their age. They'd all had some truly epic lectures from the palace staff about their antics and, on more than one memorable occasion, from the Seritarchus himself.

For most of the last five years, Rhys had been at the Navy Academy on Valon and could visit occasionally, but the last six months they'd been on their first assignment. A ship far away, patrolling the border to Kidaa space.

There was a puffiness around their eyes, a tired bent to their shoulders. Travel, maybe, but Dressa thought it was more. Navy life was hard enough for those not born to high house bloodlines. For someone who'd been partially raised with the Truthspoken . . . well. And maybe she shouldn't have hugged them. Her head was still full of the dance, too full of trying to distract herself and everyone else from what could go wrong tonight.

Dressa opened up the distance between them, nudged her movements a bit more formal. It was proper, and it would help Rhys to be seen having distance from the Truthspoken. But it didn't help her. She just really wanted to have a friend tonight.

But she watched Rhys relax a little more, and that was worth it.

Then she spotted something off in the crowd. Someone skirting the edge of the dancers, walking very much as if they didn't want to be seen.

Her focus sharpened. Moving with evaku? No, not evaku. Some other training in stealth in a crowd.

The person's face turned, just enough that she saw a coin-sized, holographic seal on their cheek.

A Green Magicker.

And then—she didn't see them at all. She lost them entirely in the crowd and could not find them even when she traced the movements of everyone that had been around them.

No, there. A disturbance a few meters past where they'd been. Heading toward Arianna.

"Dressa?" Rhys asked, alerted by her focus. And rattled—they rarely used her familiar name in public.

"Rhys," Dressa said casually. "Please go to the nearest guard and tell them there might be trouble. There is a Green Magicker heading toward Arianna, and I don't think they're on the guest list."

The Green Magickers who normally attended functions at the palace were all low-ranking and well-versed in playing down their powers to ease the minds of those around them. There were always a few, marked by the implant seals on their cheeks, but she'd already seen those tonight and dismissed them. This other magicker wasn't planned. She didn't know who they were, and they were using their stealth abilities within the palace, which carried high penalties.

They wouldn't try to assassinate Arianna—that, at least, she knew. No Green Magicker could handle killing, and most couldn't handle physical violence, either, which was the only reason the kingdom allowed their quasi-religion to continue. Her father, who'd been pushing for more acceptance of the magickers most of his rule, always pointed out the no-violence thing. Well, and that they were extremely useful in finding the truth in court cases and investigations.

But there were a lot of other ways to hurt someone than with physical violence. It was well known their father pushed for magicker rights, but maybe the magickers thought he wasn't pushing enough. Had this magicker seen Arianna wasn't well?

No, scratch that. Arianna's weakness wasn't just nerves, and that magicker wouldn't be here at all without a purpose. Were they the cause of Arianna's weakness?

Her stomach churned with a growing dread.

She glanced at Rhys for their response, itching to head toward Arianna, but Rhys had already gone to the guards, talking and pointing in Arianna's direction.

Dressa pushed herself into a light Change trance as she started toward Arianna and Lesander, growing her nails into sharpened points. She wasn't a fighter, but she was Truth spoken and trained to hold her own.

# 7

# THE MAGICKER

> *The Green Magickers controlled more than we let them, and yet they found their balance among our whole.*
>
> — ARIANNA RHIALDEN, MELESORIE X IN *THE CHANGE DIALOGUES*

Arianna hid her scowl as she watched Dressa out of the corner of her eye. Dressa was finally leaving her wild dance with that crowd of ridiculous people. To that ridiculous band.

Dressa made a show of not being impressed with court society, and yes, it was part of her Truthspoken persona of Ondressarie, and the people loved it. They certainly loved her, where they were polite and cautious around Arianna—but that was as it should be. She didn't know why their father allowed Dressa to behave so . . . so . . . like *that*.

Nevertheless. She was grateful, cocooned within her carefully gathered crowd of noble misfits, for the baleful looks they sent toward Dressa's hoots and cheers. It meant they weren't looking at her.

The music was truly getting into her skull, too, but the noise was also a distraction. She was doing all she could to direct focus away from her grip on Lesander's arm. She didn't know how much longer even that would hold her upright, but she had to endure.

Lesander was a warm and steady presence beside her that came with its own difficulties. The Javieri prince wore a cloyingly strong fragrance that made her throat burn. She'd tried to Change the burn away, without success.

But Lesander had been . . . surprisingly great with Arianna leaning heavily on her, and with carrying conversation when her thoughts wouldn't coalesce.

Lesander glanced down and asked near her ear, "Do you wish to sit? The group that took up the seats near the back wall has moved to dance."

Arianna took a careful breath to hide her annoyance. "I'm fine. Thank you."

She wasn't. But if Lesander knew that, no one else could.

Lesander didn't openly show her agitation, but Arianna could tell. And really, she probably should be more generous toward Lesander's willingness to roll with whatever she had going on tonight. She was certain Lesander had training in the nobility's version of evaku, though neither of them would ever acknowledge that fact. Did Lesander think this was a test, then, to see how well she could play along with a Truthspoken's whims without question? She'd have to after they were married and she was Arianna's consort. Better she learn those eccentricities now, or else Arianna learn that she couldn't keep up.

If she strained Lesander to her breaking point, would that be enough to get her father to call off the engagement?

Adeius, no. There was too much at stake, too many eyes

from too many political sharks watching. She had to stay in control.

Whatever Lesander thought, she'd been a near flawless cover for Arianna's missteps. Even now, as a shudder of nausea passed through Arianna, she felt Lesander pull her arm closer, a more secure hold.

Arianna clamped her jaw down on a scowl. She hated the need for Lesander's gesture, and hated the fact that she was, for the moment, glad it was Lesander beside her.

But she still didn't want to marry the prince.

And where was her father tonight? He would be watching and marking every gesture of this exchange, to be picked apart later. She hadn't yet seen him among the crowds, though. She could usually spot his tells, no matter what role he inhabited. He might not have arrived yet. Or she might just be that off her focus, and that was a more disturbing thought.

Lesander laughed politely, and Arianna tried to tune back to the conversation around her. She found to her dismay that the man who'd been talking had rejoined the edges of the group and another person, a gray-haired, nonbinary lesser lord, was saying something about the condition of their transcontinental merchant fleet. Wooden ships, of all things, as if the person had nothing but time to waste on building useless things.

"They do well in the hurricane seasons, which is always good, with steady captains to tend their ropes, and the tourist draw is high. You should come next fall! We have vineyards with the best wine anti-spin of Valon. I'd be happy to send you some bottles, Truthspoken. My best vintage."

Adeius save her from prattling fools.

Arianna smiled and made polite nonsense sounds. She wouldn't be talking to this person at all if they required more than polite nods, and that bothered her. It was as if her mind couldn't form the inner words she needed to make it run smoothly. She was safer talking to lesser nobles like this, even if it offended the mentally demanding high nobles, whom she had decided to avoid for the evening. She wasn't up to their usual games.

As the noble droned on about the technical specifications of their ships, Arianna categorized the people around her, her shield. Social unusuals, all of them—gathered on her way across the ballroom with a pointed look, a touch to the arm, while she'd ignored the attentions of the usual high nobles and hangers-on. Her whole persona tonight was off-center enough that people would attribute the group she'd gathered as part of it, though the high nobility wouldn't be happy. They'd certainly call it an insult to themselves. Would Lesander, from one of the highest houses, think it a slight against her?

That could be a problem. She'd have to work at reassuring Lesander. A Javieri prince might be willing to play along with a Truthspoken's tests for the sake of the power this marriage would give her, but she wouldn't suffer insults kindly.

Arianna paused in her perusal of her group and didn't quite freeze. There was one person approaching that she hadn't invited. Late middle-age, tall and gaunt, presenting masc. Tightly bound black hair streaked with gray. Sharp brown eyes that locked onto hers and never strayed. That alone was cause for alarm—very few would dare meet her gaze without her meeting theirs first.

But a faint green haze wafted around them, an aura as dark as the forest. And if that wasn't enough for her to tell what they were, they had the circular implanted seal of a Green Magicker on their cheek. From what she could see, the rank it showed in its dense, asymmetrical swirl wasn't low, either.

What the hell? No magicker of that rank should be at this ball, it would upset the guests. Who'd let them in? Or had anyone let them in? Magickers could walk stealthily through a crowd if they chose; the most powerful could become invisible. By their rank, this person certainly had the power for it.

They stopped on the edges of her group and didn't approach further, though they didn't have to. The people to either side parted as if the magicker was diseased, giving them a clear line of sight.

Beside her, Lesander tensed and said in a low voice, "Do you know this person?"

"No." She squeezed Lesander's arm, part support, part warning.

At least she knew Green Magickers never killed.

And why was her heart racing? Why should she be afraid of this magicker here, surrounded by all these people? She was Truthspoken. She was *the* Truthspoken Heir. She'd been trained to handle anything and knew every weakness Green Magickers possessed. They could only hurt her politically, and at that game she was a master.

Or she would be, on any other night than tonight. She needed a buffer, a break in the tension.

Arianna turned back to the shipbuilder and said without hurry, "Yes, please send us a sample of your wine. I would be happy to try it." Then she looked away, dismissing them. It was a small thing, clumsy in her current state, but it created uncertainty in the magicker's authority and redirected the attention back to her.

The magicker's eyes had never left hers, and their expression hadn't changed. They should have bowed or inclined their head, shown any sign that they acknowledged her authority over them, but they just stared.

Around Arianna, the group stirred uneasily. Would someone call the guards? She couldn't summon them without losing her illusion of control. Had any of the guards seen the magicker approach? Surely not, or the guards would have stopped them.

"Dear Magicker," she said with absolutely no emotional inflection, "how may I help you?"

The magicker's mouth twitched. When they spoke, their voice was a rasp. "Most honored of the Truthspoken, I am Sodan Iseban of the Green." They didn't give their pronouns, which was courtesy. And they still didn't bow.

Arianna's heart was skipping now, and not just from the fear, but she did her best to hold her composure and raise one brow. "Did my hand brush your arm of its own volition, Ser Sodan, that you felt privileged to approach me? Privileged to *stare* at me? Please tell me what magic this act implies."

Arianna's legs were weakening, and she wound her arm around Lesander's back, pulled her close as if to protect her. Though Lesander, who was nearly a head taller than she was and more muscular by far, hardly needed her physical protection.

A few more minutes. She would make it through a few more minutes and then find a way to excuse herself and escape. Maybe to those chairs Lesander had mentioned near the back. She could spin that outcome to the court, to anyone watching. She'd have to spin that.

Lesander, taking more than the hint, said, "Let's go. The guards are coming."

In her blurring vision, she didn't see the guards—but she did see Dressa, pushing quickly through the crowds, teeth bared.

Adeius. And what could Dressa do that she couldn't?

A lot. At that moment, everything.

Arianna shuffled her feet farther apart to brace herself against the weakness. She didn't know if she *could* walk away. She kept her focus on the magicker even while the floor threatened to tilt and the air started to shimmer and spin. It was the magicker's doing, wasn't it? Maybe the cause for all the weakness she'd had in the last few weeks, culminating in the bruising. The magicker had attacked her and they were flaunting that now, letting her know they'd won. Trying to show Arianna just how powerless she was.

But to what end? She felt a weightless confusion in the midst of it all. The magickers held a mutual peace with her father and strictly policed that peace amongst themselves. And how was this magicker causing her pain without experiencing pain themself? Magickers couldn't kill. They shouldn't handle violence well at all. Shouldn't they?

But she could not show her weakness.

Arianna clamped her teeth down and struggled against the queasiness building inside her. Whatever was happening, this person could not win.

"Magicker," she said, but her voice was small and thready. She swayed hard against Lesander.

"Stop, you stupid fuck!" Dressa slashed her hand at the magicker's face, and the magicker leaped back, turning to run into the crowd.

Arianna opened her mouth to shout to follow them, but the magicker wavered in her sight. She couldn't see them. Was that their magic, or was that her own weakness?

Were the two the same thing?

She saw guards closing in now. Adeius, she had to stay focused. She had to be in control.

The room fogged around her, and her grip on Lesander slipped. She just couldn't hold on any longer.

"Arianna!" Lesander cried, catching her as she pitched forward.

She fought against the closing darkness with everything she had, but it wasn't enough.

# 8

# THE MASK

*The Seritarchus is all. All our hopes, our safety, our reliance.*

— LORD KENVI EANO IN *THE COLLECTED SPEECHES OF THE GENERAL ASSEMBLY, FOURTH EDITION*

Arianna awoke slowly. She was lying down, the edges of a blanket tickling her chin. Her surroundings were quiet save for a soft hiss and crackling—not in the ballroom, then. She kept her eyes closed and tested the air. Familiar scents of synth leather and a hint of fire smoke. Cedar. Undertones of earthy perfume. Old, musty books, the expensive kind that were made of pulp paper.

She was in her father's study.

Safe, then, at least from the magicker.

Her anxieties turned to her father's inevitable lecture. Oh, Adeius. Had she actually passed out in the ballroom? And the magicker. The magicker who'd given her this weakness. Where were they? Had the guards taken them into custody? Would she get a chance to stare them down from the outside of a cell?

Would she get to call her first execution?

She strained to hear any signs of movement in the room beyond the soft sounds of the hearth fire. Was her father there, or Iata, his bloodservant? They both could glower enough to make little difference.

She contemplated not opening her eyes for a good long while.

But, if her father was there, he'd already have seen the subtle signs she was awake.

She could almost hear him now: "You've weakened my position, Arianna. You've allowed yourself to show weakness in public. How long do you think before we're fending off more assassins than we can handle? Before they slip into your bedroom and slit your throat while you sleep? Before they slit mine?"

She did her best to shove down her dread and quickly scanned her body and its various insistent pains. Her head was stuffed with wool and throbbed with her heartbeat. Her arms were bruised—from Lesander's catch? Yes, Lesander had caught her.

No time to be embarrassed now.

She felt around the aches, but most were the now-familiar aches of the last week, not any new injuries beyond the bruising.

Having catalogued and triaged her hurts, Arianna drifted toward the light Change trance that would quickly heal the worst of them, enough for her to think, but the trance held itself out of reach. She reached harder and found the upper levels of the trance, but when instructed, the pains in her body gave only the mildest relief.

Only then did Arianna open her eyes, doing her best to

suppress a mild panic. Whatever the magicker had done to her, it still lingered. She could barely Change.

The room with its subtly patterned beige walls was dim, the only light coming from the large hearth. It had no windows—windows were a security risk for an inner sanctum such as this. A figure stood silhouetted against the hearth. Her father, then. He loved the dramatic pose.

He stepped forward as he saw her signal she was awake. "Lights, half."

Lights around the room came on and eased the glare from the fire. And illuminated the face of—

Arianna shot up off the couch, scrambling behind it. The magicker. Had there been a coup, an impossible coup? Was her father dead, was he a prisoner? Surely there was no other way this person could be in this room.

The magicker pulled back, holding up their hands. And . . . and she saw now the green aura was gone. And the holographic rank seal wasn't on their cheek.

"Peace, Arianna." They sounded . . . tired. "I should have known you aren't well enough to see me."

They began a series of small movements—their brow creasing into subtle sternness before easing, the hint of authority in their shoulders solidifying before it faded again, the pulling of the left side of their mouth when they thought of smiling but weren't about to.

Homaj Rhialden, Seritarchus IX, Truthspoken Ruler of the Kingdom of Valoris.

Adrenaline deserted her and only left her shaking.

"Father," Arianna breathed.

She should have known. Adeius, she should have known here, she should have known in the ballroom. She'd never missed her father's tells since she was a child, and even then she'd been excellent at spotting him no matter what personality and form he wore. Was whatever was hindering her Change addling her mind that much?

Arianna's brows drew together. "But, the aura. You had an aura, I saw it. And the seal implant."

Green Magicker seals were implanted when a magicker first manifested powers—the seals were tamper-proof and extremely difficult to replicate or remove. Their rank designs were partially formed by fractals of the wearer's DNA, showing the amount of raw power they possessed. The more complex the fractal, the more power; the more contrast, the more training. The seals could only be changed by a device held by the First Magicker—and did the First Magicker know about this? Surely her father hadn't actually implanted himself with a seal. He could have, and then Changed his cheek after to remove it, to heal.

She stared at him, aghast.

He held up a small device and clicked it—the aura flared green around him again, then disappeared. He held up something else—a small disc that glinted holographic in the light.

"It's not real, has adhesive on the back. You didn't look beyond the fact of the seal, did you? Yes, the First Magicker knows," he said, answering her unasked question. "He's not happy about this but was ready enough to take some of the concessions I made in return."

But—but why? Why would he want, of all the roles he could play, to be a Green Magicker? It was the only type of role she'd never been trained for, because she couldn't replicate the aura, or the seal. Because even thinking about presenting herself as a Green Magicker made her skin crawl. Green Magics were only tolerated because of their usefulness in discerning the truth in disputes, and their protected status as a religion. But the magickers would never be accepted by the court—a court of secrets and schemes would never welcome those who could see right through them.

"Father, you can't stoop so low."

His gaze hardened. "We are Truthspoken. We become *all* those under our protection so we can see through their eyes."

"But a Green Magicker, Father—they hold too much power over us, and their magics are heretical—"

She broke off at the look on his face. Sternly disapproving. And yes, he'd been championing the cause of the magickers for years now, though she didn't know why. It was absolutely out of character for him to give anyone else a shred of his control.

"Every religion has its heretics," he said. "And you'll notice I'm not actually a magicker. And as a Truthspoken, I'm hardly one to judge the innate abilities of another."

Arianna gripped the edge of the couch, swaying on her feet. Her world was tilting again, and not just in the slow spin of the room.

Her father stepped forward. "Sit, I don't want you fainting again."

She flinched from the words and couldn't hide it.

He sighed, coming around the couch to gently grip her arm and lead her back around to sit.

"Arianna, I'm not angry. I'm not disappointed, or any of the responses you are likely thinking."

His words rang with truth, but could she trust any of her senses right now?

"I've used you too hard, too fast, I know that." He pulled a wingback chair over to sit in front of her, propped his elbows on his knees in a gesture of informality. "The nobility has been finding every crack we have as Truthspoken, trying to exploit it. The military is restless under the rule of people they will always mistrust, because they can't define us. I had to prepare you for that world, Arianna. I had to train you to be the best, because if one of their assassins gets through, if I can't stop them, then you're it."

Her hands were trembling. She clenched them in her lap,

willed a Change to calm her nervous system with everything she had, but the effort only made her headache stab harder.

"Why?" she asked. "Why be a Green Magicker?"

He sat back, those tired lines around his face becoming more pronounced. "You're ill, Arianna. And I had to do something before the court realized that, too."

## 9

## A NOBLE SLEEP

> *Truthspoken abilities are near-mythical things, almost as magical as Green Magics themselves. However, we often forget that for all their powers, Truthspoken are trained into them. And their powers are derived from genetic modification experiments carried out centuries ago. We would do well to remember that Truthspoken are still Human.*
>
> — DR. IGNI CHANG IN "DISCOURSE ON THE HUMANITY OF OUR RULERS"

Arianna clenched her hands together, her father's words hanging in the air like an accusation.

She wasn't ill. Truthspoken didn't get ill. It just wasn't possible.

"I'm stressed. It's been a difficult few weeks."

Her father raised a critical brow. "The engagement was necessary to stop the Javieris consolidating their power against us. I'd much rather have them build their power at our side. But no, it's not just stress. You've been declining for several weeks—

and you haven't sought the attentions of our private physicians, though I do understand why you haven't."

Arianna aborted a shrug. Control. Even in private, with physicians she was supposed to trust, she had to be in control.

"Then is it Green Magics? If the First Magicker knows about this, can he counter the effects?"

Her father tilted his head. "He will denounce the attack, of course. The court will be all too ready to believe you were attacked by a rogue magicker, and that's the point. The legitimate magickers will lose some credibility but gain back what they can when they're seen helping you recover. You'll lose some face and some power, yes, but it's not a fatal blow. We'll spin it to gain you more sympathy. The Heir who was attacked on the eve of her engagement."

Arianna didn't grimace. She had enough strength to keep from that. But the thought of Lesander seeing her faint, of catching her, stiffened her back. The thought of *everyone* seeing her faint made her too queasy to think about.

But Lesander—she didn't want to marry Lesander, but that didn't mean she didn't respect her.

Though as the one who had caught her, Lesander would come off as the heroic prince in this, wouldn't she? Was this a Javieri plot? Show the Truthspoken Heir as weak and give Lesander leverage and a ready-made role in court?

No. No, Lesander couldn't make her sick. No one could make her sick, no one without magics.

"So it was the Green Magickers." She stared at her father and the face he still wore. Yes, she knew it was him now, but that face loomed in her mind, that stare in the ballroom with all its intensity.

She shifted. Adeius, she remembered Dressa tackling him, raking his face with her nails. She saw no signs of injury—he would have healed those. But still. At least Dressa hadn't seen him for who he was, either. Not that it was any real consolation.

"No, not the magickers." Her father looked down. He looked nervous, and her father never, ever looked nervous. Was it an act, part of this magicker persona?

Except he'd dropped most of the act. She could see her father all the way through.

Arianna's pulse began to pound in her ears. None of this made sense. Nothing about this conversation made sense when everything in her life was supposed to. Her father wasn't one to show emotions he didn't plan. And he wasn't hesitant. He wasn't kind. He was the Seritarchus, and he didn't get afraid.

If not the magickers, then who?

"Please tell me who did this. We'll go after them with the might of the Truthspoken—"

"It's the Bruising Sleep."

Arianna sat back, the breath going out of her.

The words crystalized, unshielded by any better truths.

"What?" she whispered. That wasn't possible. The Bruising Sleep was a disease that only afflicted commoners. It had been getting worse in the cities lately, and even in the capital they'd had to set up several buildings just to house the sick. It was characterized by constant sleeping and fatigue, by bruising, by nausea and general malaise. It wasn't usually deadly, but it was debilitating. And there was no known cure.

"I'm noble," Arianna said. "I'm royal, I'm Truthspoken—I'm immune."

Her father briefly closed his eyes. "Arianna. The nobility has been contracting the Bruising Sleep for years. Commoners and nobles aren't separate races. Even Truthspoken genetics are barely a few tweaks off from the rest of humanity. *We* aren't even separate, not truly."

"We are blessed by Adeius to be their Truthspoken—"

He held up a hand. "We are Human. And I've failed you if you believe otherwise."

She shrank back into the couch, away from his weary gaze.

This—this couldn't be true. This had to be a test. Her father was . . . Adeius, he was almost sympathetic, and that just wasn't who he was. He wasn't telling her she could do better. Always do better.

Had he given her this sickness so he could . . . could what? Could weaken himself and his heirs in court? Make himself more vulnerable to assassination attempts and plots?

Was this something to do with the politics around the Green Magickers? Had they been rising too high lately and needed to be cut down? But why not tell her? Surely she'd earned that, especially on the night of her engagement, however much she didn't want to marry.

He held up his hands, his face showing more naked dismay than she'd ever seen. "Arianna, I swear by Adeius I did not give you this sickness, if that's what you're thinking. And this is not Green Magics—that was only to divert the court. No one can know you have the Bruising Sleep."

"Then it's an attack," she said. "Our enemies—"

"Possibly." His expression closed again, and she was intensely relieved. "I will do my utmost to investigate every angle. But the truth is, we don't know how the Bruising Sleep is contracted. We don't know what causes it—not a pathogen we can identify, not the water, not the air, not the food. There is not a single factor we can correlate with the cause, not age, not genetics, not existing health conditions or lack of them. Not common vectors. Nothing. We have no data on what happens to a fully trained Truthspoken who gets sick with it, because no Truthspoken ever has."

Arianna swallowed.

Until her. She was the first. She was the Heir, and she was the first.

Adeius, and there was no cure.

Nothing, with a Truthspoken, was supposed to be for life. She could Change every aspect of her appearance. Change her sex, Change her age within reason—Change everything. Heal anything.

But she hadn't been able to heal this.

"There has to be treatment. There has to be some sort of treatment if you said the nobility get it, and I didn't know about it."

Had there been any signs of these symptoms among the nobility? Surely she wouldn't have missed that.

Except . . . there'd been two this month, a high house noble and a minor functionary who'd both abruptly announced they were retiring to their estates for the summer. And many more before them—she'd thought it was just the normal flow of court. People who weren't Truthspoken had the luxury of retiring to their estates whenever they wanted to.

Adeius.

"This has been happening for years," she said.

Her father nodded. "And it's been increasing in frequency. No cure, but yes, there's treatment. Nobles will take a long and sudden leave of absence from court, and there's always a reason, almost certainly a good reason, but the pattern repeats itself. A few months to a year later, they come back and partially resume their lives. Or else retire to their estates permanently and confirm their heirs to their titles."

Arianna felt a cold sweat pass over her.

No. No, she was the Truthspoken Heir. She would not retire. She wouldn't—and Dressa couldn't rule Valoris, she just wasn't wired for that kind of responsibility. It was why her father pushed Arianna so hard, she knew that. She had made peace with that a long time ago.

"There are treatments, good treatments," her father went on. "Expensive, but that's not the issue here. And no, telling my physicians to drop everything and find a cure will not help—so many nobles have been searching for a cure for decades. Many among them, I suspect, with the same Truthspoken markers in their DNA as we have."

Arianna spread aching fingers. "Why didn't I know this?" Why hadn't he told her? Why had he come to her as a Green Magicker, and only then after there was no going back laid all this out?

He looked haunted. "I thought you knew. I thought you'd have already seen the patterns." Unspoken was the fact that he'd trained her to see those same kinds of patterns.

"You're brilliant, Arianna. You are a Truthspoken force to be reckoned with, and when you do recover, you will one day be a brilliant Melesorie, or Ialorius, or Seritarchus—whichever style of rule you choose, and *you* choose, not me—or all the above. Sometimes I think you're trying to push yourself into the dominance and control of a Seritarchus, like me, when you're much more suited to the momentum of a Melesorie rule, or the fluidity of an Ialorius. If I've pushed you there . . ."

He cleared his throat. "You will certainly regain the ability to Change as you see fit, you're too determined for me to believe otherwise. But you must learn to see beyond the surface of things. Not everything in life is about control."

Arianna let the couch hold her weight. She wasn't enough. She would never, ever be enough.

"I'm Truthspoken. My life is control. Even if you're right and I'm more Melesorie style than Seritarchus, it's still all about control—"

"Maybe it shouldn't be."

What the hell? Wasn't that what he'd been teaching her all her life?

Arianna dug her fingers into her thighs. "You're Truthspoken. Your life is pure control, it has to be. If the people saw you as weak—"

He held up his hands. "I know, Ari, I know."

"So—so you didn't give me the Bruising Sleep, and if no one

else gave me the Bruising Sleep on purpose, I, what, just acquired it? At the worst possible time? Father, surely you see that the timing of this, with my engagement and all the negotiations we've had with the Javieris—it's all intensely convenient for a lot of people."

Another thought hit her. "Lesander. Adeius, Father, the Javieris can't know I have this. No one can know. How long does it take to recover?"

"Weeks, or months. Sometimes years. Sometimes . . ." He opened his hands, closed them again.

Sometimes never.

A sob caught in her throat, a true measure of her exhaustion.

"Weeks," she said. "It will be weeks."

His lips turned up in a humorless smile.

He stood again, pacing back to the fire. She watched as his posture shifted, some of his authority as Seritarchus coming back. Arianna watched and felt smaller than she had in years. He could leave this room, go into a Change trance, and become someone else in an hour or two. He would do that. But she couldn't. She couldn't even pull herself together enough to heal the aches in her body. This sickness—this Bruising Sleep—was stealing her birthright.

"Exposing you as the victim of a rogue magicker will explain your clumsiness, your bruising, and signs of fatigue. It will explain your disorientation in the coming days, but you will make a swift and public recovery."

"But—" Arianna stopped as she began to grasp where he was going with this.

Oh, no. No, no, no.

He turned back, fully the Seritarchus now. Not her father, but the person who held the kingdom, this fragile kingdom, together.

"Arianna must show a quick and complete recovery from

the effects of this attack. The Truthspoken Heir must continue her formal engagement of Lesander Javieri and must grow even more formidable to show her enemies she's not to be trifled with."

"But . . . I will be somewhere else," Arianna said with a hollow voice. She'd lost her dignity that night. She was about to lose so much more. Maybe recoverable—maybe not.

She narrowed her eyes. No. She would recover. She would come back to the court and maintain however she could. If this was for life, she'd find a way to live with it. She'd hide it, and no one would ever know. One day, a day she hoped was long in coming, she would rule, Bruising Sleep or not.

There was a soft knock on the door.

Arianna's stomach gnawed with dread. She knew that knock.

The door to her father's study swung open and shut again with its own silence. Dressa glided in, still in her ball clothes.

But she wouldn't be Dressa much longer, would she?

# 10

# THE SWITCH

> *Life is change, and Truthspoken know that better than anyone.*
>
> — ARIANNA RHIALDEN, MELESORIE X IN *THE CHANGE DIALOGUES*

Arianna watched as Dressa stopped a few steps into the room, tensing as she took in their father. His face was still the Green Magicker's but free of the aura or the holographic rank seal. His posture still hovered on the regal authority of the Seritarchus.

Dressa's bearing shifted, closed. "Father. You sent for me."

Arianna's lips drew tight. Yes, Dressa had all the clues laid out for her here, but she'd been much quicker to identify their father than Arianna. That shouldn't have been the case.

Dressa's gaze flicked to Arianna, the smallest crease forming between her brows.

Arianna glared back. She knew she looked awful. She'd be lucky if she looked half as bad as she felt. The makeup Dressa had layered on her face earlier, the clothes and the gaudy necklace with its gaudy jewels and rock star vibe was a role she could no longer live up to.

She swallowed, fingering the titanium mesh of the necklace.

Dressa's eyes widened slightly and her gaze snapped back to their father. Ah. She got why she was here, didn't she? At least some of it. She would have to learn not to show such naked emotions when she was the Truthspoken Heir.

"Your sister is ill," their father said. "You will take her place and her duties, arranging for it to seem as if Ondressarie has traveled to one of the outer worlds. I trust you will work out the details. I want you fully Changed as Arianna before week's end. I want you public and visible, and I want you to continue this courtship with Lesander."

Dressa didn't move.

Arianna wanted to say that with her crush on Lesander, this was what she'd wanted, wasn't it? She'd get to woo Arianna's betrothed—it didn't matter if Arianna actually wanted to marry Lesander, she didn't want Dressa screwing everything up in her place. Adeius, she felt . . . she felt . . .

She couldn't muster the energy to feel much of anything. Exhaustion smothered her like a blanket. She wanted to start whatever treatment she'd need right now, not later.

"And my sudden departure will not be suspicious?" Dressa asked. A stalling, a reach for composure.

"Make it not be," their father snapped.

Dressa braced as if in a storm.

Arianna wanted to hate Dressa. She truly wanted to hate her for being the one to take over her life. But Dressa didn't want this any more than she did. Lesander, maybe, but she wouldn't be courting Lesander as herself. Arianna knew her life would be suffocating to someone with Dressa's natural enthusiasm.

Could Dressa pull this off? Could she not completely screw up Arianna's life and respectability?

Their eyes met again, and Arianna felt a chill. Dressa wasn't looking at Arianna now so much as surveying . . . all that she was.

They'd done it once or twice as children, trying to see how long they could trick their father. They never had. And those games had lasted barely longer than the time it had taken to Change and back again, which hadn't been long. Growing up, they'd kept their appearances similar.

They weren't children anymore. And while Dressa was as fully trained a Truthspoken as she was, her aptitude was not the same. She lacked the finesse and control that came naturally to Arianna.

Dressa's eyes narrowed. Oh, she'd read the contempt, hadn't she? Because that finesse and control had abandoned Arianna just now, and that was the point.

"Are you okay with this?" Dressa asked her.

"I—" Arianna cleared her throat. "I have to be, don't I?"

Her gut churned. Oh, hell. She darted a quick glance around for a waste basket in case she needed it. She'd never vomited before and wasn't eager to do so now.

She couldn't stay at court, not like this. Not with the eyes of the nobility and the military watching. Not when Truthspoken were supposed to be omnipresent, supposed to be infallible. *She'd* thought she was infallible.

Dressa turned back to their father. "How long will my sister be away?"

She hadn't used Arianna's name. Because it wasn't Arianna's anymore.

Arianna's hands clenched. She would recover more quickly than anyone else. If she was the only Truthspoken data point, she'd prove a quick recovery was possible, even if it was only the three of them in this room who knew she'd been sick. If she knew what this weakness was now, maybe she could use her Truthspoken abilities to isolate whatever was causing the Bruising Sleep internally. Maybe she could even come back with a cure. Answers, even, for everyone who'd been trying to understand what the Bruising Sleep was.

"She'll be gone as long as necessary. Perhaps months."

Dressa drew in a sharp breath. "Father—"

But she looked back at Arianna, her face pinching. A mix of anger, of worry, and . . . something else glinted in those golden-brown eyes.

Arianna's attention sharpened. Had that been hunger? Had Dressa fooled her for years, was she a better Truthspoken than Arianna had thought, was she after Arianna's position as Heir—

No. Lesander.

Hell and all the holy mandates, at least she knew Dressa would have an incentive to pull this off for Lesander. Would Arianna come back to find herself already married? Would her children not be her own?

No. She would not be gone that long, she vowed herself that.

"I will of course do what is necessary," Dressa said.

"Don't mess up my life," Arianna rasped.

"Don't stay away too long. I don't want your place as Heir. You know that, Sister."

"Good," their father said, waving away the budding argument. "Now that that's settled, *Arianna*, go and prepare. It will be let out that you—as Arianna—are not quite yourself as you're recovering from a curse of Green Magics."

Dressa touched the edges of her carefully styled hair, a nervous gesture that was fully her own. "Yes, Seritarchus." She'd have to unlearn that gesture, too.

She would Change that night. She would Change, and it wouldn't take more than a few hours, would it? Probably enough time left in the night that she could even get some sleep. They weren't as close in appearance as when they'd been children, but they were still close enough. Dressa would wake up, and she'd be Arianna.

And who would Arianna be? A claustrophobic panic clogged at her throat.

Dressa didn't look at her as she turned to go. "Get better quickly. Seriously."

Arianna didn't look at Dressa, either. "I will."

The door closed, much harder than when Dressa had entered.

Silence, the crackling of the fire.

"Ari—"

She cringed. Yes, it had to be "Ari," didn't it? They'd each been taught as children to have both a public name and a private familiar name so they could relax from their public personas in private. Except, it hadn't really worked out that way. Ondressarie's was "Dressa," though she'd been using her familiar name liberally with her friends and family for years. Half the court knew her as Dressa. Arianna's was "Ari." But she'd been eleven or twelve when she'd stated she wished to be called "Arianna" in private, too. The one thing she'd ever willfully done to contradict her father's training. He'd protested, and he'd commanded, but after she'd not responded to "Ari" for weeks, he'd given in.

The name now felt like a throwback to childhood, too small and stale. She needed a new persona to fall into, to fully become. She wasn't sure she could go back to being Ari.

Her father sat down across from her again, the Seritarchus ebbing out of his posture until he was just her father. This person he rarely was, even in private. This person who was far too open.

He took her hands, squeezed gently.

"It's not fair to Dressa," she blurted. Because it was better than saying—

"No. And it's not fair to you."

Her eyes flooded, damn them. Yes, to her. Especially to her.

"I'm—I'm—"

"You're Truthspoken. Truthspoken do what they must." He sounded tired, so tired. "You'll depart within the hour. You don't have the strength, I gather, to begin any sort of Change now, but it's a five-day journey to Hestia. Do you believe you will be able to Change?"

She wanted to say yes, of course, but over the last week her Change trances had been immensely hard, or simply hadn't worked at all.

"Don't know. Change might be possible, but not much. Not quickly."

"Then make the minimal physical Changes you'll need to be unrecognizable, both genetically and visually. For the rest, or if you can't, you'll need to rely on conventional techniques. I suggest crafting an identity around a minor branch of our bloodline. Let any similarities fall on that.

"Your document blanks will be in the packet Bettea gives you on the transport—key in your codes once you have your identity set and I'll update it in the system from here. I've already spoken to Bettea and fae fully understands the situation. Fae'll continue to accompany you as your personal servant, with faer own minor Changes in appearance, as befits the bloodservant of a Truthspoken. And Ari—you are not to break cover for any reason, do you understand?"

"Yes, Father." She hated how small her voice sounded. She'd gone on solo missions before as part of her Truthspoken training, and later as a Truthspoken to be wielded by the Seritarchus as he saw fit. Where the kingdom needed her. Those missions had always held purpose. But this? This felt like abandonment.

"What if there's an emergency?"

He let go of her hands. "You'll have instructions for emergency contact in your packet—for use in the most cosmically dire of circumstances and not before, is that understood? And you are not to break cover even if you must contact. That's essential, Ari. You—Arianna Rhialden—are still here on Valon. That fact must be ironclad if you wish to resume your life as Arianna."

Her throat clogged again. Hope, that she could one day resume her life. That Dressa wouldn't completely screw it up in the meantime, that their father wouldn't let her screw it up. She hadn't realized just how much she was losing hope until it flared again.

"Ari. You are my Heir." Her father met her gaze, held it. "I will conduct my own thorough investigation into how you contracted this illness. And I've arranged for the best and most secure care possible. Hestia is one of the worlds nobility go to when they contract this illness. It has some of the best experts on the Bruising Sleep, and they're discreet. You'll be in good hands there."

Hestia was a resort world—a "garden world" it was called, as worlds like those tended to be full of estates with reserve-sized gardens for the nobility and little else. And full of lesser nobility, as well. Another sideline.

"Trust me, Ari. Rest, and get well. I'll keep your life safe for you to return to."

"Thank you."

It was all she could say. She had to tell herself, and keep telling herself, that going away was going to save her. That Dressa taking over her life would give her the time she needed to recover. That Dressa was doing her a favor, the biggest favor. Her father wasn't sending her away, he was saving her to continue being his Heir.

Her heart still clenched in her chest. She felt raw to her

bones, and she knew it wasn't just the weakness, the Bruising Sleep.

Her father stood. "I have my own arrangements to make. I'll send Bettea in to help you through the back corridors." There was no question of whether she'd make it to her apartment alone.

"Ari," he said, then, "Arianna." He spread his hands, his expression open with no pretense. She had enough presence of mind left to read his . . . his pride? His pride in her.

Her spine straightened. "Yes, Seritarchus." She could carry that. Yes, she would be someone else for a while, but she would not forget for an instant who she really was. She never did. She never would.

He gave a sharp nod. Then, he rolled his shoulders, and through the movement shifted his posture, his expression, his personality. It wasn't back to fully being the Seritarchus. For whatever reason, he wasn't yet done being the Green Magicker. He removed the holographic seal from his pocket, looked at it for a moment too long, then gave a half-shrug before fixing it carefully to his cheek.

He raised his brows at her. He didn't have the same glare as when she'd met him in the ballroom, but his whole bearing was no less intense. She braced herself, because she knew this was her father. She surveyed the seal on his cheek and gave a small nod.

He clicked on the aura projector and the air shimmered around him, a deep and forest green.

"Ser Sodan," she said, remembering the name he'd given in the ballroom.

He stopped, raising his brows again.

"Are you . . . going to turn yourself in?"

"Child, they have already caught me. It would have been announced ten minutes ago. I'm going to go make my confession, in exchange for staying my execution."

She suppressed a shudder as he pressed open the hidden door beside the fireplace. He slipped through, leaving through the restricted back corridors.

Truthspoken. When she recovered, that would be her someday. Doing what was necessary to keep the Kingdom of Valoris safe.

No, it was her now. She was no less caught in necessity than her father.

# 11

# TERRACE GARDEN

> *Nobles in the military come and go. And some stay, too.*
>
> — HIGH GENERAL BANAMAR ABRET IN THE VID "THE GREAT GENERAL'S TOAST AT EIR RETIREMENT"

Rhys straightened from their casual slouch outside Dressa's apartment as the door swept open. Dressa came out—she'd changed from her ball clothes into a loose green pantsuit and crocheted ankle-length overcoat worked in with tiny diamonds. But her fashion sense couldn't disguise the fact that she looked awful. Deliberately, of course. Her hair was frizzed around the edges and her eyes were red, which, being Truthspoken, she should have smoothed over. But Rhys read the distress beneath the performance of distress, and it was very real.

Was Arianna okay? Rhys hadn't contacted Dressa, let alone Arianna, directly. They hadn't known if they should, but they'd come here straight from the ruckus at the ball, after doing their best to calm some hysterical courtiers who'd latched onto them as a source of information. They'd had none, of course, but they knew how to calm a crowd. Not that anyone would thank them for it.

So they'd stood here outside Dressa's door these last two hours, occasionally chatting with the guards, who weren't sure how to place them within their own social hierarchy. Was Rhys Delor, contract child of the Seritarchus Consort, who'd spent their teenage years calling these halls home, a noble to be treated with utmost respect? Or, now a serving Navy lieutenant, a comrade with stories to trade and commanding officers to gripe about? It was . . . weird. Normally, Rhys wouldn't chat with the guards at all, but they were nervous, and the guards seemed eager for information, too. It was the first time Rhys had been home since they'd shipped out after the Academy, and they didn't know where their place was, either.

Dressa nodded to the guards before approaching Rhys. "Cousin. Walk with me in the terrace garden."

Dressa rarely used that tone of command with them—or ever.

Rhys followed without comment as she led them down the main residence corridor, turned right into a side corridor, and then past more guards out onto the long, narrow terrace garden.

The moon shone as a large crescent overhead, its second a fuller but dimmer orb to the right. Soft golden lanterns glowed around and through the rows of leafy bushes, and flowers rose up from raised beds, swaying gently in the muggy breeze. Trees lined the low terrace walls and kept anyone who stood on the palace grounds below from peering too closely into their depths.

Had the ballgoers fully dispersed by now? Rhys couldn't hear any sounds of partying below. Couldn't hear any music, and the band had been loud enough.

Dressa led them down the first row of the greenery, an even

more private locale. She clutched their arm as she walked, her breaths coming faster than they should have. Her forehead sheened—the air was heavy with summer humidity, but not that hot.

Rhys's pulse spiked. They were already on edge, but now they remembered that Dressa had touched the magicker. Had that magicker gotten to her, too? And yes, they'd been around Truthspoken long enough to know that the surface of things was never as they truly were. But that Arianna had been taken down by a Green Magicker, who never should have got that far, or been in any way disposed to that kind of violence, and all in the most publicly humiliating way possible, was . . . there was something off about all of it.

Rhys couldn't wait for Dressa to speak, and they were mostly alone here, though the gardens would have security bugs scattered throughout.

They took a breath. If Dressa hadn't spoken yet, it meant either she was too distressed to do so, or she was trying to formulate a way to say what she needed to without making it obvious to any listeners. So why not just bring Rhys into her apartments, into her prep room, which had no bugs?

Rhys's skin prickled with their own non-heat-related sheen of sweat. "Is our sister okay?"

Dressa waved the question away, and their deliberate breach of protocol in naming Arianna their sister. "She's fine. Arianna is . . . fine. She'll recover. I—" She made a vague gesture in the air, like she was trying to describe a concept she couldn't picture. "I have to go away for a bit."

She stopped to look at them—she wasn't much shorter than they were tall. Adeius, but she'd grown into a poised and polished person all around, and when had that happened? When Rhys had been holed up at the Academy, cramming for exams. When they'd been on their ship near the border, watching for what baffling thing the Kidaa would do next. It felt like another universe, not this one they shared with their younger siblings. Rhys had the uncomfortable sense they didn't know Dressa as well as they thought anymore.

Truthspoken. She would always, always be Truthspoken. And they would not.

Dressa looked down to play with a loose thread on her sleeve. There was definitely something she couldn't say but needed them to know. What she needed them to know wasn't the fact she was going away.

"You're going away?" Rhys ventured. It was, at least, a starting point to information.

That she was in danger was a given—Arianna had been attacked on a vector previously thought to be a low risk. Would there be more attacks from Green Magickers? Why had the magicker attacked Arianna in the first place? It was probably wise for Dressa to retreat from court to a safer place—Rhys would have suggested it themself if they'd thought they had any right to, but they also knew it wasn't the best move politically.

Was the Seritarchus so rattled that he'd weaken an already wobbling control to keep his second daughter safe?

"Um, why are you going away? I'd think your father would want you here, to help with Arianna's duties while she recovers, if she'll need time to recover."

Dressa made a rude noise, pulling her overcoat tighter around herself—not that it was cold. "Arianna will be up and terrorizing the staff again in a day or so. Father wants me to form my own engagement, just in case Arianna totally screws this up with Lesander, or if there's another attack—the Seritarchus wants a backup plan. So I'm going on a tour to visit his top three eligible candidates—whose names will not be released publicly, just that I'm going on the tour. So no one gets jealous and gets ideas about the health and safety of the others."

Rhys cocked their head. She was lying. It was all a perfectly good explanation, and they didn't know which part of it wasn't true, but she was lying about something. And she wanted them to know she was lying.

Rhys tried, in everyday life, not to use the evaku they'd learned from being around their siblings growing up. They especially tried not to use it when they were on duty. In the Academy and on their ship, they'd gone out of their way to present a show of social awkwardness, and after a time of suspicion—people wondering if they were, in fact, a secret fourth Truthspoken—people had just begun to assume Rhys was who they presented themself to be. They hated that that wasn't entirely true. But the deception was necessary. Few people would want to serve with someone who'd absorbed almost as much about seeing through Human behavior and how to manipulate it as a Truthspoken.

Here at the palace, though, with Dressa, their senses were fully tuned. They watched every angle of her posture, ran her tone through all the arcane calculations Arianna and Dressa had taught them years ago. That were now just second nature.

Something was very wrong. Beyond the fact that Arianna, the Truthspoken Heir, had been attacked in plain sight.

And that really was weird, wasn't it? They kept thinking that was weird. They'd watched Dressa tackle the magicker and had been intensely proud of her just then. They'd been a few steps behind, but the magicker had slipped away into the crowd, flickering in and out of sight.

That had been weird, too. They'd been around Green Magickers before—there was a magicker on most ships in the Navy, though the magicker for Rhys's ship had retired the year before and their replacement hadn't come in yet. There had been several at the Academy, too, including one of their teachers—but they'd never seen a magicker disappear like that.

There had been something intensely *wrong* about that, like

the air had bent with negative energy. Had Dressa felt that? Was that part of what she was trying to say, that something was going on with the Green Magickers and, what, she was being sent to investigate it? Rhys wished they could go with her.

"So, okay, you're going on a dating trip."

"Courting," Dressa corrected. "And yeah, I'll try and actually enjoy it. I'm not as opposed to the general idea of marriage as Arianna. That's why I wanted to tell you—I'm leaving tomorrow."

Rhys's heart sank. It had taken most of a week to get to Valon from the border. They only had two weeks' total leave, and they'd been hoping to spend some time with Dressa.

"And what about Arianna?"

"What about her? I told you, she's fine. A magicker can hardly take down a Truthspoken—if you mean what are the guards going to do to protect her better, or what is the Seritarchus doing about all of this—that's up to the Seritarchus. He hasn't told me that." She took their arm again and started walking. "You should visit Arianna, after I leave. At least she'll be here to keep you company."

Lie. That last was a lie. What the hell?

A cold sweat broke out all over Rhys, and they strained their senses to the limit.

Dressa was distressed, yes. But she wasn't . . . she wasn't grieving, Rhys didn't think. Arianna wasn't . . . Adeius, the unthinkable. Arianna wasn't dead.

"You're sure Arianna is well?"

"Well enough."

True.

"Dressa, you know I'm not that close to Arianna anymore. Not like you and me. Can't you stay at least a few more days, until my leave is up? I don't know when I'll get leave again. Please don't make me spend all that time with Mother."

Not that Rhys would. They shuddered to even think it.

They'd do their one obligatory visit to their mother, like they always did. And if Dressa wasn't here, they'd just go back early.

Dressa shrugged. "Arianna's a stiff-edged brat, but I know she'll want to see you."

True, and true. Well, it didn't take a genius to know the first was true. Rhys wasn't so sure about Dressa's read on the second.

Was it Arianna who needed to tell them something and was sending a message through Dressa? But no, that didn't feel right. So why was Dressa insisting they see Arianna? It wasn't out of familial duty, Dressa's tone wasn't right for that. Though . . . she was tense enough for this to be about familial duty. Her walk was all airy graciousness, but her arm in theirs was rigidly tense.

They strolled around the far end of the garden and started back toward the doors. Rhys had marked the two guards just visible inside the glass doors, one guard outside, and one standing at the far edge of the terrace looking out over the grounds below. Not subtle, but not obtrusive, either.

Then, from one step to the next, everything Dressa had said, and everything she hadn't said, clicked. Rhys had learned to think in patterns around their siblings, in metaphors and misdirection, because that's how Truthspoken thought. Even Dressa, open as she was, wasn't the whole of herself in public, not by a long shot.

It wasn't Dressa who was going away, was it? It wasn't Arianna, at least the Arianna Rhys knew, who would want to see them. Who was so insistent on seeing Rhys, because Rhys, if few others, would know who she was.

Oh, no. Rhys was starting to understand, and they didn't like it at all.

# 12

# APPREHENSION

> *The Kidaa are the first non-Human sentients we've encountered, and though their ways are still largely a mystery to us, and they've shown little interest in helping us attain a higher level of technology, they've also shown little interest in conquering us or anyone else. I'll call that an optimal first contact scenario.*
>
> — ADMIRAL BRYNC QUACH IN HER REPORT "THE STATE OF AFFAIRS WITH THE KIDAA"

Rhys's mouth twitch was the only thing that betrayed their flash of rage. Dressa stiffened, reading the reaction.

Then they both smoothed out their postures and kept walking.

How *dare* the Seritarchus do this to Dressa. Adeius. Dressa didn't enjoy being Truthspoken. She worked hard to not be seen as so rigidly in control as that. She didn't want to be the Heir. And if she had to be the Heir, she wouldn't want to do it while being Arianna.

That's what was going on, wasn't it? Rhys had seen one of the times they'd switched as children—they'd done it not long after Rhys had started tagging along with them. Rhys hadn't had enough evaku then to tell why they kept giggling at the weirdest moments. Their performances had been nearly perfect.

It hadn't lasted longer than a day. How long would this last? Long enough, at least, for "Dressa" to plausibly go visiting potential suitors. Which would factor in travel time, visiting time, and . . . it would be weeks, at least. Maybe longer.

This certainly wasn't Dressa's idea. She was much too tense for that. Or Arianna's? Maybe. But Dressa had dropped that comment about her father wanting her to go on a trip. This had the Seritarchus's signature all over it.

"Don't," Dressa whispered, and they realized how tense they themself were getting.

Rhys glanced over, met her eyes. There was pleading in hers. There was panic.

"Yeah, I'll visit Arianna. And hope she's not too much of a brat." They attempted a smile. They weren't sure they pulled it off.

Dressa gripped their hand and started swinging both of their arms together, like they'd done as kids.

"Tell me about life on your ship. Is it good? Are they treating you okay?"

And where would Arianna be if Dressa was to take her place? Had the magicker cursed her that badly? But "Dressa's" trip would end. So that meant Arianna, the real Arianna, would be back at some point. Was she being sent to hunt down rogue magickers? Was she being sent away to keep her safe, was Dressa now a decoy for other attacks? Was Dressa expendable, was she bait?

"Oh, it's fine," Rhys said. "I'm treated like crap, which means I'm treated like the new person onboard, and that's exactly how it should be." They shrugged. "But we've got a new ensign coming onboard by the time I go back, so I won't be the newest anymore."

Was Arianna going to be Dressa, then? Was that the reason for that trip? Some sort of covert mission? They thought back to Dressa's earlier words, probing for the exact lies. They didn't have enough information. The lie could be that Dressa wasn't actually her going on the trip, or the trip itself could be the lie. Both. Neither. *They didn't have enough information*, and their job on their ship was to sift through reports and raw data, checking for errors. They hated not having enough information.

Dressa squeezed Rhys's hand as they stopped before a budding orange tree.

Rhys reached up, running fingers down the branches overhead. "Truly, Cousin, how badly was Arianna cursed?"

There was a lie in that, too, Rhys could sense it. Yes, Green Magickers could lay curses on people, but what would a magicker gain from cursing the Truthspoken Heir in public? It would do absolutely nothing to further the cause of the magickers and only bring down greater oversight on them, which they couldn't want. Even if the magicker was mentally unstable, there was too much structure to this pattern of events.

Dressa stared at them, not answering. She'd crossed lines tonight in telling them what she already had, but whatever was behind this line was something she could not tell. Or maybe something that wasn't hers to tell.

There was an orchestration to all this, but whose? Had the magicker been the pawn of someone else, maybe one of the high houses not chosen to marry into the Rhialden Seritarcracy? Was this revenge, or a plot to scare Lesander off?

Or had Arianna not wished to marry Lesander badly enough to make that kind of display herself? She'd have had no choice in the engagement. Political marriage was her duty, uniting strong bloodlines and strong politics. Their mother's match to the Seritarchus had been politics, and that match had made their mother project her misery to everyone around her. Was that Arianna's fate? Was that part of the reason for this switch?

Rhys wouldn't wish their mother's situation on anyone—Arianna or Lesander. Or their children.

"The engagement is okay? This didn't hurt Arianna's standing with Lesander?"

"The engagement is fine, as far as I know." Dressa blew out her breath, looked away.

Was that . . . oh, was that an actual blush?

Rhys very carefully didn't raise their brows. If Dressa would be Arianna, she'd have the duty of courting Lesander. She'd be signing the engagement with Lesander, if it hadn't been done already. Adeius, how would that all untangle? Would Lesander, at any point, be told?

Dressa swung their arm again. She wanted to change the subject.

So Rhys, straining to pull subjects from the air, started rambling about their pet project—which was taking more and more of their scarce free time on the ship. It had started when they'd been assigned to organize the scan data from when their ship, the border scout *Occam's Storm*, passed through the edges of Kidaa-held systems.

"I've been studying the Kidaa clans these last months, and—I don't think what our scholars wrote about them covers even the half of how complex their society is. They're really different from us, yes, but you know their technology. They're leagues ahead of us in how they navigate and manipulate spacetime. We don't know how their ships work, or why they'll decide to stay on a planet only a few months, or what might make them decide to make a permanent settlement versus moving on. They don't have cities. I know a lot of scholars think their society is on a long decline from a past golden age, but I'm not so sure about that."

Those first hours of pouring through ship data, Rhys had found a pattern that itched at their evaku senses. Then, like with Arianna and the magicker now, things with the Kidaa didn't quite add up. And from there, they'd started digging. At first just to satisfy curiosity, but then, because they couldn't find the information they needed in traditional research papers and military reports on the Kidaa. Rhys didn't think it was because the information was classified—it just wasn't there.

Could they seriously have been the only one to notice the odd symmetries in Kidaa societies? Like the way Clan Ice and Clan Hydrogen walked—it was very distinctively this forward rolling gait among their four legs, arms held stiffly to their gnarled hides. Those two clans were very different, and they lived in different sectors, one mostly planet-based and the other space-based, and they didn't even share as many common genetics as some of the other clans. But yet, among all the Kidaa clans, only those two walked the same. Why?

Dressa plucked a dead flower hanging from a branch that needed pruned and began twirling it through her fingers. "Why don't you write a book? On what you've found."

Rhys's face went hot. "I—maybe. It's just a thought. I mean, just theories. I still have a lot of research I need to do." They shrugged. And would anyone want to publish, let alone read, a bunch of theories from a junior lieutenant who was trained in the command track, not xenopsychology?

Dressa's lips quirked up. "Researching the Kidaa, of all things. Never thought *that* would be your off-hours haunt." She started singing, "In my off-hours, I haunt the—"

"Adeius, Dressa, don't get that stuck in my head again." It was a hit from last year and incredibly raunchy. Rhys had still been in the Academy, and another upper classer had made the greenies all sing the damn song for twenty-six hours straight. In their underwear. On the front lawn. The officers, of course, had ignored the whole thing.

Rhys hadn't gotten the song out of their head for months.

Dressa grinned and threw her head back, spinning out of reach, tossing the flower she'd just plucked. "In my off-hours, I haunt the bar on Sixth Street—"

Adeius, Rhys wished they'd never told her that story. She'd be taunting them with that forever.

They lunged after her and she danced another few steps back, crooning, "—and we made some music between satin sheets, with—"

Rhys abandoned the chase and clamped their hands over their ears, belting out the first thing that came to mind, that Rings of Vietor dance song from the ball earlier.

Dressa stilled, her smile fading.

Rhys stilled, too.

Because Arianna. And the magicker. And Dressa "going away" and all that was to come, whatever that might be.

Rhys cleared their throat. "So, the Kidaa."

They had to change the subject, not just in their words but in their mind. The Seritarchus didn't have an idle reputation for having eyes and ears everywhere. Rhys hadn't spotted him tonight and had no illusions that he couldn't be anyone around them. The guards, or someone listening to the garden bugs right now. Or if Rhys saw him in the corridor, that he wouldn't detect some trace of the truth that Rhys knew some of what was going on. They didn't want to get Dressa in trouble, and absolutely didn't want to get themself quarantined or reassigned for knowing a secret that they shouldn't. They weren't sure the Seritarchus would go so far with them, but they weren't willing to push it, either.

So, the Kidaa. A suitable worry to replace this one.

On their way back to Valon, they'd been trying to think of a way to tell some of their thoughts on the Kidaa to Arianna without her outright dismissing them. The people of Valoris mostly dismissed the Kidaa, because in the two hundred years since Humans had first run into their worlds, the Kidaa had yet to show any aggression. Not toward Humans, not toward themselves. They didn't seem to have wars. Their ships didn't even have weapons. Like the Green Magickers, they seemed totally averse to violence.

Well. That theory had proved pear-shaped tonight, too, hadn't it? Probably.

"Listen, though," Rhys said, "just watch the Kidaa. Pay attention to the patterns there. There's something happening there that seems . . . off. I'm not sure they're as benign as we think they are."

Dressa raised a brow. "You think they're a threat?"

"I—no. Well, maybe." They didn't know what they were finding, and that was what kept them digging, what was increasingly keeping them up at night because there was a growing apprehension, a sense of impending . . . *something* . . . that they could not shake.

They'd made the mistake, a month ago, of bringing the whole mess of theories to their captain. Who'd told them it was bullshit, and if they had so much free time, why not take on janitorial duties while they were at it?

Their captain, though, wasn't a fan of nobility. And try as Rhys might, they couldn't totally wipe their years in the palace from their speech and mannerisms. They might have been raised with Truthspoken, but they still weren't Truthspoken.

"I—I think they're dangerous, in a way we can't see or understand, because we haven't been able to understand them at all. We might never understand them. But . . . watch the patterns, okay? Please tell Arianna and the Seritarchus. I know what I'm seeing. The Kidaa aren't the people our scholars make them out to be, for good or for ill. I just—I don't want us to be caught by surprise if something does happen."

Dressa didn't laugh, not that Rhys thought she would. She didn't criticize, she didn't pick their thoughts apart. She cocked her head, thinking, and slowly nodded.

"I'll do that. Thank you."

It was another line, that moment. A line she quietly crossed. Assuming responsibility for the weeks ahead.

Rhys put their arm around her, a sibling sympathy hug—no one but the guards could reprimand them, and the guards certainly wouldn't. No one could see them from the grounds below.

Dressa leaned her head on their shoulder a moment before she sighed and moved away. "I need to get ready for my trip. I'm leaving as soon as possible. I just wanted to tell you—"

"Yeah, I know." Rhys smiled.

Dressa smiled.

It reached their eyes, but only because they'd both had a lot of practice.

They passed back through the doors into the cooler, drier air of the palace. Rhys felt their body tensing back up, their senses alert. Yes, they'd spent a significant part of their childhood in this palace, they knew its corridors inside and out, even some of the secret ones, but they'd never made the mistake of thinking it was friendly—to them or anyone who lived here.

"So what had you planned to do, if I'd been able to stay?" Dressa asked.

Rhys winced. They'd wanted to talk. They'd wanted to go hit all the city markets and binge buy a new wardrobe that they'd only see again the next time they were on leave. "Maybe go see a play, or the symphony or something." They knew what she was getting at. And Arianna would never go shopping in the city.

Dressa snorted. "That is an incredibly boring thing to want to do. But—Arianna might want to. Maybe. You should ask."

Rhys was silent for several steps, thinking through possible interactions. Social implications. "No, I know she's busy. And, yeah, I'm not her favorite sibling."

And the gap between them widened.

"Well, best get the visit with Mother over now. That way things can only get better from here."

Rhys sighed, rubbed their forehead. "Yeah."

More silence.

After a while, they paused at the door to her apartment. Rhys wanted to give her a parting hug—because it would be goodbye, wouldn't it? For them seeing her as Dressa, at least. But she was Truthspoken, and they were in full sight of the guards.

So instead, Rhys bowed. "My best to you, Truthspoken."

Would they be able to bear watching her be Arianna? Watching her do all the snubby little I'm-superior-to-you things Arianna did? They didn't know if they could, but she'd asked them to. So, they would try. It might tear them apart . . . but what would it do to Dressa if they didn't?

Dressa touched their shoulder, a brief reassurance. Her eyes were shining.

"My best to you, Cousin. Hopefully, I'll see you on your next leave."

# 13

# AN OLD FRIEND

> *Truthspoken don't have friends.*
>
> — ARIANNA RHIALDEN, MELESORIE X IN *THE CHANGE DIALOGUES*

Rhys walked the corridor of the palace residence as if in a trance. They reached out to the textured wall, trailing their fingers along the pattern as they'd done when they were younger. The sconces glowed evenly down the walls like silent sentries. The ceiling gently arched. Everything in soft, neutral colors.

They passed the door to their own apartment, in which they'd spent their teenage years—they'd never shared the same rooms with their mother. The Seritarchus had told them when they'd left for the Academy that the apartment was always open to them. They wanted to duck inside just now, flop on the bed, and drown everything that had happened that day in sleep.

This time on Valon, though, they'd requested a suite in the palace's guest wing instead. No use trying to put public distance between themself and their family if they stayed in the royal residence.

They could sleep in their apartment tonight and go to the guest suite the next morning, but, well. Their luggage was halfway across the palace. And they weren't sure they wanted to linger. These corridors held too many memories all jumbling together with the sharpness of the day.

Adeius, the memories.

It was their first time back after half a year away from Valon and its politics, and their family and their family's politics. And tomorrow—tomorrow they'd visit Arianna, knowing she was not Arianna, and they'd have to integrate that memory as well.

Growing up here hadn't been in any way normal, but it had been good, hadn't it? Rhys had to believe it had been good. No, their mother hadn't been a good mother, and yes, their father had pretty much dumped them here with her, but the richness of this environment, the never-ending games within games with their sisters, had been good. Yes, the palace had teeth, but their sisters were good. The people here, the staff and guards, were mostly good. Even the Seritarchus was decent to them, and he didn't have to be.

All of it was dangerous and bright and complicated and glittering.

But had it been *good*? The Seritarchus, now, was ordering one of his daughters to become the other—or that's how Rhys read the situation, at least. How was that in any way good?

Rhys straightened and smoothed out their uniform as they rounded the bend to their mother's stretch of the corridor. They'd get this visit over with and then retreat to their guest suite. They were too tired to think any more that night.

"Rhys!"

Rhys jumped, then broke out in a delighted grin. "Vogret!"

Ina Vogret, the former head of their mother's guards, had a matching grin. A head taller than Rhys and built like a battlecruiser, she abandoned her post at his mother's door and flung out her arms, running toward Rhys.

Rhys met her halfway in a bone-crushing hug.

"I didn't know you'd be here," they said into her maroon uniform. They pulled back. "You retired! I thought—the grandkids—"

Vogret shrugged. "Your mother asked me back. Not all the time—half hours, really. I'm not in command of her guards anymore, either, and that's a change."

If Vogret was back, Rhys doubted anyone else truly had control of their mother's household.

"Look at you," Vogret drawled, tugging on Rhys's lapels. "All grown up and shining."

Rhys bit their lip to stop a laugh. Looked up into gray eyes in a crinkling smile.

For the first time—Adeius, for the first time since they'd landed in the city earlier that day, they felt like they could breathe. For just one moment, here with their old friend, they didn't have to be on alert, or navigating tides of evaku. They could be Rhys, because that's all she'd ever seen them as.

Vogret slung an arm around their shoulder and drew them back toward their mother's door. "She's in a mood today, but not more than normal. Just be polite, as always, you'll be fine."

Rhys was aware of just how much protocol Vogret was breaking with those words, and they didn't care. Growing up, when they'd had to deal with their mother, Vogret had always been there to smooth things over. The last few years since she'd retired, visits had been much harder. Rhys had wanted to look her up in the city and visit her, too, but they'd never had the time between classes at the Academy. And they weren't sure of the protocol there, either—Vogret was security, and despite their military career, Rhys was still one of the people security protected.

Adeius, they were so glad she was here.

They lingered by the door, trading quick bursts of recent history. Vogret had married her second wife and now had a cozy triad living in her city apartment. Which, she bemoaned, was currently packed with grandkids while her second child traveled. Vogret was all aglow—she'd started a third child, twenty-odd years removed from the other siblings.

"This one will have traits from all three of us, and I told the lab tech to absolutely not let them have my nose!"

"You have a perfectly fine nose," Rhys protested.

"Too large." Vogret waved a dismissive hand. Then her smile dimmed as she studied them. "You okay, chickling?"

"I—"

Their eyes flooded and their throat closed in a flood they hadn't expected.

Adeius, but "chickling" almost broke them. Here, tonight—it was so familiar. So very true when everything else seemed so tangled.

Could they stay in this moment forever? And not have to face their mother and her disdain. And not have to face Dressa as Arianna tomorrow, knowing she was absolutely miserable.

*Had* their teenage years been so benign if they'd been inside a world such as this? They'd grown up in these few hectares of ground that the rest of the kingdom coveted. They'd thought themself lucky, though they hadn't been too happy when they'd realized just how much their peers would hate them for that privilege.

If they hadn't left to join the military, what would their life have been like? Would the Seritarchus have swept them up into his plans, too? Rhys wasn't Truthspoken, but they were already tangled in these evaku games with Dressa. They'd been tangled from the start.

They tried again. "I—"

Vogret pressed her hand to their cheek. "I know. I know what happened tonight. I know."

Rhys drew in a shaky breath, nodded. She'd know it was more than just the attack by the Green Magicker and the fallout from that attack. A whole lot more. Vogret had been around Truthspoken too long to not know that everything was always complicated. And that if Rhys knew anything more, they couldn't share.

She pulled Rhys in for another hug, and for a moment, Rhys clung tight, struggling with all they had to get their emotions under control.

They'd been hoping for a happy visit home. They'd wanted to spend time with Dressa, to dip into this world just long enough to recenter and take off again. Life on their ship was good, but it was so different, the people so different from the people they'd known here. Rhys had to use their evaku just to present themself as reasonably ordinary, and that was a strain they'd been hoping to shed for at least a few days.

They hadn't wanted, and hadn't expected, to come home to an attack and a crisis. But, well, no one had expected that.

Rhys pulled away and attempted to smooth out their uniform. It was rumpled and—ugh, a little ripe from the stress of the night. They should have gone back to their suite to change into something else before coming to see their mother. Well, no fixing that now.

Vogret fussed over their uniform, then gave up with a shrug that seemed to say, "Some days you lose some."

She knocked once on the door to their mother's apartment and another guard poked their head out. The guard saw Rhys, nodded, and disappeared back inside.

Rhys's shoulders tightened again as they waited. Could they just visit Vogret and leave? Not, for once, endure a visit with their mother?

"I'll be right in the entry, chickling. Right in the entry."

Rhys nodded.

Or, they could come back in the morning, when they could

better handle their mother's acid. But they were here, and if they waited until tomorrow, they'd be dreading the visit all night. It was late, but their mother seldom went to bed before dawn. And she was usually mellower at night.

Best chances were now, Adeius help them.

The door opened again, and the other guard beckoned them inside.

# 14

# LEAVING

> *We never realize how strong we are until we have to face our fears in the mirror.*
>
> — ARIANNA RHIALDEN, MELESORIE X IN *THE CHANGE DIALOGUES*

Ari sat on the bunk's thin mattress with her knees drawn up, shivering despite the two blankets she'd pulled around herself. The ship lights were dimmed to amber—she hadn't been able to take the harsh white lights when they'd boarded and Bettea had put the tiny passenger section on emergency lighting when fae had gone to spin up the engines. That had been ten minutes ago, and now Bettea, her bloodservant, hadn't yet called back over the comm, and Ari's panic was threatening to tear apart her heart.

Around her, the ship's engines whined as it prepared to lift.

How? How had she ended up here?

Yes, she knew the mechanics of how she'd gotten from the palace to this ship inside the city port. It was one of any number of ships that were paid a constant retainer—they could be called upon for use by the Seritarchus at any time, and he'd chosen to call this small trade ship now, temporarily displacing the usual captain and co-pilot.

She knew how Bettea had sat her down before they'd left, in her own apartment, which wouldn't be hers again for a while, and fussed over her in faer no-nonsense fashion. Bettea had deftly handled makeup, scarves, and clothing until Ari at least didn't look royal anymore. Her face was rougher, hard used. She looked ten years older and decidedly androgynous. She wore a yellow spacer's jacket that had seen better days, a plain gray undershirt, and green skintight trousers.

It had taken only minutes to cut her hair—they hadn't needed it stylish, just spacer short. The false tattoos on her neck and hands had gone on quickly, if not as expertly as they might have.

Rough up her nails, pop in lenses to shift her eye color.

They only had to get to the port in the dark, get through customs with pre-cleared documents. They didn't have to fool a roomful of nobles, but anyone could be watching. Anyone could be reporting, and so Ari had done her utmost to make everything about her body language scream "ordinary!"

She'd barely made it from the aircar through the customs check without holding onto Bettea's arm.

Bettea faerself had Changed just enough to not be recognizable, wearing faer own rough jacket, faded enough it was only black around the seams. Fae had decked faerself in a modest amount of cheap jewelry, faer makeup inexpertly applied. Fae looked to all the world like a trader who'd had only slightly more good luck than bad.

Bettea, as a bloodservant to Truthspoken, was born from a service branch of the Rhialden line. Fae had been with Ari since they'd both been children, though Bettea was a few years older. Fae had just enough ability to Change and training in evaku to help Ari when needed, in any situation. But fae couldn't easily make a full Change, and couldn't read people and manipulate even as deftly as Rhys could.

For this trip, though, Bettea's training was enough. They'd sailed through customs, they'd boarded this ship. Bettea had deposited Ari here, and here was where she now sat.

She knew all of that, could retrace all of those steps a thousand times over. But how, by Adeius, had she come to need this trip at all? How had she contracted the Bruising Sleep, and how had she let it get bad enough that she'd have to be sent away?

All she could think was that she should have known sooner. She should have known it wasn't just stress slowing her down, hindering her Change. She should have been so much more terrified that she was having trouble healing herself.

But she'd thought herself invincible, hadn't she?

She shuddered in a wave of self-loathing so intense it threatened to destabilize her volatile stomach.

A noise from the door brought her head up. Bettea brushed in, sitting down next to her.

"You—should be in the cockpit," Ari said through chattering teeth.

"We're lifting in a moment. Everything's set—I'll keep the lights on emergencies as long as we need to. Just wanted to check on you. Get you strapped in."

Ari pulled the blankets closer. "I'm not a child."

"No," Bettea agreed, "but you're sick." Fae hesitated. "Do you want to lift in the cockpit? Or strap into bed?"

Cockpit, Ari definitely wanted the cockpit, and to avoid the indignity of being strapped in like an invalid.

But she was an invalid, wasn't she?

She was . . . sick.

She, a Truthspoken, was sick. And she couldn't heal herself.

How could she even call herself Truthspoken?

"Hey." Bettea crouched in front of her, gripped her hand. "You. You stop blaming yourself. This isn't your fault."

"I'm yanking you out of your life, too. Dressa's bloodservant will have to be you, too, for this all to work."

Bettea's lips thinned. "I'm with you. I'm here. We don't have to worry about what's happening there—"

"Don't we? They're taking over our lives—" Ari stopped, gasping for breath, clutching at her pounding heart. She didn't have the energy to be upset. She just didn't have the energy.

"They're taking over illusions of our lives," Bettea corrected, and tugged at Ari's arm until she scooted back to lie down. "They're not taking over us. We are going on a vacation, you and I. We're just going to take a little trip, get a little treatment, and then we'll be back. It's just a mission, same as usual."

"Different parameters," Ari said, wincing as Bettea reached over her to fasten the safety straps across her chest, stomach, and legs.

"True. But still a mission." Fae tightened the last strap and stood again. "It'll be educational."

What her father always said about difficult missions. But he hadn't this time, had he? He'd just bared too much of his heart to her. Too much of his own distress.

Bettea squeezed her hand one last time. "I'll be in the cockpit. Launch in five minutes, and I'll keep ascent as steady as I can. You shouldn't feel anything—at least we've got a decent enough ship."

"Then do I really need the straps?"

"Yes," Bettea said, and faer tone brooked no argument. Ari might be the Truthspoken, but her bloodservant had never been afraid to call her on her bullshit. She liked it that way.

Ari settled back, trying to ignore the pain throbbing through most of her bones. Trying to ignore the nausea and the fatigue. Trying to just . . .

She had no strength now to construct a persona around herself. She hadn't even seen the documents Bettea had used to get them through customs. Bettea had done all the talking.

The engine pitch rose, and Ari felt the slightest tug to one side before the ship's gravity stabilized. They were off Valon. Not her first time off Valon, certainly, and not even her first time off on her own. But everything else—absolutely everything else—was different.

She wasn't the Heir anymore. Not right now, at least. Later, maybe. But not now.

Her whole life, her entire purpose, was about being the Heir. Yes, she would throw all she had into the persona they'd create in the next few days, but when she played into a persona, she always had herself to anchor back to. Arianna Rhialden, Truthspoken Heir. She always, always knew who she was. Her father had taught her that was the key to never losing herself in a role, even if it was sustained over time.

Would she lose herself if she had no life to go back to? Or, more terrifying, had she already lost herself the moment the Bruising Sleep had taken hold?

She couldn't even claim her name anymore. She was using "Ari" only because she had nothing else. She wasn't Arianna anymore. She just . . . wasn't.

Feeling the fatigue close in, Ari resigned herself to let the bunk hold her, the straps hold her steady in the minute shifts of the ship's gravity field as Bettea made course adjustments.

Five days until she started another life. She told herself maybe that would be a good thing.

But she couldn't stop thinking about Dressa. Tomorrow, Dressa would *be* Arianna Rhialden. And what Dressa did in the next weeks and months would shape Ari's life forever.

Adeius, Dressa, you had better not screw this up.

# 15

# MOTHER

*My ten contract children have been the light of my heart, my source of joy in my old years. And a way to bind some younger lovers to me that wouldn't otherwise have looked my way. And then there are the territories I've bound to me, too, and the influence I've expanded. It was so good to get the Jjat family's dyes for my wools. But I do love the children, too.*

— LORD IVANNA GALSERI, IN PRIVATE CORRESPONDENCE TO HER SISTER

The entrance to their mother's apartment was lit by soft rose mood lights. An enormous fragrant arrangement of different flowers in shades of yellow dominated the large space, making Rhys's nose twitch. Abstract paintings that Rhys had once described to Dressa as gilded sock puppet dragons hung around the cherry paneled walls.

While Vogret positioned herself by the door and gave an encouraging smile, the second guard slipped out into the corridor. A night watch butler arrived and gave Rhys a bow.

"Ser Delor, if you will follow me."

Rhys followed through a formal receiving room and into another parlor, and this one—this one was the lion's den, wasn't it?

"Lieutenant Rhys Petrava méron Delor to see Seritarchus Consort Haneri ne Delor Rhialden," the butler announced.

Haneri Rhialden looked up from her holographic light-weaving as Rhys entered, her light pick in one hand. She was intensely beautiful, her brown skin flawless—which, okay, Rhys was glad they'd inherited from her—and a face that had all the right angles in all the right symmetries. Large, golden-brown eyes. Flowing, round figure. Of Arianna and Dressa, Dressa most resembled their mother, though Haneri would outshine anyone in a room, even the Truthspoken.

Her brow creased with annoyance, as if that was all the expression Rhys warranted from her. As if, coming home after six months away, they were simply distracting her by their visit.

Rhys made their very prettiest formal bow. "Ser Consort."

She wouldn't suffer to be called "Mother."

She lifted her chin and resumed plucking and pulling at the holographic light of her art.

"Ah, Rhys. You've come back to Valon, I see." Her tone implying that she wondered why they'd bothered.

"Yes, Ser Consort, I came back to attend Arianna's engagement."

One sculpted brow rose as she continued to weave her light pick. "Is she engaged now?"

She wasn't that unaware. Once, she'd absolutely dominated the court of Palace Rhialden, playing the people around her with exacting precision. Truthspoken consorts were not chosen for their connections alone—she'd certainly had the nobility's version of evaku training, and Rhys suspected a little illicit Truthspoken training as well. Few people were that unerringly beautiful from genetics alone.

But five years ago, the year before Rhys had left for the Academy, she'd suddenly stopped going to court functions. She'd holed up in her apartments and took up lightweaving, receiving a few guests, but those guests trickled as they realized she'd extracted herself from everything to do with the court and could do little for them. Plus, her already-biting personality had turned cruel.

Rhys and Dressa and Arianna had all tried to understand what had happened—was she sick? Was she depressed? They'd bullied one of the royal physicians into admitting that Haneri had seen him, but that he hadn't found anything physically wrong with her, and she'd refused any medications he wanted to try. The Seritarchus had summarily dismissed the physician when he'd found out the man had given away even that much information, even to members of the royal household.

So what had happened? Rumors had run the course of everything from the Seritarchus ordering her retreat to her having an emotional breakdown to several scandals around nobles she'd been known to have flings with. She hadn't been bound exclusively to the Seritarchus since Dressa was born, but that didn't mean the court didn't still want to believe that illusion.

Rhys and Dressa thought it might have had something to do with Lord Chelsa Fadira, a dour matriarch of a lesser house who'd been killed in an aircar accident a month before Haneri's retreat. Haneri had had two contract children with Chelsa before Rhys, and she hadn't had more than one child to anyone else except the Seritarchus.

Rhys drew in a long breath, all of this running through their thoughts, conflicting their reactions.

"No, Ser Consort, I don't think the engagement papers have been formally signed, but they should be within the next few days."

Maybe. Rhys hardly knew what would happen now or how the Seritarchus would play this all out.

Should they bring up the attack? Would their mother know about it?

Rhys didn't dare wonder if she would care. Of course she'd care. To not care would be . . .monstrous.

No, she had to know about the attack. She seemed secluded in her apartments here, but she was by no means uninformed. Whatever had made her retreat, Rhys was absolutely certain she had full command of her wits as well. Her cruelty was far too calculated.

She looked up, focusing more fully on Rhys. Her eyes flicked up to their hair. "That looks atrocious."

*Well thank you, Mother, just come right out and say it.*

Rhys felt their face heat and resisted the urge to touch their phosphorescent hair. "It's in fashion."

"It shouldn't be." She turned back to her weaving, flicking another few strands of light into place.

Rhys didn't know what she was making, beyond knowing it would be a sculpture. Her works, which she'd started soon after her seclusion, were popular viewings in galleries and private halls all over the worlds of Valoris, and not just because of her status. They had odd, abstract geometries which caught and held the eye. At the Academy, Rhys had to walk past one exhibited in the entry hall every day for a year, and had wondered every day of that year if she'd sent it there as a message to them, and for what purpose? To remind them of her? To intimidate?

Their cheek twitched. If their mother didn't know about Arianna's attack, she had to be told, didn't she? And if she did already know, Rhys wanted to know that, too.

They watched her face as they said, "The engagement ball didn't go well."

"I can see that. Your uniform is less than optimal."

They wanted to stomp their feet like a child. Adeius! Grant them the ability to stay calm.

"Arianna was attacked by a Green Magicker," Rhys hissed through clenched teeth. "She's recovering now, but Dressa assures me she's okay. She's not well, but she'll be okay."

"Is that so." She didn't even look up from her weaving.

"The—the Seritarchus has it under control." Presumably. Rhys hoped. And did she even care about that? They were wasting their time here.

They distinctly remembered that day when they were twelve, when their father had said they were taking a trip to the palace. Rhys had been to see their mother several times before, but on that day, their father had let go of their shoulder, backed away, and told Rhys they'd be staying.

Haneri had studied Rhys for a long, long moment. It was like she'd been looking through them. In those days, she was still a force to be reckoned with at court, but she'd never been warm. She'd never been friendly, or anything other than critical and demanding. She'd gotten worse over the years, but the bar had been low to begin with.

Haneri tilted her head, the nova hearts woven into her hair catching the lamplight and the soft silver glow from her lightweaving. She studied Rhys again now, not quite that same penetrating stare, but Rhys did their best to make themself opaque. They hadn't had evaku when they'd been twelve, but they had it now.

"Does he," she finally said, and resumed her work. "I imagine my daughters will be quite shuffled about in the days to come."

Rhys blinked. She knew about Dressa becoming Arianna?

No. She knew the ways of the Truthspoken, and she knew how they dealt with problems. If she didn't know the specifics, she at least knew that a threat to the Seritarcracy or its Heir would be met not with force but with illusion and intrigue.

She could extrapolate with razor precision, and Rhys wasn't exactly doing well at hiding their own emotions around all of this. How much had they let slip? They were absolutely certain no one else had told her.

Dammit.

She hated this world, Rhys knew. Hated absolutely everything the Truthspoken stood for. She used to go on rants about how she'd given up her high house princedom to marry the Seritarchus, and all it had gotten her was two children who were like him. She hadn't said those things in public, of course. But Rhys had been present more than once. So had Dressa and Arianna.

Time to go. Rhys could not take a moment more. Didn't have the energy left to parse out what all of this meant, if anything. Their mother was bent on loathing her life and making things miserable for anyone who cared for her.

Rhys gave a shallow bow, a familiar bow. "Goodbye, Mother."

She'd hate that.

But she didn't actually contradict them this time. She didn't throw insults after them, and they resisted the urge to turn around and see if her gaze followed them out.

Haneri Rhialden had five contract children beyond her two children by marriage with the Seritarchus, and Rhys was the only one stupid enough, or maybe masochistic enough, to keep visiting her whenever they were here. To keep thinking that maybe, at some visit, she'd say something extraordinary, like that she loved them. Or that they were more to her than the amount of wealth and influence the contract of their birth had brought her.

Or even that she approved of something they did, anything. Anything.

"Rhys."

They stopped just short of the door, heart pounding.

Adeius, their heart couldn't take any more daggers that night. It just couldn't.

But they turned, slowly. Haneri had set down her light-weaving and was watching them intently.

"Rhys, don't come back."

Rhys closed their eyes. They would not cry. *They would not cry.*

"You have a choice to leave this world. It's a choice I wish I had, and you shouldn't have come back. Don't come back again. Don't look back at all."

They opened their eyes. What? Was this her way of saying she actually did care? But—

They bit their lip.

She stood slowly, smoothing out her casual gown, and walked with measured steps over to them. Rested her hands on their shoulders, which—which she just never did.

She looked into their eyes, hers fierce and intent.

"Forget the evaku. Forget the Rhialdens. Forget the palace." She touched the rank pins on their collar. "You are *this*. You use Petrava as your name in the military, correct?"

"I—I thought it was better there than using Delor, and I have a legal right to both names—"

"That's good," she said. "Keep it. Forget Delor."

"Mother, I can't—"

She stopped them with a glare.

They froze. They didn't know how to act, because their mother hadn't paid them this much attention in years. Certainly not since before her seclusion.

She seemed to brace herself in her grip on their shoulders. "This court devours people. I should never have let you stay here to begin with. That was a weakness on my part. I have lost two children to the Truthspoken tyranny. I do not want to lose another."

"I'm not Truthspoken—"

"You're halfway there. You can think like them."

Which . . . which wasn't untrue.

"But I love Dressa. Even Arianna."

"Their lives have no room for love," she said. "You will not get love here, only that which drags you under."

They stared at their mother, studying, up close, the fine lines on her nearly perfect face. Reading the weariness, the grim determination of a life lived past a breaking point.

They swallowed hard, swallowed again. The question was on their lips: "Mother, what happened to you?" But they didn't ask. They didn't dare ask.

She smiled, though, a bitter smile. "I don't play the game," she said, as if in answer to their unspoken question.

Rhys suppressed a shiver. Yes, she certainly had evaku. And maybe more than what the nobility trained themselves in.

"I choose not to play the game. I could retreat to my family's estates, but then, I would be forgotten. I would not be the bitter sore in the Seritarcracy that I am now. And then there would be no one to stand between my children and the lives they were born to live."

Rhys blinked. What was she saying? She didn't protect Dressa and Arianna. She was hardly a part of their lives at all.

She reached up, drew their head down, and kissed their forehead.

Or did she mean . . . them?

Rhys's eyes flooded despite all their earlier willpower and their breath caught.

This moment felt suspended, the colors a little too bright. This moment was an ending, wasn't it?

Haneri turned, strode back to her chair, and picked up her lightweaving. Her eyes narrowed, her smile twisting cruel again. Arrogance etched itself back into her posture. Was that cruelty truly her? Or was it the armor she wore to survive? Or was it . . . something else?

She hated the Truthspoken, but she was playing their games right here and now, she'd just shown Rhys that. Games within games within games.

So why had she retreated from the court, and for whose purpose? Rhys had thought, of all the people they might see on this trip, that their visit to their mother would be the most predictable.

"I . . . thank you—"

She didn't look at them, only raised an arched brow.

They couldn't say they'd never come back. But, Adeius, they didn't know what to think. They didn't know what to feel just then.

So Rhys turned and, without another word, left the room.

# 16

# BECOMING ARIANNA

> *Do they change their personalities? I've heard they even change their genetics. How do they still know who they are?*
>
> — XINANDER, VID COMMENTATOR, IN A VIRAL VID ON THEIR FEED

In the end, the Change had taken less than an hour. Dressa had always been quick to Change. She hated the process, hated the discomfort and disorientation of forcing her cells into different patterns, of forcing her body into a different shape. It was a familiar shape, though, a familiar genome she'd inhabited before, even if those times were only in play.

Dressa sat in the center of her bed in rumpled, sweaty sheets. Her skin felt too tight, her body too thin. She could change that, in time, but not right away. Arianna couldn't suddenly go from being fairly thin to graciously curvy.

She didn't need a mirror to know exactly what she looked

like. She didn't need to speak to know how she'd sound. She'd made no mistakes.

Long, straight hair fell loosely over her shoulders, and she pulled it around in front of her, inspecting the texture. Well, and that was mostly the same as her own.

As hers *had been.*

This was her body now. This was her hair, her face, her voice.

She rolled her shoulders, and with the movement, began layering in the nuances, all the tells and clues of a lifetime of observation. If there was one role she would never have to prepare for, it was this one.

In the night-dimmed bedroom, she glanced toward the door that led into her bloodservant Pria's room. Pria, being trained but not actually Truthspoken, would be awhile in her own Change to Bettea, possibly most of the next day. Dressa resolved to check in on her as she could. It was stretching Pria's limits to Change that fully, but she'd assured Dressa she could do it. The Seritarchus himself had allowed a full Change where normally that would be forbidden to anyone but an Adeium-sanctioned Truthspoken.

Pria hadn't been happy about it, though. Neither of them had. And being Bettea—that might be interesting. Bettea's fluidity ran a spectrum of genders, but Pria preferred a butch presentation. Well. They'd manage, wouldn't they? Pria could change Bettea's presentation over time, just as Dressa could change Arianna's overall appearance, too. Maybe not as ideal for the actual Arianna and Bettea when they came back, but they weren't the ones who had to deal with this in the meantime, were they?

Dressa stretched, feeling every centimeter of her musculature and body. Different, yes. Not quite comfortable. But, workable.

She got out of bed and poked her head into Pria's room—

she was lying still in bed, breathing steadily, her face not yet Bettea's but also no longer her own.

Dressa gently closed the door.

It was just shy of midnight.

She pulled on a robe—one of her favorites that was now too roomy on her frame, dammit—and headed for the hidden door to the back corridors.

She slipped into the narrow space, touching a plate in the wall. Soft lights came on down the corridor, and she followed them toward the back door to Arianna's bedroom.

The thing that always wigged her out about being in a new and different body was the way she walked. Different bodies forced you to walk differently, and she knew Arianna's walk—she found herself falling into it, because it was the most natural walk this body could make. And that, more than anything, gave her a jarring sense of wrongness that took her several minutes to breathe through. It always passed for her as she got used to it. But that didn't make it any less unpleasant.

By the time she reached her target door, her walk felt more natural. It would be mostly her own by the end of the day. By the end of the week . . . would she even remember her original walk?

She would practice it, as she'd been trained. Once a day, for at least several minutes, she would be herself, with all her own tells and gestures. It would feel intensely weird over time, she knew that, but it was essential for keeping her own self and personality intact through a long role.

Arianna's bedroom smelled faintly of the cedar sculptures she liked to hang around the corners, a folk ritual that predated the Adeium. Dressa wondered if the Truthspeaker knew about Arianna's non-canon decorations—well, and if she knew, would she care? The Truthspeaker was remarkably chill as far as religious leaders went.

Dressa rewound that thought through her head. No, not

"chill." That wasn't something Arianna would think. "Remarkably relaxed." Better.

She walked slowly around the bedroom, touching everything. Most things were familiar. But there were a few pieces here and there—a new painting on the wall, a blue-green glass on the bedside table—she hadn't seen before. She touched everything, and in touching it, brought it into the universe she was building where it had always been hers.

Finished with the bedroom, she wandered out into the prep room and into the closet. She grimaced at the rows and rows of extremely well-tailored, expensive, and entirely bland clothes. Hardly any dresses, but then, Ari had never been one for dresses. That wasn't a huge problem. But if Dressa wouldn't go insane the next few weeks, she'd have to introduce just a little more flavor.

If anything was an excuse for more spice in one's life, it was nearly being killed by a Green Magicker, wasn't it?

She stopped in her perusal of the already-familiar clothing.

Adeius. Adeius, she still couldn't believe the magicker had been her father. And she'd razor-clawed his face.

Fucking hell.

With unsteady hands, she pulled a pajama set off the rack —an absolutely boring gray silk top and pants—and dropped her robe to pull it on. She didn't, not yet, linger on her body. That would come later, when it felt more fully her own.

But she did look up to the mirror between two racks of clothes. Her fingers slowed as she buttoned up the top.

That—that was her. That was her in the mirror, her.

Arianna.

Her.

She took a shaky breath, rolled her shoulders again, relayered what gestures and posture she'd lost in the last few minutes as her mind had wandered.

And . . . most dangerous of thoughts . . . what had Lesander thought of her? Of Arianna. Had she thought Arianna was beautiful? She certainly didn't have to for them to be married. Political marriage had nothing whatsoever to do with physical attraction. But it could be a bonus, couldn't it?

Her stomach churned. Yes, she was Arianna. But she wasn't her older sister. She wasn't the one Lesander was truly meant for. She had to remember that with all she had, because Lesander melted her.

Adeius, how was she supposed to survive these next few weeks?

Treat it like a flirtation only. She had to. Lesander was not and never could be hers. She had to keep the Javieri Prince at a respectable distance. Propriety only. *Only*.

She closed her eyes, turned away from the mirror.

Swore again and turned back, moving closer. What would Ari do in this situation? Ari would power through, because she had to. Because it was her duty.

Lesander was marrying the Truthspoken Heir, and right now, that was her. Legally, as Truthspoken, she could claim this name as hers until the Seritarchus ordered otherwise. Legally she, Arianna Rhialden, could court and even marry Lesander if it came to it.

She hoped, oh Adeius she hoped it didn't go that far.

And also, she hoped a little that it did.

She bit her lip—then quickly licked her lips to smooth them out again. That had been her gesture, not Arianna's.

Hers. Dressa's.

Ari might be able to immerse herself fully without losing herself, but Dressa had always struggled with immersion. Her father knew that, and yet he'd ordered this.

But then, what choice did he have? It was this or expose whatever weakness Ari had to the court.

Dressa. She was still Dressa inside her head. She was

Dressa being Arianna, not Arianna herself. That might be doable.

Dressa drifted back to the bedroom, pulling back the sheets. They were fresh, but Arianna's scents, her shampoos and lotions, lingered. Those would be Dressa's too.

Her throat tightened, and she closed her eyes against the tide that threatened to overwhelm her.

She could do this. She must.

There just . . . there just wasn't any other way.

She set her sights firmly on Lesander—and it wasn't fair to Lesander, she knew that. But there were casualties in any battle, weren't there? This battle was to save the Seritarcracy from scandal and ruin. From falling under the reality of how fragile it truly was.

Dressa slid between the sheets, plumped the pillows, and lay back.

"Lights off," she whispered in Arianna's voice. The room lights dimmed, leaving only the very faint night lights in the corners.

Truthspoken bedrooms didn't have windows. The threat of assassination was too great.

Her eyes adjusted to the dimness, and she could pick out patterns of flowers on the ceiling. Unfamiliar, and never seen from this vantage before. Ari had redecorated a few years ago. She'd wanted it all to be more stately, and it was.

Dressa stared up at the ceiling, her heart racing.

*Come back soon, Ari. I don't want your life—I want mine.*

## 17

# THE SPY

> *Truthspoken serve a purpose in our society that in other nations and in times past was traditionally occupied by the head of an intelligence service. Truthspoken gather information, deploy people who gather more information, and assess all of that information for whether it's in the best interest of the kingdom to act now or gather more.*
>
> — DR. LASHONDA KOJIMA, MILITARY HISTORIAN, IN *THE RISE OF THE NEW INTELLIGENCE SYSTEM*

Still reeling from the conversation with their mother, Rhys ignored the butler who led them back out of their mother's apartment and almost barreled into Vogret in the entry in their haste to get out the door.

"Hey, chickling, you okay?"

They'd blinked back the first tears and were trying hard not to cry. They were trying so fucking hard not to cry.

Vogret's arm wrapped around them, but they felt their whole body stiffening at the touch.

"Oh, Rhys," she said and let go, but she propelled them gently out into the corridor. Which was hardly better—there was so much more surveillance out there. But at least they weren't in their mother's apartment anymore.

Rhys pressed their lips tight. What could they even say? That their mother had just told them to leave and never return? That she thought that was a kindness?

That she'd shown any kindness at all.

Vogret hovered, brow furrowed, but didn't try to hug again. Rhys couldn't tolerate touch when they were really upset.

Rhys sniffed hard because she was just so kind, and so very different from the mother they'd left inside that apartment. And they were so, so confused.

They let out exactly three gasps before they inhaled sharply and forcefully pulled themself together. They didn't have their sisters' ability to will away tears with a thought, but dammit, they could pull themself together.

"How long are you staying, chickling? Do you want to come back to my place in the city, come have dinner with us tomorrow? Do you want to stay at my place? It's pretty full right now, but we have a good-sized couch."

Adelus, that did it.

Rhys sniffed hard again and swiped at their eyes. "I—I don't know how long. Not long. Maybe not that long."

They wanted that time, so wanted that time with Vogret and a normal, healthy family. But there was still the issue of social boundaries and lines being crossed between those who could live in the palace and those who guarded them. They didn't know how to sort anything out right now. And they were pretty sure staying at Vogret's place would cause some sort of trouble with their family at the palace—just too many people knew who Rhys was for it to go unnoticed and unremarked.

And if they stayed here—Rhys didn't honestly know if they could stay at this palace a moment longer than they had to.

"I'm leaving tomorrow. Morning, probably. Thanks, Vogret, but—"

She smiled, a wide and blazing smile. "Any time, chickling. I hope you have fun out there on your starship."

Rhys snorted, and some of the tension eased in their gut. "I will. I absolutely will have fun."

And they would. They hadn't just joined the Navy to separate themself from a world that only had dead ends for their career. They loved the routine, loved being out on the edges of known space. Absolutely loved researching the Kidaa—and that was important.

They'd visit "Arianna" tomorrow. They would, because they'd promised Dressa. But then they'd grab their duffel, board a shuttle, and catch a ship out-system. They'd been so eager to come home, but . . . was this home? All the edges of the corridors felt too precise, and they missed the cool, quiet lines of their ship. They missed the few friends they'd been gaining among the other junior officers on the *Storm*. They missed just being Rhys, not this multi-faceted pawn in half a dozen people's plans. People whom they loved and would play along with because they loved them.

Rhys did dare to hug Vogret one last time, bracing against the touch. But it was worth it. So worth it.

"Love you, Vog."

"Love you too, Rhys. Come back safe."

They swallowed hard again and nodded. And tried not to think of their mother's words drumming through their head: "Don't come back again. Don't look back at all."

How? How could they ever do that? And should they do that?

Rhys turned and started back toward the main corridor.

Their mother wasn't wrong about this world eating people up. Rhys kept trying not to see that, but it was true, wasn't it? This world of Truthspoken and secrets had devoured their mother, and Arianna, and was taking Dressa now. If Rhys kept coming back . . . would it take them, too?

They weren't Truthspoken and didn't want to be, but they were evaku trained. They did their absolute best to hide that fact from everyone they met—everyone but the actual Truthspoken—but that training wouldn't just go away. They didn't want to get entangled more than they were in the Truthspokens' lives. They had their own life now. It wasn't always roses, but they were happy enough.

They loved Dressa. They loved Dressa so much, and they loved Vogret, and Arianna, but could they stay a part of their lives in this place and not be drawn in? Dressa meant well, and yes, she'd asked for help, but Rhys's gut was knotting back up thinking about tomorrow. About how they'd have to act differently to her face, as she would act to theirs.

Why couldn't the universe just be simple for once? Just . . . simple.

A shadow fell over them and they stopped abruptly, looked up.

"Rhys."

The Seritarchus? No—Iata, the Seritarchus's bloodservant.

"Adeius, Iata, you scared me."

He was tall, his tan face angular and severe. Thick dark hair pulled into a knot, thick dark brows. Iata had always scared Rhys a little. The man was just . . . intense.

But Iata smiled, reached out and gripped Rhys's shoulder. "I wanted to see you before you left—I know you'll be leaving tomorrow."

Because of course he knew. Everyone in this whole residency knew much more than they reasonably should.

"Yeah," Rhys said, "yeah, tomorrow."

Iata nodded. "You warned Dressa about the Kidaa."

Rhys swallowed. Should they be surprised that Iata knew that as well? Maybe he'd been at the listening post for the gardens that night. "Yes." Was there any need to elaborate if Iata had already heard all they'd said?

"I just wanted you to know I'll pass that directly to the Seritarchus. Thank you, Rhys—your eye is good. If you have any more observations about the Kidaa while you are on duty, please send them to me here, and I'll give them directly to the Seritarchus. He is not as settled with them as the rest of the nobility." Iata pulled a thin plastic chip from his jacket pocket and held it out.

Rhys took it gingerly, glancing at the nearly transparent circuit pattern. Did Iata want Rhys to spy on the Kidaa? On the military's handling of the Kidaa? And was it spying if the order came from the Seritarchus himself?

Or did it come from Iata?

Iata pulled out another plastic chip, this one bearing the seal of the Seritarcracy. Iata would absolutely not use that without it being a legitimate use—it could only be activated by the Seritarchus's genetics, voiceprint, and personal code, and that verification would only last for two hours. Rhys had played games with these credential chips with Dressa and Arianna—they knew their limitations.

Iata handed it over. "This is calibrated for the seal to disappear within the hour, but if you are ever questioned, it will activate again at your touch and saying your full name."

Well, Rhys didn't know it could do that. They carefully took it as well, folding it into their hand before they slipped it and the other into their jacket pocket.

They wanted to protest, but what could they say? Could they possibly say no, Iata, please tell the Seritarchus I don't want to spy for him?

They were too late. They were already too late to unentangle themself from this palace and its webs. If the Seritarchus couldn't find a use for them here, he'd find a use for them elsewhere. They did have the training. Their mother wasn't wrong there, either—they weren't Truthspoken, but they were halfway there. An asset not to be ignored.

But Rhys was finding out things others didn't know about the Kidaa, and they needed someone to tell them to. Their captain wouldn't listen. Iata's first chip would likely have protocols to get a message to the Seritarchus at minimal risk to Rhys's—or the Seritarchus's—involvement being discovered. The Seritarchus didn't work any other way.

This was what Rhys had wanted, wasn't it? To get their information heard? To get it into the hands of someone who'd know how to use it?

But at what cost? At what cost to their personal autonomy? The chips felt like fire in their jacket pocket.

Iata patted them on the shoulder, his gaze steady but grim. He knew what he and the Seritarchus were asking of Rhys. Rhys thought they even saw sadness there.

They swallowed hard, shaken to their core.

"How's the tour going?" Iata asked. "Border patrol all it's cracked up to be?"

Rhys's smile was crooked. Not a smile, really. Because there was surveillance everywhere here. Because this conversation could be made public record if the Seritarchus wanted it—in Rhys's favor or against it. And they didn't think for a moment that the ties of family would ever stop Homaj Rhialden from getting what he wanted.

Would it stop at the Kidaa? Or would the weight these chips carried follow Rhys forever? The need for more and more information. Oh hey, Rhys, can you go here for me? Oh hey, Rhys, can you do this for me?

"Boring enough. But I like the company, and the places we see, and the duty. It suits me."

"Good, that's good." Iata smiled again, which also wasn't really a smile.

He moved on. "Keep us posted."

## 18

# THE CELL

> *The Adeium mandates that Truthspoken keep ever-constant watch and control over their kingdom, as Adeius does themself. Some interpretations—albeit, highly disputed—even say that Adeius can only observe and experience the kingdom through the Truthspoken, and that's why we must be everywhere and everyone. But if that was true, what flawed perspectives would we give our god?*
>
> — HOMAJ RHIALDEN, SERITARCHUS IX IN A PRIVATE LETTER, NEVER SENT; PUBLISHED IN *THE CHANGE DIALOGUES*

Homaj Rhialden, in the persona of the Green Magicker Sodan Iseban, squinted up as the dark cell flooded with light. This cell, in the basement headquarters of the Palace Guard, was supposed to be lit, but the guards had turned the lights off when they'd thrown him in, plunging him into darkness for the last . . . hour? He wasn't sure.

He uncurled from the cell's single hard bench and planted his slippered feet gingerly on the concrete floor, glaring at that crack of light for whatever would come through next. He'd withstood everything they'd thrown at him so far, and he was ready to go again, damn them. He'd already confessed, but he'd already confessed when the beating had happened the first time.

He'd given Jalava, the Commander of the Palace Guard and one of the very few people who knew who he was right now, instructions not to interfere with their juniors' actions. Sodan Iseban absolutely had to be seen as the person who'd made the Truthspoken Heir as ill as she'd been.

Jalava hadn't obeyed him during the interrogation—they'd tamped down their juniors' enthusiasm, and they'd forbidden the use of slurs against a magicker. Well, and he was glad for that last.

But the guards who'd taken him to the cell hadn't been as discerning.

Two maroon-uniformed members of the Palace Guard hurried in now, not the ones who'd worked him over in the corridor earlier, but they still held their stun batons at the ready.

Sodan flinched back before holding steady, sneering at the guards.

One of them shouted, "Don't move, Magicker!"

He didn't, but the guard touched his shoulder with the baton anyway. He stiffened, his whole body clenching up with the shock. And then shuddered when the baton withdrew.

"None of that," a calm voice said from the open doorway, and Sodan looked up.

He'd given his bloodservant, Iata, instructions to come get him a few hours after giving himself over to interrogation. Iata's excuse would be the Seritarchus also wanted to see the magicker who'd attacked his Heir.

But he didn't think it had been a few hours yet, and the compact woman dominating the doorway wasn't Iata.

"Truthspeaker," he slurred through a swollen lip.

The cell's lights finally came on—Adeius, he was sick of the darkness, but did they have to be so bright?

Truthspeaker Ceorre Gatri stood with her hands clasped firmly in front of her, regarding him with an expression of steel. Her gray hair framed her dark brown face like a halo. She didn't wear her red and violet robes of the Adeium but instead a cream linen pantsuit. She wore the sigil of her office, though, a heavy pendant inlaid with diamond stars that made up the Kingdom of Valoris. And there was no one in the palace, on all of Valon, who didn't know who she was.

"Get them up," she said. "Without abuse, please."

"Why are you here?" Sodan spat, because a radical magicker would be expected to hate her. "Are you here to try to convert me? You can't. You can't force a magicker to bow to a false—"

"No!" Ceorre said sharply as the stun batons moved in again. The guards hesitated but backed off.

Ceorre knew his tells. It was her job, as the Truthspeaker of the Adeium and counterbalance to the Truthspoken. He'd buried himself in this role, but the edges had leaked sometime after they'd thrown him in this cell, and he'd had to find a way to smooth out the worst of the beating without making it look like his injuries had actually healed. Verisimilitude.

But then, Ceorre would have only seen the recordings of the interrogation, wouldn't she, not what had come after. Or maybe she'd only heard reports of the captured magicker. And still she'd known who he was and come.

"I'm not going to convert you, Ser Sodan," she said coolly. "You're remanded to my custody. The Adeium has questions for you."

He stood, then sat again just as quickly as stun batons

closed in. He held up his hands. "I gave my confession to the guards. They said I'll be transferred to a prison ship. We agreed. You can't take me to the Adeium, they agreed I'll be transferred to a ship—"

"And you will be. The Adeium is not in the habit of interfering with the Palace Guard. I have questions only, no more. You gain nothing by fighting me on this and lose nothing by coming with me."

"I could kill you where you stand," he hissed.

He saw fury flash in her eyes and knew—and knew he'd miscalculated. He read the signs now, so carefully concealed because she was as expert at the art of evaku as he was. She wasn't here to get him out. Oh, hell. She was here to chew him out.

"Could you, Magicker? Because I've never known a Green Magicker who could do that."

That was a lie. They both knew that was a lie.

And there it was, wasn't it? That was the source of her fury, and she wasn't wrong to be upset. He'd spent much of his time as Seritarchus trying to rebuild the relationship between the Seritarcracy and the Green Magickers, to ease the prejudice against magickers and boost public perceptions. Anyone, absolutely anyone, could suddenly manifest the ability to use Green Magics, and Green Magickers could see through all lies, among other abilities. People generally feared that kind of power. They ostracized anyone who developed Green Magics even in their own families, and it had a tendency to run in families once manifested, which brought even more fear. With social pressure on the side of that fear, the cycle of prejudice continued.

He'd made good progress in breaking that cycle, but it would be set back by what had happened tonight. But he'd had no other choice but to see this through. He'd repair what he could, do what he could, he would fix this. But tonight, he'd truly had no other choice.

"Yes, I could." But his protest sounded hollow, and the guards didn't even flinch. He held her gaze, then looked away. "But I'll come with you, if you get me to a planet-side prison, not a ship. Or a mining ship. I could serve on a mining ship, I'm good for that. I'm a decent mechanic. That's my price. I'll give you what you want, if you give me what I want. A mechanic on a ship."

Ceorre's brows rose, and she took a moment just to regard him. Her eyes traveled to his right eye, nearly swollen shut, and his split lip. To the blood staining his arm under the short sleeves of the red prison shirt. To all the bruises she could not possibly see but would be imagining.

He stared back with the force of Sodan Iseban. With the force of Homaj Rhialden.

"Oh, Magicker," she said, "you'll offer me your cooperation because I *can* interfere with the Guard, if I so choose. If I say you're too unstable, you won't get to any ship at all. You won't leave the palace. Are you that unstable, Ser Sodan? Or did you just get a little carried away tonight, attacking the Truthspoken Heir?"

He narrowed his eyes, and that wasn't a part of the act. Her words were a threat—not just to Sodan Iseban, but to Homaj Rhialden. As Truthspeaker, she oversaw the Truthspoken. She had the authority of the Adeium to revoke a Truthspoken ruler's mandate if she determined them unfit or dangerous to the kingdom. But that had only been done once before, more than a century ago, when a Melesorie was found to have grossly abused their Truthspoken abilities.

What he'd done tonight, he'd done to protect his kingdom.

The guards, of course, only picked up on the sarcasm. He tensed back as a stun baton came dangerously near again.

The guards weren't just brutes, they were afraid of him. Afraid of his magics.

Adeius. This whole night was a mess. Ceorre wasn't wrong to be furious.

"I'll come with you," he said, as if it was his decision.

Ceorre's lips twitched. It wasn't a smile.

The guards hastily pulled his hands behind his back and cuffed his wrists with stun cuffs. It was a barely adequate measure against a magicker of his supposed rank—the guards could only stop him after the fact if he decided to risk his soul and sanity to kill. Not that he could, and not that he had any magics at all, but they didn't know that. The cuffs at least made them feel better.

He suffered the cuffs with dignity.

As he'd suffered the cell with dignity. If he had been a magicker of the rank marked on his cheek seal, the walls of the cell wouldn't have held him. They were thick plastic, difficult for even a high-ranking magicker to manipulate, and the best option for holding a magicker at all. But, not impervious to Green Magics. There was no material anywhere that didn't have its roots in nature.

Ceorre motioned out the door, and the guards marched him out of the cell, stun batons on each side and hands on the cuff triggers.

She started toward the stairs that led up to the main floor of the headquarters, but then glanced at him again, at his obvious bruises, and changed direction.

His stomach tightened. He knew where they were going—Commander Jalava's office. Ceorre could ruin everything he'd done here tonight, did she know that?

Of course she knew that.

Down the corridor, up a different flight of stairs, down another short corridor. At Jalava's office, Ceorre pressed her hand to the door plate and said, "It's Ceorre."

After a short hesitation, long enough for Jalava inside to swear, the door clicked and opened.

Ceorre turned to the guards holding him. "Leave us. Stay outside."

They both looked in for their commander's approval, and Jalava, their eyes on Sodan's swollen eye, nodded. Their own face, pale under cropped dark hair, was turning a dark red.

Ceorre pulled Sodan inside, not gently, and shut the door.

## 19

## CONSEQUENCES

> *They fear us because they think we hold their secrets captive, but we fear them because they hold our lives in their hands. If they could just let go, they'd see we're not as interested as they think in destroying them.*
>
> — FIRST MAGICKER MARIYIT BRODEN IN AN ADDRESS TO THE GENERAL ASSEMBLY

"Soundproof the room," Ceorre snapped.

Commander Jalava went back to their desk and hit several toggles set into the surface. The air tightened with the layers of security that had just been put into place. The office had been secure before, but now it was a vault.

Ceorre still gripped Homaj's arm, but she didn't shove him down into a chair with the violence she might have if he was actually the magicker Sodan Iseban. Instead, she dragged over one of the two chairs facing Jalava's desk and pressed him down. He didn't protest, but carefully shook off her hand on his arm.

The Truthspeaker backed away, hands up, face pinched. She didn't take the other chair but opted to pace instead.

"Seritarchus, they beat you," Jalava said. "I will cashier their asses so fast—"

"I told you not to interfere," Homaj said. "Which you didn't do, by the way. You know I'll heal myself. I suppressed the pain. This was necessary."

He could fairly sense Ceorre boiling as she paced.

"So did you think punishing yourself would make up for punishing the whole damn kingdom?"

He forced his tone to remain calm. Truthspeaker or not, she was out of line. She didn't know all of it. There hadn't been time, and it had been his decision. It was always, in the end, his decision. "I'm saving my kingdom, Ceorre."

She brushed his answer aside. "You—when you made your bid to rule, when you were still young, you had a magicker verify your sincerity, not the Truthspeaker. That upset a lot of people, but you know what, you changed how we view Green Magickers. You've spent your rule bringing them up to parity in society, and we have a ways to go yet, but prejudice and hate crimes against the magickers are down by far.

"But you know what happened tonight after you performed your little stunt in the ballroom? A kid in the city was brought into protective custody because her family thought she might be a magicker and was threatening to beat her. Another magicker, sealed and everything, was attacked in the Financial District. And that was just in the last hour, Homaj. What these guards did to you now—" She stopped, because she was trembling. Because she was having trouble getting out words. "What the *fuck* were you thinking?"

Homaj glanced at Jalava, whose lips were pressed so tight as to be invisible. Jalava was shaking their head, just shaking their head.

Homaj narrowed his eyes. "I'm saving my kingdom. The

Green Magickers will recover—I talked to the First Magicker before I acted. We agreed to look at the laws restricting magicker children from attending ordinary schools."

"The—schools—" Ceorre spluttered. "Homaj, you bargained with children? Where the hell did you go? Where did you, the idealistic Homaj who was absolutely going to use his power for good go, because I don't think I've seen him for a while now—"

"Don't play that card with me, Ceorre. I don't act without purpose. I never act without purpose."

"Yes, but when you act, you should actually think about those who are the most vulnerable!"

He glared up at her. "Arianna's sick. It's the Bruising Sleep."

Ceorre rocked back.

Jalava stiffened.

He had been intending to tell them both—Ceorre, because she'd need to know about Dressa's role for the next few months, and Jalava because they had to know what was happening in order to best protect the Truthspoken. But he'd been wanting to tell them in his own time, in the right time. This absolutely wasn't that time.

His shoulders twitched with the need to move, but the cuffs restrained his hands. Jalava cursed and came around behind him, waving a key fob over the cuffs. They clicked and opened.

Ceorre's lips thinned. "The Bruising Sleep." Oh yes, she'd be calculating the damage to the Seritarcracy if that got out. She'd be weighing it against his actions.

And she wasn't wrong that he'd made some colossal mistakes tonight.

"I didn't know until today," he said, rubbing his wrists. "Even then, I only suspected, and I was only intending to put some doubt in people's minds by approaching her as a magicker, I wasn't expecting her to actually faint. She's —Arianna."

Ceorre turned, massaging her temples with vigor. "And then you had to see the whole damn thing through."

He opened his hands, a silent agreement.

"You could have just let this magicker escape."

"Could I? Or would that have inflamed the paranoia even more? How many magickers would be attacked if people thought a rogue magicker, one known to have attacked the Truthspoken Heir, was free?"

He hadn't been paying enough attention these last weeks. His focus had been on the reports coming in about bizarre attacks happening on some of the border worlds—attacks which people were blaming on the Kidaa, though that was, on the surface at least, ludicrous. He was more inclined to think those attacks were a campaign from one of the high houses either against another high house or to destabilize some portion of the government, not actually the Kidaa showing violence for the first time in two centuries. But he couldn't rule anything out, and he'd been requesting and managing information all across his network.

He hadn't known his Heir was sick until that night. He'd missed all the signs. He'd been giving her more responsibilities leading up to the engagement and would have continued to give her more. He'd thought she could handle them—and no, that wasn't fair. She could handle them. But her ability to handle was being curtailed by the illness. Their kingdom couldn't afford such a gap in control just now.

"The Bruising Sleep," Jalava said, sitting down heavily in their chair. "That's the fifth case we know or suspect among the nobility this month. And the Truthspoken Heir. We can't keep this quiet much longer, Homaj."

"So what now?" Ceorre asked. "I'm assuming she'll need treatment. And if you're playing this out with the magicker, then—ah. You'll have her bloodservant fill in for her."

"No, I won't ask that of Bettea—faer sense of faer gender is too strong to fit into Arianna for any length of time. Dressa, then, is the only other option. I've already set that in motion."

Ceorre finally pulled out the other chair and sat down with a sigh. "Months of having to be her sister will break her. That is no good option."

"I don't agree. Dressa's well-trained. And she knows what's at stake."

"Training doesn't—"

"Doesn't what?" he asked flatly.

"Doesn't negate abuse, Homaj." She held his gaze, tight and focused. Her eyes flicked pointedly to his own injuries again.

His jaw tightened. "We're Truthspoken. You're the Truthspeaker. This is how it's done. We can't have Arianna disappear from court; we will lose the kingdom. We are so close to losing it now. The Delors and the Javieris aren't being subtle about their moving in on our power."

Ceorre looked like she wanted to say more, but she just shook her head. She looked up to study the pictures Jalava had hung on the wall across from their desk. Flat images they'd taken of their three children.

Homaj's throat closed. Yes—yes, he absolutely knew the system was rotten. He knew that. His life was a testament to that. But it was the system they had. He was changing what he could, but he could only steer the ship, maybe make a few retrofits. He couldn't tear the whole ship apart and rebuild it while it was in motion. And it wasn't all bad. Every system had both good points and flaws.

"Dressa will need help, Ceorre. Lots of help."

Ceorre sighed again, nodded. "No, I won't deny her that. And when it does, inevitably, come out that the Bruising Sleep is an epidemic among the nobility as well, this stunt as a magicker will link Green Magics with the Bruising Sleep in people's minds. You know that, don't you?"

He'd figured that out in the dark of the cell, along with as many paths to repairing it as he could think of. He wasn't unaware of his flaws, but he didn't know what else to do. He'd had an intense argument with his bloodservant, Iata, when Arianna had been brought to his study—they'd both, in the end, concluded that neither had a better idea than to play this all out. The damage had already been done at the ball.

He should never have thought to use a magicker's guise to approach her in the first place. But, well—well, that had had another purpose he wasn't going to discuss here.

"I'll set a meeting with the First Magicker tomorrow," Ceorre said. "The Adeium will absolutely unite with the magickers on this—that the actions of this one magicker were rogue and not indicative of all magickers. I suggest you release an official statement that the Seritarcracy stands with the magickers at your earliest, and that you won't tolerate hate for the magickers."

He nodded. "Yes. I agree." He glanced down at the dried blood on his arm. He was blocking the pain, but he could still feel it like a distant itch. He looked up at Jalava.

"We'll turn me over to the magickers and their justice. That will be better, I think, than parading me around the palace like this." He grimaced. "The prejudice against the magickers isn't as gone as I'd hoped. From there—"

"From there, ask the magickers," Ceorre said. "You said you talked to the First Magicker, but that was before the ball, wasn't it?"

He sighed. "Yes. I will. This decision—this might not be a popular one with the people. To hand me—to hand Sodan Iseban—over."

"You're also the Seritarchus, and that's your call, not theirs," Ceorre said, some of her steel coming back. "And you'll need to run damage control there as well. But it's a step to repairing the damage. Don't give up what you've built because you're running scared."

She understood. She knew he'd done what he'd done that night to protect not just his kingdom, but his daughter.

And she knew he couldn't fully pull himself into the Seritarchus just now, not while they still sat in the Guard headquarters, him still in prison clothes and the pain of a beating a distant throb on his awareness. He'd have to fall back into Sodan Iseban's persona soon.

At least the magickers, being repelled by violence, wouldn't attack him. And the more powerful among them would know who he was, or at least that he was Truthspoken, on sight—not that they would tell the others. That part of his long-standing agreement with the magickers was solid, if he hadn't completely botched it that night. They'd never out him, but they certainly wouldn't be happy to see him.

It would be a long night—he glanced at Jalava's wall display and corrected himself to long morning—full of arguments, full of apologies and promises. But he owed them that. Adeius, he owed the magickers much for what had happened at the ball, and after. He did not look forward to this particular conversation with the First Magicker.

He was so tired, and not even a Truthspoken's ability to heal themself could wash away the fatigue of a long night. He ran a hand through his hair, grimaced as it snagged on dried blood.

Jalava saw it. "Ser Seritarchus, that will not happen again. Not with my people, not ever, not to anyone. Especially not a magicker."

He'd been expecting it—well, at least some of it. The guards who hadn't been able to stop the magicker's attack on the Heir had taken it out on their prisoner. The prisoner had confessed, had given a twisted manifesto. He had done his best, his absolute best, to separate himself as Sodan Iseban from the rest of the magickers in public record. But that didn't make any of this right.

Homaj nodded to Jalava. “See that it doesn’t.” He stood, holding his hands behind him again.

“I don’t think that’s necessary,” Jalava protested.

“You’ve been around me far too long to think I can afford to take anything for granted.”

Jalava waved their concession and snapped the cuffs back into place. The night hadn’t been kind to them, either—their eyes were bloodshot, their shadows darker than usual. “I should take you to the magickers personally.”

Homaj weighed that, then nodded. It was both protection and a bridge.

Ceorre stood, too. “Send Dressa to me—not right away, I think, but maybe in a week. We will weather this, Homaj. However we must, we will.”

He nodded. Then let Homaj fade as he pulled back the magicker Sodan Iseban.

# 20

# THE CHANGE

> *To Change is to embrace a possibility of a person you could be. We are none of us just one person.*
>
> — ARIANNA RHIALDEN, MELESORIE X IN *THE CHANGE DIALOGUES*

They were four days out from Valon, one day yet to go until they broke out of Below Space over Hestia. The hum of the trade ship's engines was now a permanent soundtrack in Ari's bones. Did Bettea feel it, too? She didn't think so.

Ari gripped the post of the double bunk and stared at herself in the holographic mirror. Bettea, sitting on the bunk, studied her with faer head tilted to one side. Ari didn't have to be Truthspoken to know Bettea's expression wasn't good.

Her Change wasn't enough. It was hardly enough. It had taken her two days of exhausted tries at the Change trance to get just enough concentration to move her eyes slightly farther apart, to thin the shape of her lips. Hair was another day—

she'd grown her brows thicker, grown more fine dark hair on her upper lip.

And then, exhausted from those Changes, her body had mostly refused to do more. She'd nearly passed out trying to give herself another few centimeters of height—she hadn't gained a single millimeter. She'd given up on any modifications to her body shape—the effort and energy it had taken to attempt the Changes had thinned her too much, anyway. She hadn't been able to Change her skin color more than a few degrees in either direction and had settled on slightly paler, mostly because she was too exhausted to do more. She'd nudged the brown of her eyes a few shades lighter, too. She hadn't been able to Change the color itself.

"All right," Bettea said slowly, "we can work with this."

"How?" Ari gasped. "Seriously, how?" She waved at herself in the mirror. She was dressed in a loose robe Bettea had packed, rumpled from two days of alternating trying for trance and sleep. She hadn't showered in three days and badly needed it.

"I'm a mess. I look Rhialden. I don't even look that far off from how I did at court."

Bettea ran faer hands through faer short hair. "Well, we already agreed that would be best. You'll be from a minor branch of the Rhialden line."

Ari stabbed a finger at herself in the mirror. "This doesn't look minor. This looks like me, but . . . off. I'm a living vid filter."

Bettea reached for her hair. "We haven't done this yet."

Ari fought the urge to swat faer hand away. Hair wouldn't change her base appearance.

"And we can use cosmetics. That will do much."

"I've never needed cosmetics."

Bettea arched a brow. "Yes, you've never needed, but you do now." Fae grabbed faer hair kit from the bed. "We'll do it in the bathroom. I don't want to be cleaning hair from the bed."

Ari kept a hand on the wall as she followed Bettea to the ship's single bathroom. It wasn't as tiny as it might be and even had a small tub—a decadent luxury for a trader. Ari sat on the lip of the tub, away from the mirror hanging over the sink, and closed her eyes.

Bettea combed faer hands through her hair, feeling out the lines, then stopped.

"What gender?" fae asked.

Ari let out a soft breath. She'd been heading for an androgynous presentation from the start of all this—first because it was the quickest way to the most effective change in her appearance, and then . . . well, Ari liked it.

She gripped Bettea's arm, turning to stand up again and look in the mirror. Yes, she had thickened her brows, and grown back the hair on her upper lip. In all her years of creating personas, feeling out what would be best for each circumstance, that had felt right. The few Changes she'd made to the shape of her face didn't lend to either femininity or masculinity. She was still short, and presenting farther masc with her body type and face shape would make her look younger than she was. Was that desirable in this circumstance? She might be able to state her age as fifteen or sixteen. That would certainly distance herself from Arianna Rhialden.

But she had no idea how long she'd inhabit this new persona, and she didn't want to settle into a gender presentation that wasn't hers. She wasn't particularly tied to any gender—she'd spent a summer a few years ago as a boy to see if that was who she was, and had found out it wasn't, but it wasn't disagreeable to her, either. She was mostly agender, but with a light flavor of female, though she'd never been particularly femme like Dressa. That makeup at the engagement ball—no. She could not do something like that in the long-term.

A comfortable androgyny felt good, though. She could do that.

Reading her mood, Bettea combed through her choppy hair a few more times, then pulled out the clippers and began to cut.

At the end, Ari ran her hands over the fresh fine stubble of her undercut, a smile tugging up her lips.

Adeius. It really was good to be free of Arianna's long hair.

Another half hour of gagging on chemical smells and her hair was a rich, dark blue with tones of teal and violet. Even a minor Rhialden would have an excellent stylist.

Ari sat back on the bunk while Bettea pulled out clothes from the bags fae'd packed. Ari's closet had always been stocked with clothing from many different styles, presentations, and body types. Bettea would have to alter some of what fae had brought, but that was doable.

A flowy midnight blue jumpsuit. A casual brown and green cardigan. A white silk dress shirt, black trousers, teal tunic vest. A deep red full skirt with a tight-fitting, militaristic jacket.

Eh—no. She liked the jacket, but not the skirt. Ari skimmed into the midnight jumpsuit.

They both frowned at her reflection in the mirror again. Holding onto the bunk post to steady herself, she tried shifting her body language to something more open, less flowing. She was still elegant but in an edgier way, not the carefully controlled lines she cut as the Heir. But Adeius, even with the haircut and color, she still looked too obviously Rhialden. She looked like she could be her own sibling, or close cousin. This new persona was supposed to be from a more distant family branch. She'd get far too many close looks, too many questions. People would wonder why they hadn't seen her before, because anyone who looked that Rhialden and wasn't Truthspoken would be remarked upon.

"Piercings," Bettea said. And fae was right, but Ari sighed. She'd always hated when her personas required piercings. They hurt up front and would only be healed over later. And she had to make a conscious effort not to accidentally heal them over in her own daily self-heals—though that wouldn't be a problem this time. She couldn't heal herself at all just now.

Bettea got out another kit and began prepping local anesthetics and piercing instruments. Two rings on her right brow, a septum ring, large hoops in her already-pierced ears, and a waterfall of studs up one side. Fae finished with a small sparrow tattoo beside her right eye shifting holographic blues and greens.

Ari stared again at her reflection through the sting of the anesthetic wearing off.

Bettea unpacked a medical booster and waggled it in the air. "It's all going to swell, and you can't heal it."

Ari sighed as fae got to work—she wouldn't need it if she could still Change with any reliability.

"She and her pronouns," Ari said. "I'll keep that. But list my gender as agender." Which was true enough, though not many people knew that.

Truthspoken were generally seen as nonbinary unless they said otherwise—her father was a fluidity of mostly male but a full spectrum of presentations, and she'd gone through a number of presentations herself as Arianna before she'd settled on her controlled slightly femme a few years ago. She hadn't changed it since, wanting to build a picture of constancy as part of her public image. Her father had said she should build more variation into her public persona, for her own sake, but that rigidity of presentation was serving her well now. Going off-brand was a lot easier.

She fingered the row of rings and studs up her ear. They didn't signal a particular gender so much as . . . not the rigidly controlled picture of sedate power she usually projected. Few people at court had facial piercings beyond a few ear and nose piercings.

"Have you decided on a name?" Bettea asked, coming around to run the med booster on her tattoo.

Ari had been sifting through several names in the long hours of trying to push her trance. Reciting through them, trying out combinations and variations, had fallen into a trancelike rhythm of its own.

She ran through them again now, matching them to the person she saw in the mirror. Names had different personalities attached all on their own. A name could make her bolder, or quieter, or more audacious.

"Imorie," she finally said, tasting the name. It hadn't been her first choice. But it fit the sleek punk vibe she was putting off. Imorie wasn't quiet, but wasn't the first to take a risk, either. She was fierce, but cautious. "Imorie Rhialden méron Quevedo."

Bettea paused to look at her again. Fae slowly nodded.

"And you?" Ari asked. "What about your name?"

"Jis Ameer," Bettea said without hesitation.

Ari snorted. "That was quick."

Bettea shrugged. Fae had also made more Changes to faer appearance since they'd left, in between shifts in the cockpit to make sure all was well with the ship on autopilot. Fae had sharpened the lines on faer face, softened faer lips, put on another thirty pounds. Faer hair was a light gold now, not brown, faer eyes the deepest burgundy. It was more of a Change than Ari had expected or thought fae capable of as a bloodservant. But then, it had been managed in many smaller bursts, so maybe that wasn't so surprising. And the stakes were higher. This wasn't just a few days or a weeklong mission. This was . . . this could be months of the deepest sort of cover.

Ari tilted her head, watching the mirror. Imorie Quevedo. Or Rhialden, depending on who she was talking to. She could legally use both names.

She leaned back more heavily against the bunk post as Bettea finished with the med booster and clicked it off. She'd had enough rest for this short burst of energy, but her body was weighing her down again. The air was weighing her down. She'd need to lie down again soon, and she hated that.

She enjoyed the process of creating a persona, she always had, but knowing she would have to be this person for months sat like a lump in her throat. She could do it, she absolutely could do it, but . . .

They'd done their best, and yes, the piercings pushed her in a different direction than the conservative royals and nobles usually showed at court, but she still looked Rhialden. She could cover some of that with cosmetics, but—she didn't want that. It suddenly felt important that she not have yet another mask on top of this person she was going to become.

She wasn't going to just play a role for a week or two at most. For the next month at least, she would be Imorie Rhialden.

She was trying to still believe whatever treatment she got on Hestia would heal her quickly, but she was just so tired. And recovering within weeks was a shrinking hope. It had already been the better part of a week since she'd left Valon.

If she looked Rhialden and couldn't Change that anymore, she'd just have to lean into being that minor, contract Rhialden—make it a quirk, not a feature. Make it blatant, make it tacky.

She swallowed.

Bettea, packing away faer tools, raised a brow. "Nervous?"

Ari huffed. "Hardly." She pressed her lips tight, still studying her reflection. "I want to be at court. I should be at court."

But she didn't want to be tending to her engagement with Lesander. And . . . was it horrible, even with how she was feeling, that the thought of not having to juggle all the weights of the kingdom for a few weeks or months made her feel almost giddy? She'd been trying to identify that sensation for the last few days. That sensation of not having things to do. Immediate and dire expectations to meet.

She rubbed at her chest. Her breaths were coming short again—she definitely needed to lie back down. But—

"Is it horrible that this feels . . . I don't know . . ."

"Like coming out of a dark room? Like being able to breathe?"

Ari turned to Bettea and looked at faer, really looked. Bettea's posture now fit faer new persona as personal servant to Imorie on this trip. A little less regal, a little less rigid than faer demeanor as a bloodservant.

Bettea was just always there. Ari hadn't thought—well, she hadn't stopped to think, as her own schedule was increasing, as her life was changing, how that might affect her bloodservant. Because Bettea would always be there. Wouldn't fae?

Bettea stood, gripped her hands. "I'm fine, Ari. But I needed this, too." Fae hesitated, then shifted faer weight and said, "Maybe we shouldn't play this out like a mission. Maybe we should play it like what comes after a mission. Like this is normal. I really want, for a few weeks at least, to know what that's like."

Ari swallowed. Normal. Normal for her, as Truthspoken, was being other people. Was tending to the dire needs of the kingdom. Was always, always being aware of every word she spoke and gesture she made so that she and the people around her were in a dance she was leading. She knew what categoric states of normal were for a lot of different types of people, but . . . could she even have a normal outside of being the Heir? Was that possible for her?

Could she pretend it was possible, for a time?

Bettea kissed her forehead. Fae was her bloodservant, yes, but also her friend. "Sleep. Right now, you need sleep. We'll plan out the rest tomorrow, right?"

Ari nodded and let Bettea help her back into the bunk.

She still smelled faintly of the hair dye, of antiseptic.

Normal. Could she possibly find a different normal in the weeks ahead? And what if normal, for her, meant being sick?

She could treat the Bruising Sleep, but it wasn't curable. What if normal came with never being able to Change without exhaustive effort? What if normal meant she'd never be the Heir again?

She was exhausted, but it was a long time before sleep came, lulling her with the slow, persistent hum of the ship's engines.

# 21

# THE CHOICE

*Truthspoken are the vessels of governance that Adeius uses to direct the kingdom, and so some would argue are beyond such common things as having autonomy over their own lives.*

— DR. KIRAN STRIGEN IN "THOUGHTS ON THE NATURE OF TRUTHSPOKEN PSYCHOLOGY"

Dressa set down a tube of violet lipstick and surveyed herself in the mirror.

Smoky eyes with rhinestones beside them. Sharpened angles. Those violet lips.

She smirked—which wasn't like Arianna at all, so she changed her expression to a more sedate smugness. With the heavier makeup, deliberate and artistic, it made her look edgy and mysterious. She was rocking that rock star vibe she'd given her sister the night before, the night of her collapse.

Let that night be known as Arianna's mark of a new era—Truthspoken did that now and then, pairing changes in their appearance or demeanor to major events to establish an acceptable reason other than that they just wanted the hell to change.

She'd suffocate if she had to wear Arianna's usual natural lip gloss only. If she couldn't let out her own personality through the cracks.

She ran a hand through her long black hair—she hadn't done it yet, but she planned to dye it red at the tips.

Okay, yes. She could do rock star Arianna much more than fussy, uptight, I'm-the-Heir Arianna. Maybe this wouldn't be so bad. She'd slowly gain back her own comfortable weight the next week or so, and people wouldn't bat an eye. They'd see it as part of this new and improved version of Arianna. It would play well in the vids, too, and public opinions—this version of Arianna could stand against Lesander's fashion model poise and not be outshone.

She could stand in a way that drew the eye through presence, not domination and control.

Dressa suppressed a shiver as she studied her face, turning her head from side to side.

She was Arianna. And what kind of Arianna would she be? She couldn't stray too far, but she'd thought it through while she'd been making up her face. She had a lot more room to play in after a public event like that than she'd thought the night before.

She glanced toward the bedroom. Her bloodservant, Pria, hadn't come in yet through the back passages from Dressa's—Dressa's *old*—apartment. She'd still be in her own Change trance, then, and likely days after orienting herself to a full Change, which she'd never done before. Pria was way past the bounds of what she'd been trained for in making a full and exact Change to be Bettea. Dressa wanted her bloodservant's company, her quiet input, but for now, Dressa was on her own.

There was a soft knock on her prep room door—not from the bedroom but the hallway.

Dressa froze. She hadn't yet shown herself to anyone, not even the servants of Arianna's household.

She swallowed her rising panic, checked herself again in the mirror. Adjusted the small details of her posture.

Arianna. She was Arianna. And she was Truthspoken—she could handle this. She knew she could.

She rose smoothly, and so did her panic.

She would fail. She would make some fatal and obvious error, she would laugh at the wrong moment, at the wrong joke—Adeius, she would laugh at all—she would come up to someone Ari knew, and she would slight them by not even knowing their name. She would give herself away by her walk, by the different rhythm of her speech, she would—

Dressa closed her eyes and said, "Enter."

The handle turned, but then stopped. Rattled.

Adeius, that damned genetic lock. Dressa strode to the door, smoothed out her expression, and pulled it open.

One of Arianna's staff stood just outside looking nervous. She'd have to learn all their names, pronouns, and positions quickly, wouldn't she?

The servant bobbed a bow. "Ser Truthspoken. The officer your sibling is in the sitting room. They asked to see you. I told them you were still recovering, but they insisted."

Rhys—oh Adeius, Rhys. Why had she asked them to come? It would be too weird, far too weird, with them both knowing who she really was. And with her trying to feel her way through these sharper edges she'd given Arianna, too. Should she send them away? That would certainly be in character.

No. No, she'd asked them to come. Begged them, really, when she'd sensed their reluctance. Yes, it would be an act. But the relief was in that they both knew it. Rhys would be leaving again soon, and then the only people who knew she wasn't the original Arianna would be so very few. And none of them her very favorite person.

Who was not, she had to remind herself, Arianna's favorite person.

"Thank you. Tell them I'll be out shortly and will see them."

The servant shut the door, and she braced herself against the frame, drawing in deep breaths. She had to regain her composure.

But, okay, who better to first try all this out with than Rhys? Their command of evaku was excellent—they'd be able to spot her mistakes. They could signal her, they could play along. Correct her if she was straying too far. And if she made a big mistake—well, they already knew who she was. It wouldn't matter.

She pulled her composure back around her like a cloak. She checked her posture and adjusted it again, checked her internal gestural language and adjusted it. Checked her speech patterns, checked her mental response flow. Then she opened the door again and strode through the short hallway, entering the sitting room.

Rhys was perched on a chaise lounge near the windows, staring out at the palace grounds. They wore their dark blue Navy dress uniform with pale blue piping—not the formal tunic of the night before—rank pins polished but slightly askew. Their posture was stiff, jaw tight. But they stood and faced the door as she entered.

"Truthspoken." Then, less formally, "Sister." They took two steps toward her, then stopped and bowed more deeply than they ever had to her. To her as Dressa.

Dressa blinked several times, slotted Arianna back into her mind.

"Rhys," she said simply, taking the wingback chair Arianna usually used in her sitting room. She smoothed out the creases in her flowing black trousers. Waved Rhys back to their own seat.

"Uh," Rhys said, awkwardly looking behind them as they

backed up again to the chaise. "Uh, you're looking well. I was worried, I mean, after last night—"

Dressa narrowed her eyes. "Last night was an aberration."

"Yes, but—" Rhys spread their hands. "Adeius, Arianna. I saw you fall, and I couldn't get there in time."

The best evaku, always, was playing on things that were true. Dressa heard the break in Rhys's voice. They were truly anguished that they hadn't been able to reach Arianna in time.

It took all of Dressa's training not to open up herself. She couldn't. She could not. She was Arianna. Rhys was not her favorite sibling right now, they were just a sibling she'd grown up with. A onetime friend and confidante who could no longer be that, because she was the Heir.

Her heart pounded an unsteady rhythm. Her stomach filled with a nausea she couldn't smooth away. Was this how it was going to be from now on? She'd have to push away anyone even remotely close to her?

"Thank you, Rhys. Thank you for checking on me." She gave the barest of tolerant smiles, managed to make even that look condescending. She saw the hurt flicker across Rhys's face, but it was quickly buried.

She wanted to fling herself onto the chaise next to them, wrap her arms around them, and pour out all of her rampant fears.

Instead, she watched the stuffed smile they always wore when around Arianna curve their face, and she made inane small talk. Arianna didn't know enough about Rhys's life to do more. Arianna didn't actually care.

And she felt the tear escape before she could do anything about it.

Rhys, who'd been tightly contained, vaulted off the chaise and was over to her in an instant. "Sister. I ran out of silver eyeshadow. Can I borrow some of yours? In your prep room."

Rhys's voice was calm, but their jaw was tight. She knew

that expression, that particular brand of rage. She'd seen it in the garden the night before.

Dressa fought for composure. She had thoroughly botched this. She knew her father would watch this encounter later and tell her everything she'd done wrong.

Rhys flexed their hands. They looked like they wanted to drag her to the prep room, but they waited for her to stand, waited for her to catch a breath and then lean on their arm. Well, and she could do that, because of Arianna's illness.

Rhys was a solid, anchoring presence beside her. Adeius, she wished they'd never leave.

In the prep room, Rhys shut the door, then braced against it as if holding back the world. They stared at her, their eyes red-rimmed and intense.

"This is wrong, Dressa. All of this is wrong."

## 22

# THE PLAN

*A knee bruised during play*
*A pastry left because it's your favorite*
*A loud song you can't change*
*A blanket after a storm*
*That is a sibling.*

— EXCERPT FROM "SIBLING," A POEM BY LAKSHA BENONI, TRANSLATED FROM THE ORIGINAL INDRI VARSI BY ELINE KODRARE

In the prep room, where there were no microphones, no cameras, Dressa sat heavily in the chair in front of Arianna's vanity. Caught another glimpse of herself. She was going to ruin all her work on that makeup if she didn't get a hold of herself.

Rhys crossed the room, pulling out the seat at the other vanity—Bettea's.

"This is wrong," they said again. "All of this, and you know it. Your father shouldn't be making you be Arianna."

Nothing in this room was hers at all. Nothing. Not even the clothes she wore. Not even the scent she wore.

"I'm Truthspoken," she said with a wavering voice. "It's my duty—"

"Dressa. How badly was Arianna cursed? You didn't tell me last night."

She took a breath. "Not—she's sick. Really sick, I think."

"Okay. Okay. How long will she be away, then?"

Dressa looked down at her hands, picking at her cuticles. She sat on her hands to stop. "Probably months."

"Okay. So, what would happen, really, if people knew Arianna was sick? Long-term sick, not just a thing that's supposed to heal quickly. Would the nobility tear down the kingdom like your father wants you to believe, or is that just his fucking paranoia talking?"

She drew back, looking around her. No, there were no microphones or cameras in this room. But it still felt too dangerous to say things like that out loud.

Rhys leaned forward. "Look at you. Look at you, Dressa, you're afraid to breathe because of him. You can't even be who you are, you're not allowed to be—" They ran their hands over their neatly styled hair, mussing it up. "Dressa, I don't think Ari should have been sent away at all. That's what happened, right? She's still sick from whatever the magicker did to her, and so your father sent her off somewhere to recover in secret where she can't embarrass him."

"So she wouldn't endanger the kingdom," Dressa corrected. She shifted. And yeah, said out loud, that sounded . . . well, it sounded like her father. "But you don't get it. I watch the nobles. They are just waiting for the barest hesitation, the smallest show of weakness to exploit it and bring our dynasty down."

"Are they, really? Or is that what you've been taught to see? Is that a way for the Seritarchus to exert his control over you?"

She pressed her lips tight, looked away. But the problem was, there were too many mirrors in her line of sight. Too many reminders of just how messed up this all was.

"I have to do my duty." Her stomach tightened. "The plots of ambitious nobles killed my father's father, the Seritarchus before him. The history of the Truthspoken is filled with assassinations and coup attempts—you know this. Rhys, you have to know this. I have to be Arianna, to keep some semblance of balance—" Her throat closed, and she shook her head.

Rhys pulled their chair closer until they could grip her hands. "Hey, hey. I'm sorry. I know—but listen, Dressa. Why do you have to be Arianna? Yes, she went down from an attack by a Green Magicker. Maybe that will play like weakness, but then, why can't you just be strong to compensate for that? Why must you, Dressa, be Arianna, and not be Ondressarie? Why can't you take over Arianna's duties as yourself?"

She opened her hands, and the damned tears were pricking again. "Because I'm—because Ondressarie isn't that kind of person. I've built too much into being Arianna's foil. And I don't want—"

She didn't want to be the Heir. But she didn't see a way around it right now. She didn't see a way out. Right now, she was going to be the Heir as Arianna. She was going to sign that engagement contract as Arianna. She was going to present herself as Arianna.

"I can't," she said, testing out the words.

Her whole body shuddered with the truth of them. "Adeius, Rhys, I can't do this as Arianna."

Rhys let out a shaky breath, held her hands tightly.

"But my father—"

"What can he do? Seriously, what can he do if you, as Dressa, go out and give a speech or something about how you're stepping up to be the Heir temporarily, or something like that?"

It was much more complicated than that. So much more complicated. Rhys wasn't remembering the engagement and all the political maneuvering that entailed. Rhys might know a lot, but they hadn't been in the palace these last few years, when she'd come to see just how many thorns grew in its gardens.

"He can make my life hell," she said.

"As opposed to . . ." They waved at her, at her Arianna-ness. "Dressa, he's not going to make a move that will further undermine the kingdom. You make it clear that what you're doing is with his approval, and he won't contradict that publicly. Get—get the Truthspeaker behind you. Ceorre's good, I've always liked her. I've always read the tension between her and your father. She knows what he's like. He's gone too far, Dressa. She will see that, it's her job to see that."

Dressa wasn't so sure. Truthspeaker Ceorre Gatri kept her own counsel, to be sure, but that didn't mean she wasn't allied with the Seritarchus. Then again, she was the Truthspeaker. She was the only one with the power to check him if he went off course.

Had he gone off course now? Was what he was doing, the decisions he was making, endangering the kingdom? Could she prove that?

She swallowed. His order for her to be Arianna was endangering her. It was endangering her mental health and sanity. And right now, that meant endangering the only Heir he had on site.

Dressa shifted, sitting straighter. She let go of Rhys's hands, grabbed a tissue, blotted at her eyes.

And Lesander? What—what would she do about Lesander? Lesander had been promised to Arianna. She knew this alliance between the Rhialdens and the Javieris was important to holding the balance of power in the kingdom. And she didn't want to let Lesander go, either. Not without—

Not without seeing if her crush was more than a crush. If

this marriage could be something that neither of them were trapped into, like it would have been with Ari.

Oh. Oh, Adeius, her father was not going to like this at all.

Rhys, watching her, relaxed some of their tension. They didn't ask what she was thinking, but they knew it was in a different direction than when she'd come into this room.

Finally, they asked, "Do you want me to stay? Put in for a transfer, or take extended leave?"

She drew a sharp breath. "No. Rhys—I won't ask that of you." It would bomb their career. She wouldn't do that to them, no matter if they were willing. And from the lines of their shoulders, they weren't truly willing. They didn't want to stay here in the middle of this mess—they would, if she asked, but it wasn't what they wanted.

Which . . . hurt more than she would let show. She understood, but it still hurt. Rhys wanted to live their life independent of the machinations of the Seritarchus. And so did she.

So would she be alone in the maneuvers she was now planning? If she had her way, absolutely not.

She stood, slowly smoothing out her silk shirt. Smoothing the creases from her trousers.

Rhys stood, too. "I can stay while you Change back, if you want. I've already booked a shuttle up to Orbital, but I have a few hours yet."

Dressa shook her head. "No. I'm not Changing back yet."

Rhys's jaw twitched. "But you're going to Change back, right—"

"Not that you'll be here to care," she snapped, and immediately regretted it. "Rhys—"

They held up their hands. "I know. Stress. And it's probably better I don't know."

She wrapped her arms around them, hugging tight. "I think I've got a plan. And no, I don't need your help."

They pulled back. "I don't have to go back this early. I can—"

"You stay, and the Seritarchus will find a way to use you against me." It was true, another fact she'd never fully acknowledged. And that hurt, too. Hurt because Rhys was right—all of this was very wrong. And it wasn't that she hadn't known it. But she hadn't thought she'd had the luxury of acknowledging it. She still wasn't sure she had.

What she was planning, the hope that was forming, was treason, no matter if she thought it was better for the kingdom than the option she'd been given. To disobey a direct order from the Seritarchus was treason. And it was a betrayal, too. Of her father, and of her sister.

She prayed—oh, Adeius, she prayed—Ari wouldn't hate her for what she was about to do.

Dressa stretched to kiss Rhys on their cheek and pulled back just as quickly. She couldn't linger or she wouldn't let them go.

"We're going to go back out there. I'm going to be Arianna—just for a little while longer. And then you'll leave, and you'll be out of the Seritarchus's reach."

Rhys shifted uncomfortably. "I won't, actually." They touched their jacket pocket. "Your father asked me to send him information on the Kidaa."

Dressa swallowed her curse, smoothed out the worst of the frown. They both knew that request would not end with information on the Kidaa. And maybe it wasn't even about the Kidaa at all. Her father knew how close she was with Rhys.

She held out her hand, and Rhys pulled out two chips. One had no markings—a comm chip, maybe? The other bore no seal, either, but she knew what seal would be there if activated.

"Report to me," she said. "Find a way to route this back to me. Tell my father what he wants, but—also tell me."

Rhys took the chips back, sliding them back into their jacket pocket. They gave a tight nod.

And they stared at each other, knowing that in the last minutes, something fundamental had changed. Not between them, not really. But in the world around them. A world they were pushing back against with all their might.

## 23

# HESTIA

> *On Hestia, you'll see only the best in curated natural views from every vista. Set in Finnan System, a quiet system with prohibitions against large-scale trade, industrial mining, and formal infrastructure, Hestia promises you days, months, or a lifetime of leisure!*
>
> — A TRAVEL BROCHURE FOR THE RESORT WORLD OF HESTIA

On every display, the countdown to coming out of Below Space ticked down. It shone red on the bulkhead in Ari's and Bettea's shared cabin. It shone red in the narrow corridor that led to the cockpit and aft to the ship's small cargo hold. Which, Ari had discovered, still held an actual cargo.

Ari ran a hand along the bulkhead as she made her way to the cockpit, rapping once on the hatch before thumbing the automatics open.

The cockpit hatch opened with a metallic grinding sound, and Ari grimaced. Well, and no royal Rhialden would let a ship fall into even mild disrepair. It would all be part of the disguise.

Bettea looked up from where faer hands were over the control boards. "What are you doing out of bed? We agreed that you'd be strapped in when we landed. It's safer."

Ari gave faer the side-eye while she slipped past faer into the copilot's seat. Bettea had upgraded faer role in this farce from personal servant to a minor noble to *servant companion* to a minor noble. The difference was a much sharper tongue and a parenting way about faer. Which, okay, wasn't all that different from how Bettea spoke to her at the palace, true. And yes, Ari was glad Bettea was with her—she didn't truly have the energy to pilot the ship, let alone wade into whatever awaited her on Hestia on her own. But she'd been feeling out the boundaries of Imorie's personality, and Imorie was a lot less tolerant of people trying to parent her—of authority in general—than Ari.

"I'll strap in here," Ari said, and pulled the restraints over her lap and chest.

Bettea made a sound, not a pleased sound, but sighed. "Right, fine." Fae flipped a toggle and the copilot's controls lit up. "I might as well have a backup, just in case. Not that anything will happen. I've been reading up on Hestia, and it's not in the major shipping lanes. Quiet as far as worlds go, which I guess is the point of a garden world."

Ari leaned forward as much as the restraints would let her. She could still reach the controls fine, just not hover over them as she might have if she were actively flying the ship.

She was an adequate pilot—her father had made sure she and Dressa both, along with their bloodservants, had those skills. Rhys, too, and that had been one of the few times Rhys had been allowed into active training with them. Of all of them, Dressa's bloodservant, Pria, had been the sharpest. Then Rhys, then Bettea, then Dressa. It rankled Ari that she had not been able to excel in piloting—she just didn't have as good of spatial processing, and she hadn't worked out a way to give it to herself without changing her core personality.

Bettea glanced at her, and Ari knew fae was reading her, likely guessing her thoughts. Fae said nothing, though. They'd had the argument before that even though she was the Heir, she didn't have to excel at absolutely everything.

Ari took a long breath. She wasn't the Heir now. And that thought let her slip further into Imorie, into a persona that had known only the periphery of power, secondhand and scraped for all its worth.

The countdown, hovering above the center of the control boards, reached sixty seconds.

Bettea clicked faer own restraints into place. "Ready?" Fae checked Ari's. "Tighten the chest belt."

"I'm fine."

"Ari—"

"Imorie," Ari corrected, pushing her words fully into Imorie's tighter, leaner accent.

Bettea's lips drew taut, but fae didn't argue. The act started now.

Their ident info would be flashed out to populate in all networks as soon as they emerged from Below Space. They'd already made the hard copy documents. Everything was set.

Forty-five seconds.

Ari stared at the comm displays, which would be lighting up shortly with any in-system beacon messages and urgent news. Would there be urgent news from the capital? Would she see the announcement of Arianna's formal engagement to Prince Lesander Javieri?

Her throat tightened.

Thirty seconds.

"Don't open the news," she said. "When we get out, look at the beacon only. Don't open the news from the capital."

"And if there's something urgent we need to know?" Bettea asked. "Seriously, Imorie, we can't not read—"

She shifted. Met Bettea's eyes. "If it's urgent enough, we'll find out on Hestia. And urgent or not, we can't go back until—"

Until she was better? At least well enough to function as a Truthspoken. To be able to Change.

Bettea nodded faer understanding. "Okay. Beacon only." Fae turned back to the boards. "Neutral space in three, two, one."

The engines made a brief, high-pitched whine, the feeling of space itself had a stuttering hesitation, and then the smudge outside the cockpit windows turned into stars.

The comm lit up. Ari reached for the comm controls, configuring receipt to beacon only.

". . . to Finnan System, home to Hestia, the resort world for all your vacation needs! Please send identification . . ."

"Do you want me to get it?" Bettea asked as fae checked the ship's position in system as well as any nearby traffic. Ari glanced over. They'd come in far enough from Hestia to be out of the worst of the congestion, but "congestion" was only a relative term. This looked nothing like the tightly packed commercial and military space over Valon. She could count the number of ships here—twenty, thirty at most?—and at least half had intra-system tags, not interstellar.

Ari was feeling tired again. Adeius, everything tired her so much—but she shook her head and clicked out of the restraints. She pulled up the comms and saw another message come through—a network notification that the request for contact had been accepted. Which was code that their ident update had been sent and received, and their new ident documents were now fully entered in the inter-system network.

Ari called up the documents in the ship's systems, glanced them over—their ship, now named the *Jade Crescent*, held Imorie Rhialden méron Quevedo, with a commercial small vessel piloting license, and Jis Ameer, also with a commercial small vessel piloting license. She peered at her ident image, taken that morning. She had, after all, gone with the heavier cosmetics. Imorie was just too recognizably Rhialden otherwise —it wasn't necessarily better, but it was safer.

She sent the documents to the beacon address with the ship's ident credentials to be disseminated in the system's network. Hestia, being a resort world, had a single small administrative and commercial trade station in orbit, and smaller craft were cleared for surface landing without pre-docking at customs. They'd be heading straight to landing once they reached orbit.

The comm chimed with a request from an administrative channel.

Ari flicked it open.

"This is Hestia Orbital Control. *Jade Crescent*, we have you on scan, we've got your idents. Everything clears. What's your business in Finnan System?"

"Hestia Orbital," Ari said, "this is Imorie Quevedo. My companion and I have private business on Hestia."

"Any cargo to declare?"

Ari took a breath, found she didn't have as much breath as she'd like, and grimaced. "We have cargo, but we're not offloading. Nothing on the interdiction lists. Here for leisure."

"Ah, good. All looks in order, Ser Quevedo, and . . . and receiving your flight plan now, good."

Ari glanced at Bettea, who nodded. Fae'd just sent the flight plan.

"Okay, *Jade Crescent*, you're clear. I'm sending an updated flight plan—please follow this unless Orbital tells you otherwise. Failure to do so will result in a mark on your record in this system and a request to comply. Failure to comply will result in a fine, and resulting failures to comply will accrue increasing penalties up to and including incarceration and impoundment of your ship. Please verbally sign that you agree to these terms."

Ari rolled her eyes. "I agree. Thank you, Orbital."

"Thank you, *Jade Crescent*. Enjoy your stay on Hestia."

The comm clicked off.

"Well," Bettea said, "that part's done." Fae locked in the updated flight plan. The ship's engines kicked in as Bettea spun them around until they faced the planet directly. It was a tiny blue marble out the cockpit window. Almost not visible among the stars. It would be home for the next . . . however long. Hestia.

"Done," Ari said, nodding. She ran a hand through her hair, which had fallen over her face. And if nothing new had erupted at the capital, nothing that she wanted to know, maybe she could treat this like a vacation. She'd certainly never had one before. Truthspoken didn't get to go on vacations.

The comm chimed softly. The news lines had pinged again and at least one from the capital was marked "urgent."

Ari's stomach tightened. But that could mean anything. That would almost certainly mean the engagement. It had to mean the engagement.

"Imorie," Bettea began.

"No. I can't be Imorie and also worried about . . . about Arianna. I don't have energy for both."

Yes, she desperately wanted to know what was urgent in that news. But she also knew she'd be sorely tempted to abandon this course of treatment, run back to the capital, and seize back her life however she could. And she could think of no way that wouldn't end in disaster.

She usually had more control than this. This illness was unraveling her to the core.

"Then will you let me see at least and I'll let you know if—"

"No!"

Bettea stared at her. Maybe that wasn't in character, for herself or for Imorie. And it wasn't wise, going down to the planet without knowing the state of the kingdom. But the news wasn't anything as drastic as military action or a state of alert—she was sure of that, or else their greeting into the system would have been a lot more hostile.

"It's just the—" She couldn't say "engagement." And why was she so upset about Dressa doing something she hadn't wanted? Because the engagement, and that life, would be hers again, eventually. She couldn't control the narrative if Dressa started this all.

She couldn't think about it. Not about Dressa, and what Dressa might have done in the five days she'd been traveling to Hestia. Not about her life, her real life, which she'd had to leave behind.

Ari cut her hand through the air. "No. Just land. If you need to find out then—well, find out. Don't tell me what it is unless it's—unless it's life-threatening to us here."

Which it wouldn't be. Yes, she still had Rhialden features, obscured as artfully as she could manage, but she absolutely was not Arianna.

Ari dug her fingers into the blue leather of her pants. Her heart was pounding too hard, and she had to calm down. She couldn't smooth away her nerves with a thought anymore.

"All right," Bettea said after a minute, and Ari hated the concern in faer voice.

But she bore it. As she would bear what would come after she left Hestia. After she was well enough to resume her life.

Fatigue passed over her and she growled inwardly. She couldn't face whatever she'd find on Hestia like this. She checked the flight clock—they were on a leisurely path in, with three hours until they landed at the country estate where she was to stay. It was time enough for a nap. The world and everything else could wait until then.

# 24

# THE ADEIUM

> *Adeius is the essence of the stars. Adeius is the connection between the stars and the star material in each of us. Stars never forget who they are.*
>
> — ANONYMOUS, IN *THE ESSENCE OF ADEIUS*, CONSIDERED TO BE A HERETICAL TEXT

Dressa stole out of the palace residence in the late afternoon, taking the back corridors. She'd told Arianna's staff she was resting—she was still recovering from a curse of Green Magics, after all. She dressed in generic clothes that might read anywhere from upper tier serving staff to down-dressed lower noble. Bundled all her hair under a cap. Redid her makeup to re-contour her face, an invisible heavy layer meant to look natural and plain. She changed her posture, changed her walk, kept her eyes on the cobblestones of the broad palace courtyard as she passed various workers and nobles chatting in groups. She carried a plain canvas bag over her shoulder and a stack of what looked like linens under her arm.

No one stopped her. Few people looked. No one looked twice.

At the far end of the courtyard, in the open side of the palace's "U", the Adeium loomed before her. Tall with dramatic, triangular peaks, cream stone and silver-blue steel. She opened the metal gate past the two maroon-uniformed guards, then past two more red and violet uniformed Adeium guards inside. She kept her head down as she crossed the Adeium's own courtyard, narrow and paved with tiles of lapis lazuli.

She pulled open the heavy door and stepped into the entry, with its open arch to the sanctum beyond.

Dressa took a long breath and blew it out slowly. The Adeium had always had a hush that drove out all other noise.

Natural light filtered through various tinted windows. The cream walls of the entry were austere, but the wooden framework around the walls was intricately carved with constellations. Through the arch into the sanctum, the carvings ran along the massive semi-precious stone pillars, around and up the walls, and framed a ceiling full of painted stars.

There were a few petitioners kneeling on mats inside the sanctum. From where she stood in the entry, Dressa could see that the holographic representation of Adeius at the front, which flickered and changed to reflect those viewing it, was hovering on a semblance of a dark-skinned person giving off a clash of gender signals. If she walked quickly on the edge of the sanctum, she thought she could reach the door to Truthspeaker Ceorre's offices before the image of Adeius shifted to anything like a Rhialden Truthspoken.

"May I help you?"

She jumped, then let the response amplify, crafting the persona she needed in this moment around it. A speaker in the indigo, form-fitting robes of the lower rank tier stood in front of her. Black hair cut short, dark eyes concerned. There was no overt signal of gender, so she didn't assume.

"I, uh, I need to see the Truthspeaker," she said. "Was sent by the bloodservant, Bettea."

She watched the speaker for any signs that they recognized she was Truthspoken, but there were none. Speakers often had no evaku training unless they were much higher ranked, or particularly promising. Ceorre kept those she trained personally close, too, not assigning them tasks like door duty.

"I can see if the Truthspeaker will see you, but she's very busy, I'm afraid."

Dressa held up her shoulder bag, as if that was proof of a good reason. "On business for the Truthspoken Heir, the bloodservant told me."

"Ah." The speaker opened their hands, frowning. "Well, I'll check. Wait here, I'll check."

Dressa waited while they retreated into the sanctum, then found a bench to sit on, because she was too conspicuous just hovering by the door. She didn't have long to wait, though, before the speaker returned and motioned her to follow.

Dressa shouldered the bag, which held wads of random clothing, tucked the linen stacks under her arm again, and followed the speaker into the whispering acoustics of the brightly lit sanctum. She craned her head back, gawking at the indigo and violet ceiling covered with stars and constellations. The ceiling would glow softly at night like the sky itself.

She glanced at the likeness of Adeius as she passed, but it barely flickered, rippling more to the features of the speaker than her own.

Through a side door at the front of the sanctum, through a short corridor, past a secretarial suite. They reached the door to Ceorre's office, and the speaker knocked once, then pushed the door open.

"You're expected. Make sure you bow to the Truthspeaker."

"I will. Thank you."

She slipped inside and made her deep bow to the woman behind the desk while the door clicked shut.

Then she straightened.

Truthspeaker Ceorre Gatri had always had power in her presence. Not just a thing learned from evaku, but something held within herself. A weight of knowing, of having more insight into the world around her than anyone else in the room. Or maybe it was just that she'd seen too much in her lifetime. Ceorre wore her tightly coiled gray hair in a bun today and wore a looser, more casual version of her red and violet robes. The heavy pendant of office sat on a stand on her desk, not around her neck. She had a pair of reading glasses perched on her nose and studied Dressa overtop them.

The Truthspeaker waited.

Dressa waited—she absolutely knew Ceorre recognized her. But Ceorre didn't seem to be in a hurry to open the conversation as she always did when they'd met for training before.

Finally, Ceorre sighed and set down the stylus she'd been holding. She waved at one of the chairs in front of her desk, and Dressa sat.

"This isn't training. You're here for a purpose. Open with it."

## 25

# THE TRUTHSPEAKER

> *The Truthspeaker is a balance to the Truthspoken. One is a conduit of Adeius's presence in this physical universe; the others are Adeius's active will among the stars. Those two elements must absolutely work together for the kingdom to have prosperity in the will of Adeius.*
>
> — TRUTHSPEAKER ADUWEL SHIN MERNA IN "STRIVING FOR PROSPERITY"

Dressa stiffened at the Truthspeaker's tone. No, this wasn't training anymore, was it? She was Truthspoken. She was here wearing a face and body that weren't her own, with a purpose that outweighed any of the identity games she'd played growing up.

She was here as someone who was going to be the Heir. At least, that was her plan, and she couldn't do it without the Truthspeaker's help.

Dressa folded her hands together, squeezed tightly. Absolutely did not let that tension show anywhere else. "My father told you what happened?"

"Enough," Ceorre said. "Do you wish to retell it?"

She fought the urge to fidget in her seat. Ceorre had always made her feel like a wayward child.

"Cards on the table?" she asked.

Ceorre's brows rose. "Cards on the table."

"Okay. The Seritarchus wants me to be Arianna until Ari can return. That is likely for weeks or months. Doing so, however, will be damaging to a vital asset to the kingdom—me. Therefore, I propose that this order is against the kingdom's best interest, and have come to you, Truthspeaker, to judge this situation."

She saw the faintest twitch of Ceorre's left eye, the only hint of any emotion beyond her projected calm. Ceorre was a master of evaku, rival to her father in the art. Dressa would get little more clues than that twitch, which could mean anything.

Ceorre took off her reading glasses and folded her own hands in front of her, mirroring Dressa. "How is this order damaging to you, Truthspoken?"

Dressa eyed Ceorre's hands, considered smoothing out her own. She didn't, though. Ceorre was signaling her willingness to listen, to come into rapport.

Carefully, she said the words she'd been rehearsing in her head. "While I am Truthspoken, my personality is not suited to long-term immersion in a role. The Seritarchus himself has said this multiple times." Along with admonishments to do better, as if she could change her personality. "And—and I physically dislike, strongly dislike, having a body other than my own. I can do missions for the Seritarchus, yes. I accept that is my duty as Truthspoken. I do not accept that my duty as Truthspoken is to replace another Truthspoken entirely, especially when there is another way that offers less damage to the kingdom and its assets."

"And what way is that?"

Now she did press her palms flat on her thighs. Her hands were sweating more than she could quickly smooth away.

"That the kingdom acknowledges Arianna is not currently fit to serve as the Heir, and Ondressarie steps up to serve as the Heir instead."

She met Ceorre's penetrating gaze. Saw the smallest hint of a grimace on Ceorre's lips.

"Dressa. There are several factors to consider here. First and foremost being that you have never wished to be the Heir, and while your training is adequate to the task, I'm not sure establishing you as the permanent Heir is in the best interest of the kingdom."

Dressa sat forward. "But it could be temporary. Until Arianna returns."

"Second," Ceorre said, holding up a hand, "is the matter of the engagement to Prince Lesander Javieri. The terms agreed upon in the negotiations stated that the contract would be signed within the next week. If we try to change that, the Javieris will play offended and maneuver for much more gain, or use it as an excuse to cancel the contract and rally support in their victimhood. And third, once an Heir has been declared unfit, that decision can't be undone. Legally, yes. But in the eyes of public opinion? The damage has been done. There will always be doubt in the minds of the people. If Ondressarie becomes the Heir, it is a permanent decision. Are you willing to do that, Dressa? Are you willing to set your whole life to being the Heir, and the ruler after? And are you willing to do that to Ari? She has set her whole life to this task. Are you willing to take it from her?"

Dressa's fingers dug into her pant legs. Part venting tension, part a tool to move this conversation in the direction she wanted, as Ceorre would see that tension. She had thought of all of these things. Separately, and in great detail. She hadn't yet presented Ceorre with the whole of her plan—she wanted to see where the Truthspeaker stood, first.

"I don't know how long Ari will be gone," she said slowly, measuring her words with care. "I don't truly know what's wrong with her."

"It's the Bruising Sleep," Ceorre said.

"What?" The sickness that inflicted mostly commoners in the city? That rocked Dressa off course. She hadn't known. "How? How could she get—but she's Truthspoken. She can't get a disease like that, she should be able to heal it."

Why hadn't her father told her? And—well, did it change anything? Ari was still sick. She'd seen just how sick Ari was and knew how bad it must be if Ari couldn't heal it away. But the Bruising Sleep had a lot of social baggage. Adeius, for a Truthspoken to be sick with the Bruising Sleep. And was there a cure? She knew the hospitals and permanent housing halls for the sick were always overflowing with it. Nobles complained about housing halls asking for more funding, because their patients weren't getting better enough to leave.

Horror bloomed like a midnight flower in her stomach. "There's a cure, right? Ari's not—"

"No cure, but there's treatment."

Ceorre sighed, and some of the stiffness left her posture. She was setting evaku aside. They'd played their games, they'd probed for information. Now it was time to get down to the matter at hand. Dressa silently agreed, discarding her own controlled posture in favor of an anxious fidget.

Ceorre reached for a glass on her desk, likely water, but looked like she wished it was stronger. "This isn't isolated, Dressa. The nobility has been getting the Bruising Sleep for years. It's a well-kept secret with far too many people keeping it. And the cases have been increasing in the last few years. Ari can get treatment, yes. But will she ever be at full capacity again? Will she ever be well enough, sharp enough, have the acuity needed to run the kingdom?"

The question hung in the air, cloying, too heavy. And they both knew just how little weakness Truthspoken could show—as the Heir, and especially as the Ruler. Her father was tireless. She'd thought Arianna was tireless. A Truthspoken had to be tireless to be effective.

She would have to be tireless. But if she had to do it, she'd do it on her own terms.

# 26

# TIRELESS

*Witness the death of the honored*
*Witness the truth of the living*
*Witness the strength of the stars*
*Witness the whisper.*

— DIRAN VAM, "PROVERB 286," *SECOND BOOK OF THE HOLY MANDATES OF ADEIUS*

"So, if Ari comes back," Dressa said flatly, "she might not be able to be the Heir anyway. Is that what you're saying?"

Truthspeaker Ceorre set her glass down. "We don't know. We simply don't know. She might be fine. With her Truth-spoken abilities combined with treatment, she might cure herself. But we don't know." She eyed Dressa. "And in the meantime, what you need to ask yourself, and what I need to ask myself, is can the kingdom afford to wait? Can the kingdom afford, as you claimed, to have an unstable Truthspoken masquerading as the Heir, if that's the only buffer we have between the Seritarcracy and all the people of our worlds?"

Dressa's shoulders drew tight. "So . . . so you agree with me, that I shouldn't be Arianna."

"On that, yes, I do agree. But here's the choice at hand: do you hold out these few months, be Arianna, buffer yourself for your mental health as best you can, but then be free of the duties of the Heir the rest of your life after? And meanwhile, the kingdom is at the most vulnerable it's been in years. The Seritarchus has only one Truthspoken at hand, and that one is not a viable resource for anything other than the task assigned. Or—"

Dressa leaned forward. "Or, Ondressarie steps up, becomes the Heir, and then . . . that's it. That's my life. But the kingdom has something stable, at least. I'm not the best choice. I know that, Ceorre. I don't want to rule the kingdom. It's . . . not my first choice, at least. But if I'm me, and I'm not trying to twist myself into knots to be Arianna, then I'm aware. I can do what the Truthspoken Heir needs to do. And if Ari doesn't ever get well enough to be the Heir again, then there's continuity. And now, while everyone thinks she's gone down with a magicker curse, people won't question if she steps down, will they? Not as much as if she'd have to step down later."

Ceorre tapped the edge of her cup with one lacquered, violet nail. "If the Seritarchus declares Arianna unfit—which he won't, as that's a blow to his own power and pride—he'll need to state a reason. The Green Magicker's curse will be that reason, and the prejudice he's already stirred up against the magickers will inflame if the people think a magicker successfully took out their Truthspoken Heir." She looked up. "But you have a better plan than that. Or else, why would you still be in Arianna's form?"

They hadn't discarded games after all. They never discarded games. People seeped in evaku didn't know how.

Dressa steeled herself. This was her life already, but as Dressa, as the second heir, she'd been able to forget the full weight of being Truthspoken, for a time. To let Ari carry most of it. She'd immersed herself in her groups of friends, in palace parties, in the enthusiastic vapidness of her public persona. But when she became the Heir—she wouldn't have the luxury of forgetting who and what she was. Every moment, absolutely every moment for the rest of her life, she would know that she was part of the force holding the kingdom together. That would be her role, played to the fullest.

And still the thought was better than forcing herself to be Arianna. She knew herself. She had so few barriers between who she was and who she would become in a role. She would lose herself in the role of Arianna, always suppressing her own self until there was nothing left but Arianna.

She met Ceorre's gaze. "This will only work—well, work best—if Arianna steps down herself. If she says she'll need a longer time to recover than she thought, and she doesn't wish to marry, and she's had the time to reflect that she would rather remove herself from the succession." She swallowed hard around the words.

Adeius, Ari would kill her. Might literally try to kill her. There would still be pushback if she did this, people questioning why Arianna suddenly decided not to be the Heir if not just for the Green Magicker. There would still be pushback on the Green Magickers, too, but not as much as if this didn't look like Arianna's own decision.

"I'll need you to witness," she said, "when I do this. Witness that I'm Arianna, and that I'm telling the truth."

Ceorre looked away. And this was the biggest thing to ask. Ceorre's sacred duty was to tell the truth as it concerned the kingdom, the Adeium, and the Truthspoken. And yet, it was also her sacred duty to protect the kingdom and its rulers.

"Be Arianna in that moment," Ceorre said finally, "fully Arianna in that moment, and I'll witness that this is Arianna's truth."

## 27

## THE TRUTHSPOKEN HEIR

> *There are ten rulers for every dynasty, ten chances for a dynasty to rise to glory or ride out history as an immense failure. We've yet to see a dynasty that did not, overall, rise to glory. And our Twelfth Dynasty, I dare say, has been the most glorious of all!*
>
> — LORD MYNIN JADIAR, FROM *THE COLLECTED SPEECHES OF THE GENERAL ASSEMBLY, FOURTH EDITION*

Dressa sat back, her whole body feeling shaky, wrung out. Ceorre would do it. If she gave her all for just those few moments, when Ceorre would need to confirm that she was, in fact, Arianna and telling the truth, and not under coercion, Ceorre would do it.

Dressa could do that, too. Be Arianna in truth. She could fully, *fully* be Arianna for those few moments, and then never again.

Dressa reached for a light healing trance to calm her body's responses, but it only soothed some of the pieces, not the whole of it.

None of this was fair. It wasn't fair to Ari, certainly, but then, it wasn't fair to Dressa. Why should her father punish her when it was Ari who was sick?

No, that also wasn't fair. It wasn't Ari's fault, and she didn't know who to blame, and that was part of the problem. Why should Ari have to lose her position through no fault of her own? Why should Dressa have to be the Heir, when that was the very last thing she'd ever wanted?

Was this the right choice? Couldn't she just hold out for a few weeks or months, be Arianna, and then resume her life? But what life, after those few months, would she have to resume? She couldn't make it that long. And Ceorre's arguments that Ari might not get better, or might always have a weakness for the nobility to exploit, were valid. Her father had also maneuvered hard for the marriage contract with the Javieris—it was vital that contract be signed.

She couldn't marry Lesander as Arianna. Absolutely did not want that union to be poisoned from the start. She'd seen the results of a sour marriage with her parents and would never do that to Lesander if she could help it. So none of this was fair to Lesander, either. Adeius, where did the unfairness end?

She pressed her hands to her lips, holding in the tension, trying to think. She had thought of this before, in her prep room—no, Ari's prep room—no, it would be her prep room anyway if she became the Heir, wouldn't it? That was always the Heir's apartment. And she'd thought of it on the way to the Adeium, and she'd made her decisions, but Ceorre had given her information she hadn't had before. But was there truly enough time to think it all through? This was the rest of her life. This was the future of the kingdom, and if she was going to do this, she'd have to do it now before her father could stop her.

What if Ari did recover? She'd come back to a life that no longer existed.

And what of Dressa, as the Heir? She would assume all of Ari's duties, and she'd have to take up her Truthspoken training again in earnest. Her father had let her training lapse these last few years—given up on her as a useful Truthspoken, she'd thought, and that didn't speak well for any of this.

She would, one day, rule the kingdom. She'd been trying not to think about that part of it, she'd set it aside as a problem that had years left to be solved. But here, in Ceorre's office, she couldn't ignore it. No matter what she'd said about this being temporary . . . she'd known it wasn't. Could she do that? Could she rule the Kingdom of Valoris and its one hundred and eighty-seven worlds, and all their various nobles and people and . . . everything?

Adeius, how did she possibly think she could do that?

Did she have a choice? If the only other choice was to traumatize herself so much she couldn't function, and the only other choice for the kingdom was to have an Heir and ruler who had a vital weak point their enemies could exploit, and the only other choice was to break or poison an engagement contract with the person who would be half of the next generation of Truthspoken—no, she didn't have a choice.

But it was wrong, all of it was wrong, as Rhys had said. The whole system was rotten—why couldn't Ari come back and resume her place when she was well again? Why did they have to hide the fact she was sick, and why should weakness matter? Why were the nobles such sharks, and was Rhys right there, too? Were they as bad as she'd been taught to believe?

She had to think so. She, and the kingdom, couldn't afford to think otherwise.

"What about my father?" she finally asked. "This will go against his orders."

Ceorre sighed. "I won't formally contradict him—and there

are, of course, no formal orders to contradict. This is between Truthspoken, and because of that, within my purview and mandate to alter his course here. Though he certainly won't be happy about it. But again, publicly, there is little he can do."

That was a lie. Dressa sensed it, and had to know Ceorre was trying to convince herself. This was a much, much bigger risk than it looked like on the surface of things. While Ceorre did have the power as Truthspeaker to gainsay a Truthspoken ruler, a Truthspoken ruler certainly had the power to make her life hell, and to undermine her in any way he could. He could make a bid to replace her as Truthspeaker with someone else, too, if he could bring enough public evidence to justify the move. He would need to have a lot of unsubtle evidence, and he'd be airing his own ills in the process, but it was possible. Dressa had learned long ago not to underestimate her father in anything.

And her? How would her father retaliate for Dressa? She wouldn't be able to avoid him—they'd have the meetings on the direction of the kingdom, and training, and she just knew he wouldn't be pleasant for any of it. But then, he never had been.

A new thought took hold, a very dangerous thought. What if, if she did eventually become the ruler, she could choose to do things differently? Choose not to be her father. Choose to raise her children and train them with kindness.

Or not train them at all.

"I have to talk to Lesander," she said. "She must know what's going on. She must be able to make her own decision on if she wants to transfer the engagement contract to me. As the Heir." That, Dressa had already been planning to do after she left here. Truly, for all Ceorre had said, it hadn't changed her plans much at all.

Ceorre nodded. "We have spent enough time talking—haste is prudent now." She stood, picked up the heavy pendant, and slung the gold chain over her head with practiced ease, letting it drop into its authoritative place. And then, she was fully the Truthspeaker. The counterbalance to the ruler. The person seldom acknowledged to at times hold the most power in the kingdom.

She touched a button on her desk. "Ien, come back in, please."

A minute later, there was a knock, and the speaker who had brought Dressa in earlier came back inside.

Ceorre didn't look particularly happy to see them, but she motioned them over to her. "Forgive me—the others are in the city trying to quell the anti-magicker panic. You'll have to do for this. I hold you to your oaths of discretion and secrecy. Absolutely nothing you witness in this office will be repeated unless and until I tell you to do so."

Speaker Ien's eyes widened. They bowed. "Yes, Truthspeaker. I am ready to serve."

"Good. Witness." She tapped another control on her desk, and a holo popped up with a red recording symbol, along with the official knotwork seal of the Adeium, the same as on her pendant. "I, Ceorre Gatri, Truthspeaker of the Kingdom of Valoris, do hereby privately and officially relieve Arianna Rhialden of her duties as the Truthspoken Heir, though she will remain Truthspoken and second heir. This is my decision in light of present circumstances, and the safety and wellbeing of the kingdom. I now officially appoint Ondressarie Rhialden as the Truthspoken Heir, with all the titles and responsibilities that position ensues. This appointment shall be effective from this moment forward. A public ceremony with oaths will follow. So be it under the breath and will of Adeius. Decreed this day of Enei the Eighth, in the rule of the Ninth Seritarchus of the Twelfth Dynasty, 2968 New Era. Witnessed by—" She motioned, and Speaker Ien haltingly said their part.

Ceorre tapped the recording off. It felt like an ending, a seal on the life Dressa had lived before.

Dressa swallowed. And swallowed again as the gravity of what had just happened tried to settle around her. She was the Heir. Not as Arianna, but as herself. That was already done.

Speaker Ien had stiffened like a board and was now trying not to look at Dressa—they had of course by now recognized her as Arianna through the makeup. Cosmetics could only go so far, and she hadn't been trying to hide her own bearing in the last few minutes. Well, and whatever they made of that, in light of what Ceorre had just said, was up to them.

"Thank you, Speaker Ien. And I remind you again: utmost discretion. Dismissed."

The speaker bowed again and slipped out.

The door closed. And Dressa found herself caught in the Truthspeaker's gaze.

## 28

# FOR THE GOOD OF THE KINGDOM

*I worked in a high house palace for years, and I saw actual Truthspoken twice—that I know of. The way they interact with people is . . . strange. They're very attentive, even though it doesn't look like it at first glance. And they'll ease their words in and out of the conversation, like they're playing an instrument, not actually talking to people. It's all very subtle, and I don't think most people would notice it, except most of the high house nobles I'm around act like that, too. You start to see the patterns. So, do the Truthspoken have those same exact patterns, or are they now projecting what the high houses do as part of a deeper act? If I saw a Truthspoken who wasn't obviously a Truthspoken, would I know they were Truthspoken?*

— ANONYMOUS89445-B7 IN THE CHATSPHERE
*VALON CITY HOUSE STAFF/DEEP MUSINGS*

It was done. It was done and Dressa was having trouble breathing. Slow, measured breaths.

There was no going back. Was there? There was no going back?

Ceorre came around her desk and held out her hands. She seldom offered anything in the way of gentleness—it wasn't in her nature. But Dressa found herself taking the older woman's hands, found her throat burning, found it hard to swallow as the Truthspeaker squeezed tight.

"Dressa. You will do well. I know you will. And while these are the circumstances now, they might not remain that way forever. We'll proceed on the course we've laid out, but if it changes, if Ari comes back and we find a way and you wish it, we will do what we can."

No, that couldn't be right. Ceorre had said when a Truth-spoken Heir was declared unfit—but her father wouldn't be declaring Arianna unfit. If Dressa didn't use the magicker attack as her only reason for Arianna to step down, it wouldn't be as sharp of an obstacle for Ari to return to. Dressa had a chance. If Ari came back and could handle being the Heir, she could get out of this.

Dressa's heart hammered.

But—Lesander. The engagement contract would absolutely state Lesander would marry the Heir. The Javieris would have it no other way. And the engagement contract had to be signed within the week.

Ceorre leaned forward, shaking Dressa's hands. "This will be your choice, Ondressarie. This is your choice from here out. You are the Heir. That will only ever change if you wish it to be so."

But that wasn't true, was it?

She stared up into Ceorre's dark eyes and knew it wasn't

true. Ari had been the Heir, and that had just changed, and Ari hadn't wished it.

She wasn't on stable ground. She'd never be on stable ground—that wasn't in any Truthspoken's future, let alone an Heir's.

But Ceorre's eyes shone with as much truth as Dressa could read in them. Ceorre was serious. Deadly serious. What had just happened to Arianna would not, within all of Ceorre's power, happen to Dressa. And what was she supposed to make of that? Did Ceorre actually favor her as the Heir? No one favored her. She was hardly a functional Truthspoken, according to her father.

"Do you wish me to call Prince Lesander here?" Ceorre asked.

Dressa shook her head, withdrew her hands. "No. No, I'll—I'll go and see her."

She took a breath, one more thought. "I know the agreement with the Javieris is important politically, but—how important? What will happen if—" If Lesander took objection to her, or to the situation, and didn't agree to get engaged to and eventually marry her. Her stomach clenched at the thought. But Lesander would have to agree, wouldn't she? Their families had negotiated this contract for weeks, or even months now, or even years? She had no idea how long her father had been planning this. And Dressa actually liked Lesander, where Ari hadn't. They had maybe the smallest bit of a chance at happiness. Surely that would count for something.

Oh Adeius, what if Lesander said no?

Ceorre leaned back against her desk. "Hm. You haven't spoken to your father—well, of course you haven't spoken to your father. The Javieri and Delor families have been consolidating their power for some time. It was my view and your father's both that one or the other, in alliance with each other, would make a bid to rule in the next five years if we did nothing to curtail it. Both high houses have the genetics for Truthspoken training. Some among them may be illicitly trained—they certainly have some evaku training, the nobility's version at least. Your mother, I suspect, has some of both Truthspoken and evaku, though I don't see her as a participant in this venture rather than a pawn who didn't live up to her usefulness—forgive the bluntness."

Dressa stiffened at the part about Lesander having Truthspoken training. "Have you seen that?" Because of anyone, Ceorre would know. "Lesander—did you see she has Truthspoken Change training, or evaku?"

She herself had watched Lesander's social ease and suspected the evaku. Lesander had adapted to compensate for Arianna's illness with effortless grace. It was unlikely any child of a high house wouldn't have evaku.

"Some evaku, likely, I don't know about Truthspoken Change training. I haven't been able to read that yet either way—she's beautiful, but she doesn't have the perfect beauty of some of the nobles I suspect of cosmetic Change training. If she does have any Truthspoken training, it will be much more subtle than that." She pressed her lips together. "If the Javieris have gotten so bold as to send an heir with illegal Truthspoken training to be the next ruler consort . . . that is certainly something I will watch for."

"Did Ari know about this? The politics, I mean?"

Dressa hadn't paid much attention. Adeius, she hadn't thought she had to. She usually made a point of not paying as much attention as she should.

And didn't that seem childish now, that small defiance of her father? Now, when she needed to hold all the threads, she found her hands empty.

"Some. Arianna would of course have worked out about the evaku training and would have been watching Lesander closely. It was part of our plan, the Seritarchus and I, that this not have a chance to form into a love match and so compromise her." Ceorre eyed Dressa. "Which I fear will be different for you."

Dressa's pulse pounded in her ears. Oh, Adeius. And here was a wicked new twist. She liked Lesander, a lot. And yes, she knew it was a crush, and didn't know if it would become more. But how was she supposed to engage and then marry someone who could be trying to bring down her family? She had to think—no, had to trust that she'd be able to read Lesander enough as time went on to see if that was the case.

She hoped it wasn't. She hoped so much that Lesander was just as miserable about marriage as Ari had been, that her family was only her family and pushing her into something she didn't want.

Which sounded implausible even in her own head. Whatever else, like Dressa herself, Lesander would be a product of the world she was raised in.

And what would Dressa have to give up, too, in her private negotiation with Lesander? What would it take to make Lesander agree to marry her? If these were the stakes, she doubted Lesander would refuse her outright. But she could demand so, so much or threaten to drop the contract. Just how much of a shark was Lesander in this game, too? And how much of the future ruler's animosity was Lesander willing to risk?

"Okay," Dressa said tightly. "Noted. I will be on my guard."

"Always," Ceorre said, voice sharpening. "You will always be on your guard with Lesander Javieri. This is not a time to indulge a childish crush, do you understand me, Truthspoken Heir?"

Dressa snapped her mouth shut, cheeks warming in anger. "I said, 'noted.'"

Her father hadn't told her about the politics of the engagement when he'd ordered her to be Arianna. Had that been bad timing, had he hoped to brief her later? Or had he been hoping to get her hooked to Lesander, or them hooked to each other, and then play her against the Javieris?

Dressa closed her eyes, thought quickly. He could still do that. And she would not be played. Time to move again, one more step ahead. She had to start establishing herself as separate from him, even if not out from under his rule. The best way she could think to do that was to solidify her own household.

"I think—I think to keep the good will of the Javieris, we should push this marriage quickly, not just the engagement, but the marriage. And not publicly yet, that will come later, but so the Javieris will know that we won't change or break the deal again. And bind them to us now so they don't have time to take advantage of any perceived weakness."

She would have to argue like a hurricane.

But was that the right approach? How would Ari handle this?

But she wasn't Ari. That was the point. That was the whole fucking point.

Ceorre tilted her head. "That gives you significantly fewer options should Ari return early and well."

Yes, this was a very permanent choice, but she'd already been headed for that permanence. The small hope that Ari would return and take over had been hollow, she knew that. She knew, and Ceorre knew, that the future of the kingdom would be decided in these next few days, not when Ari returned. She had to help stabilize the kingdom now, and the change would have already settled by then. The kingdom wouldn't want to be shaken again.

And with what Ceorre had just told her about the Javieris and the Delors, who the Truthspeaker and Seritarchus both considered a present threat, Dressa wondered if Ari would have a kingdom to return to if Dressa didn't act now. At least, not the same kingdom, ruled by the same family as when she'd left. The Rhialdens had held onto Valoris for the last three hundred years. And that hold, year by year, was slipping. That hold right now was just fingertips.

Testing. Ceorre was testing her, gauging how she felt. How she might react when Dressa truly understood, understood in her bones when she was alone at night, when she knew she'd wake up in the morning to a kingdom that would be hers and a wife, that this was the choice she'd made and she'd have to live with it. That what she was deciding now was truly, world-shatteringly important.

She would marry Lesander, no matter what it took, and she would continue to be the Heir. And Ari . . . would Ari try to kill her, out of revenge, or to reclaim her position? Was that in her sister's nature?

She wasn't sure. And that chilled her to her core. Certainly, if Ari could fight this decision, she would, unless she saw it would harm the kingdom. Dressa, set on this course, would have to armor herself at every turn.

She met Ceorre's eyes again, and this time registered Ceorre's grim smile. Yes, the Truthspeaker had been testing. And somehow, Dressa had passed.

Dressa raised her chin. "For the good of the kingdom. This is what I must do, Ceorre."

After a moment, Ceorre nodded. "Go, then. Talk to Lesander. Come back with her if she agrees, and we'll go from there."

"And if she doesn't agree?"

Ceorre's look didn't change, but Dressa felt the gathering tension. "We'll go from there."

## 29

## BLOODSERVANTS

> *Would I consider my Green Magics a curse? If you're talking about my own beingness and how I relate to the world, then no. I have extra senses, and that's how I see the world. Would you call one of your senses a curse? I can see and sense in a different way, that is all. It doesn't make me more or less.*
>
> — ETIENNE TANAKA, AS QUOTED IN *THE CHANGE DIALOGUES*

Homaj Rhialden slipped through the back passage door to his bedroom, shutting it silently behind him. The panel blended back into the wall as if it had never been there.

He glanced around the palatial room with its enormous bed, two large, overstuffed couches along one wall, and no windows. He reoriented himself back to a sense of familiarity, of safety.

He paused, his breathing growing heavier.

Homaj could feel the exhaustion of the last . . . what, had it only been last night that Arianna had collapsed? And he'd been gone from the palace most of that night and now the day after. He hadn't slept. He'd held the pain at bay and healed the worst of his injuries from the guards' beating, but he'd been unable to reach the thorough healing trance he needed while the Council of Magickers strode around him, arguing over how best to proceed. Blaming each other—and never him, never openly, but he'd sat there among them, wearing the face and body of a person who'd just set the magicker cause back so far. Whose face and body still bore the visible marks of that fact.

Oh no, they hadn't scolded the Seritarchus, who had been their greatest champion in centuries. They'd done absolutely everything but yell at him, and he'd heard that lack exactly as loudly as they'd wished him to. He'd just as loudly not admitted he'd done wrong—as the Seritarchus, he couldn't. But he'd made more promises than he probably should have, and he'd have to spend the next weeks convincing the nobility, the military, and the General Assembly to see those promises through. He'd have more promises to make, chipping away at his own power base. Everyone, always, wanted as much of his power as they could take.

The bedroom door opened from his prep room. Only one other person had access to the triple lock on his bedroom door—genetic, biometric, and a pin code which changed daily. Iata came in, balancing a tray with wrapped sandwiches in one hand and a large thermos giving off the aroma of coffee in the other, with mugs dangling from various fingers.

Homaj swiped a hand through his hair. "Oh, thank Adeius. Yes. Coffee."

He sat heavily on the bed as Iata set the tray next to him, uncapped the thermos, and poured them both a mug.

Homaj didn't say any more until he'd had a sip. And another sip. He was Truthspoken, yes. He could hold exhaustion at bay for longer than ordinary Humans, and he could push the pain aside. But he was still Human. And he'd need to rest shortly. Heal himself before he could Change himself out of the guise of Sodan Iseban.

"How goes the palace?" he finally asked.

Iata sat down on the other side of the tray, considered the sandwiches, and picked one. "Uneasy. I Changed after you went with the magickers last night, and I've been putting out fires all morning. The nobles are demanding assurances they won't come under attack from the Green Magickers. Some are going so far as to insist the magickers be banished from the capital. Or at least the palace."

Homaj looked up into dark brown eyes. His own brown eyes, in his own face. While he had been with the magickers, he couldn't have left the palace and the evolving crisis unattended. He'd needed to be more than one person—and he had been.

Iata, as his bloodservant, was only officially supposed to have the ability to Change in small measures. He was only supposed to assist the Seritarchus, not actively *be* the Seritarchus and make policy himself.

The truth was far more complicated, and known to very few. Among them, the magickers he'd been treating with, because no one could hide that kind of truth from the highest ranked magickers. Magickers, especially the ranking magickers, could touch a person, or even just look into their eyes, and know their deepest truths. They could see the layering of personal truths when a Truthspoken played a role as plainly as Homaj could read a person's features. While Homaj and Iata were always careful around magickers, the highest ranked magickers would know when Homaj was actually Homaj, or when Homaj was Iata.

That knowledge hadn't been played on the table today. That knowledge would never be a threat. If the magickers let out the Seritarchus's greatest secrets, they would be trusted by absolutely no one.

Iata raised a dark brow at his silence. One of Homaj's own gestures. But they'd done this often enough over the years that the sensation of seeing himself mirrored back to himself had stopped being strange. When Iata was him, it was like watching a twin, not an exact mirror of himself.

"Maja," Iata said, frowning. He gestured at a bruise on Homaj's cheek. Sighed. "I could have done this part, too."

Homaj looked down at the tray and selected his own sandwich, carefully peeling back the wrapper. "No, Brother, you couldn't." Which they both knew to be true.

"So," Homaj said, taking a bite. "Is Dressa settling? Has she Changed? What about the Javieris, has there been any unrest about the contract? I want that engagement contract signed as soon as possible."

"She's Changed," Iata said, and Homaj read the wariness in his tone. And they'd had that argument the night before in shouted whispers, while Arianna lay sleeping on the couch on the other side of the room. She'd barely roused when the guards had set her down. She hadn't been unconscious at that point, only sleeping. The Bruising Sleep living up to its name.

"Dressa is trained," Homaj had hissed to Iata. "She knows her duty. You have no trouble being me—"

"I'm not you without cease for weeks at a time, not usually. And we've made our choices. This will not go well, Homaj, for her or the kingdom—"

"She's Changed," Homaj repeated now, thoughts back in the present, echoing Iata's wariness. "Have you seen her? Have you spoken to her?"

"You know I don't like to do that. I have to bury deep to show your tells, not mine."

Homaj finished the last bite of his sandwich, started on another. "Yes. Fine. And Ceorre? Has Ceorre been to see you?"

"Remarkably, no. Commander Jalava told me you spoke last night, and that she ripped you a new one." Iata didn't sound disapproving. His lips thinned. "You were with the magickers for longer than I expected."

He watched Homaj carefully. Watched with his evaku-trained senses. And watched with senses every bit as acute as the magickers Homaj had been with that day.

Homaj set the sandwich down. Faced his brother. Faced the only person who knew the whole of things. The only person he could never lie to, not even when he was lying to himself.

Iata was his bloodservant, officially a distant cousin in a branch of the Rhialden family raised into family service. But they'd found long ago that this truth was also complicated. There was no service branch of Rhialdens, at least not anymore. Bloodservants were the same children of their parents as the Truthspoken they served. Every bit as capable of Truthspoken abilities. Genetically, they were full siblings.

And Iata's truth had grown even more complicated nine years ago.

Nine years ago, when Iata had manifested Green Magics.

# 30

# BROTHERS

*Who cut me most, my brother;*
*Who healed me most, my brother.*

— CHIKE USMAN, IN FAER POPULAR SONG
"WHO IS MY BROTHER"

"I'm sorry," Homaj said, and knew Iata would see and feel and hear his sincerity. "I am sorry for dragging the magickers into this. I'm sorry I asked you to test Arianna last night, I'm truly sorry for the outcome."

He'd been in his prep room, finishing his cosmetics before he went to the ball as a minor noble. He'd gotten an alert from the guards that the Truthspoken Heir had been attacked by a magicker—he hadn't asked for details, he'd just ordered her to be brought to his study.

He'd known. Even then, he'd known that what he'd sent Iata to do had ended in disaster.

Iata had returned quickly through the back corridors, shaken at what had happened.

"She has it, Homaj. I saw it. She has the Bruising Sleep."

"You have to be me when she comes in," Homaj said. "Tell her you were me, as the magicker—she has to know, has to not be afraid of a magicker attack."

Adeius, he hadn't thought she'd collapse. He'd just wanted to see how she'd handle the situation and put doubt in the minds of the people as to why she'd looked fatigued. She'd covered it well, but the signs that something was wrong were too obvious for a nobility largely trained in some form of evaku.

He'd wanted Iata to look at her with all of his magicker senses wide open and see if there was any of the faint sludge in her aura that seemed to go with the Bruising Sleep. Not many magickers could see it, and Iata had only ever been able to detect it in others when he wasn't holding back his own forest green aura, which had posed a problem. Iata couldn't approach Arianna as himself with his aura visible, and as a magicker who wasn't himself, he couldn't very well ask that he scan her in public, having no position at all for that presumption. Not without far too much explanation.

Iata had fought the need to scan her aura as an invasion of privacy—but they both knew the risk if one of Homaj's physicians made the diagnosis. No diagnosis outside the family was ever a secret safely kept, no matter how many security gag orders the physicians were under. Not for a scandal this big, not when there were so many high house politics in play and a marriage alliance on the line. So, reluctantly, Iata had agreed to all of it.

Homaj knew that all of this, this whole plan, had been born from his own panic. He hadn't noticed how fatigued his Heir had been until he'd feared it was too late—and it had been. He'd known others would have noticed by now, too, and started putting the pieces together. The truth of the Bruising Sleep among the nobility was not as well-hidden as anyone would like. He'd had to do something drastic, he'd truly had to.

Convincing Iata to go that far had taken much. And

convincing the First Magicker had taken the first of what had become a long, long list of concessions.

"I can't," Iata had said in the study. Eyeing the other end of the room where Arianna lay sleeping. "I can't pretend to be you. Homaj, I can barely be myself right now. I used my magics to disappear in the crowd, and you know what that does to me. It will take days to recover fully. And this was far too close to violence, Homaj. What you're asking me to do now—it's more violence."

So Iata had stumbled away, through the adjoining hallway toward Homaj's prep room, shedding his magicker robes, pulling off the temporary rank seal on his cheek, dropping them all on the floor and kicking them away as if they were on fire.

"You do it," Iata rasped. "You made this mess, you tell her what you've done."

He slammed the door to the prep room, and Homaj had been worried it would wake Arianna—but it hadn't.

He'd gathered up the robes, checked on Arianna—still asleep. Then he'd sat down hard in a chair out of Arianna's line of sight and pushed into a dangerously fast trance to Change his face and voice to the same Iata had used as the magicker Sodan Iseban. The rest of his body had come after, once he'd already sent one daughter off and set the other to his new mission.

In his bedroom, in the afternoon now, the memory glittered like a jagged shard of glass.

"I'm sorry," he said again. And fuck, he meant it.

Iata slowly nodded at his apology. And the fatigue, the wear around his edges, the toll from using his magics the night before showed deeply on his face when he wasn't actively trying to hide it.

Iata carefully set his sandwich down. "I won't use magics for you anymore."

Homaj frowned. "I apologized. I mean it, Iata, I'm truly sorry. But this was an isolated incident—and while yes, the results were not what either of us wanted—"

"No, Maja. We've been over this too many times—there's always an exception. What we're doing is unethical in the extreme. And—reckless." He nodded at Homaj's bruises. "Those should have been mine. That all should have been mine, and rightly deserved, because I never should have said yes to that. You're Truthspoken. You have to use the tools at hand. I'm as like to Truthspoken, but I can't use this tool. I can't use my magics against my own heart and judgement. You know what that does to me, and you know what it did to my people today—"

"Your people, Iata?" He half rose from the bed. "You're my brother—"

"Not in anything like fact," Iata snapped, then paused, closing his eyes.

No violence. He could not do violence, even emotional, even to himself, without pain.

"Yan," Homaj said, using Iata's private name, the name they'd worked out when they'd found out Iata was his full brother, not just a distant cousin. Not just a bloodservant. A Truthspoken, a Rhialden, needed a private name.

"Yan—" He held out his hands. "You're my brother. You know that. I know that. I know exactly who and what you are. And—" Adeius, it was not the time to push. But he couldn't help himself. He needed Iata to see that he needed him. He needed his magics. Couldn't Iata see that they were just barely holding onto the kingdom as it was? They needed every single edge.

"Yan, you have your duty to me, and to the Seritarcracy—"

Iata stood, holding up his hands, and Homaj drew back.

"Adeius, Homaj," Iata said. "You're saying that to me, right now, like this?" He jabbed at his face. Which was still the face of the Seritarchus. "You think I don't know about duty? Has this all been vastly different than I thought?"

Homaj pushed himself fully to his feet. He was tired. He knew he'd gone too far. But they'd both made this mistake with the magicker at the ball, and he was the one who'd been beaten for it. If Iata had been more careful with Arianna, or—

He closed his eyes, pinched the bridge of his nose.

He was tired.

"I know my duty, Brother," Iata said. "And what you're asking of me lately is beyond my duty. You want me to read nobles without informing them they're being read. You want me to give you insight on people—Maja, this isn't just unethical, it's illegal. Yes, we need the edge. We need every edge, and so I've done it. But this is too far. We've gone too far. We've gone too far for a while now."

That had been roundly hinted at when Homaj had spoken to the magickers. A pounding not-lecture on the ethics surrounding the uses of Green Magics. No one at all was happy at what Iata had done at the engagement ball—and whether he'd taken the punishment for it or not, none among the Council of Magickers had believed Iata was acting on his own initiative. Magickers didn't do things like that on their own initiative.

The magickers only just barely tolerated that one of their own was actively hiding his abilities within the palace. Iata certainly hadn't asked to manifest Green Magics, but if he was found out by the general public, the consequences would be devastating. So the Council tolerated it, because having a Green Magicker at the Seritarchus's side—a Green Magicker who was sometimes himself the Seritarchus—was too valuable to outweigh the detriments and the risk.

Homaj reached into the pocket of his shirt and pulled out the rank seal and the aura projector. The projector he put back—Iata certainly wouldn't need that—but he handed the seal back to Iata. It was his own, after all. Not implanted as magicker seals were legally supposed to be but made with bio-adhesive, to be worn whenever Iata used magics in public, no matter what face he wore. That seal must, at least, show the truth of who he was as a magicker, and those among the Council of Magickers would know who he was.

Iata stared down at the seal in his palm, swallowing audibly. He was distressed, and not trying to hide his aura at the moment. It shimmered a thickening deep forest around him, dense enough it blended into the dark blue of his silk jacket.

"All right," Homaj said. "No more using magics. Not unless it's your choice."

"Not unless I'm wearing the seal," Iata corrected, closing his palm around the seal. "Then it's at least approved by the Council, and I'm not reading anyone covertly. And I don't have to nearly swallow myself not to let my aura show."

Homaj leaned back against the bed, his heart starting to pound with the adrenaline leaving, and his injuries still waiting to be healed.

Iata saw and nodded. "I'll leave you. I have a meeting with Joint Command in half an hour. I didn't think you'd be up to that yet."

"No," Homaj agreed. "But are you, Yan? Truly? I know it takes a few days, when you make yourself unseen."

Iata paused. Struggling with his emotions, and Homaj tried not to feel too much guilt at that.

"The Seritarchus must be present, regardless," Iata said. "Of the two of us, at the moment that means me."

He gave a tight smile and reached a hand toward Homaj's forehead. He hesitated only long enough for Homaj to nod permission before he pressed his cool palm to Homaj's forehead, and the warmth of a summer breeze flooded into Homaj.

It wasn't healing in a physical sense, not like Truthspoken

Change healing. But the magics pushed back the worst of his fears, the gnawing stress, and he breathed out slowly.

"Healing first," Iata said, "then sleep, then Change. I can certainly handle the rest of today. You can be the Seritarchus tomorrow, and I don't envy you the task."

Homaj didn't protest, feeling his limbs growing heavy as he climbed into bed.

"Yan," he said softly, "thank you."

Iata's aura slowly faded, suppressed again by his will. "Always, Brother."

## 31

# NOT YET

> *It has always been the Truthspoken Heir's sacred duty to make an alliance through marriage, to create children who would one day rule, as they would one day rule. That sacred duty brought me so much grief.*
>
> — ARIANNA RHIALDEN, MELESORIE X IN *THE CHANGE DIALOGUES*

The palace's secure back corridors were mainly in the residence and administrative wings, and since Lesander was not yet family—not *yet*—and was staying in the guest suites and not the residence itself, Dressa fit herself back into her servant's persona. Bag over her shoulder and stack of linens in hand, she wound her way through the service corridors of the guest wing, passing staff and the occasional guard.

She held her emotions tightly contained, letting only a relevant amount show through her servant's persona so she would be believable. Her fear was turned into trepidation at being in the palace on a new job. Her frustration at the state of her life was turned into frustration that she was having trouble finding the right corridors. Ari might make a habit of impersonating staff for various missions and training, but Dressa only grudgingly did anything like that these days.

She found her way to the second floor and out to the main corridor with its largest and most luxurious guest suites. Rhys's suite would have been on this floor, and truly, were they fooling anyone by getting a suite here instead of using their own apartment in the residence wing? Rhys wasn't always as attuned as they thought they were.

Dressa found the door to Lesander's suite, paused to consider a servant's knock, and tapped two soft, brisk taps.

The door opened on a young person in green and gold High House Javieri livery, who eyed her suspiciously.

Dressa held up the stack of linens she carried. "I have these for the prince's rooms, along with new toiletries. And table linens." Best to cover all corners of the suite. "May I come in?"

"The cleaners don't come until four," the young person said. But then shrugged and opened the door. "We are almost out of towels. Just don't disturb the prince. She's in the study."

"Absolutely." Dressa hefted her bag and strode inside. She looked around at the suite—more like apartment in its own right—that rivalled her own in the residence wing. Yeah, Rhys was absolutely not helping themself if their own suite had been this luxurious.

Through a sitting room with the curtains pulled back and afternoon sunlight streaming in, through a dining area that could host a small formal party, through a pantry and night kitchen—she'd taken note of the closed doors along the way, any of which could have been the study. The Javieri servant had gone back to whatever they had been doing before, and she couldn't ask them, anyway. As a servant here, she should already know, even if it was one of her first days.

She deposited some of the linens—tablecloths she'd stolen

from her own pantry closet—on a pantry shelf here. She tried to think how best to approach Lesander if she wasn't supposed to disturb the prince. She turned, and—

Lesander was there, and close.

Dressa inhaled sharply, biting down hard on any other sounds of surprise. She stared up at Lesander, who was almost a head taller than she was now, and Lesander stared back down, a frown creasing between her brows.

Her perfume was the same as the night before, juniper on an ocean breeze. Adeius, Dressa could get lost in that scent. She was tempted to steal a shirt, a pillowcase, something, just to take that scent back with her.

Recognition flashed in Lesander's sharp blue eyes, and her lips, a calmer shade of red than the night before, pursed.

"In my study, please," she said, and spun, leading the way.

Dressa passed the young Javieri servant on the way, who stared back with trepidation. And what did that mean? Did Lesander have a temper? If so, that would be good to know now.

"I brought towels for the bathroom," Dressa said, holding up the bag. It wouldn't be safe to talk in Lesander's study. It wasn't truly safe in the bathroom, either—microphones from other rooms could pick up sound, enhance and filter it. But the bathroom was safe enough for them to have a quick conversation, at least, and for her to convince Lesander to go somewhere more secure.

But Lesander said, "My study." She didn't turn, and waited for Dressa to enter before she shut and locked the door.

She held up a hand, went to the desk, and pulled out a portable scrambler, a chunky gray box with an inordinate number of toggles and controls. And that was not a cheap piece of tech if Lesander knew it would thwart the palace's very aggressive surveillance systems.

Would Dressa gamble her future on that tech defeating her

father's surveillance? Her father absolutely could not know what they talked about here.

Lesander turned the scrambler on, and the air grew tense with the static of signal cancellations.

Then she crossed her arms, staring blandly at Dressa from where she stood behind the desk. "You're supposed to be sick, not traipsing about the palace like a servant."

When Dressa didn't answer, Lesander sighed. "This box is military grade of the highest caliber. Flag war room grade. I didn't come unprepared. There's nothing the Seritarchus put in this room that will get out through this, or be able to make a recording. You have my word on that."

"Okay," Dressa said. There was every sign Lesander wasn't going to budge, so she would have to give that small bit of ground and trust. She also had to walk the finest line between asserting her own authority and asking for Lesander's help. Trust worked both ways.

"Okay," she said again. She kept her posture relaxed, but not open. Held some of her Truthspoken presence in her stance and voice, but not an overbearing amount. "I'm not Arianna."

Lesander tilted her head. The sun from the window painted a bright triangle across the pale skin of her neck. Wisps of red hair curling around her ears.

"No," Lesander said slowly. "You're not. But you also are, aren't you? So, give over. Are you her bloodservant? Are you Ondressarie? Adeius help me, please don't say you're the Seritarchus."

"Oh, hell no." Dressa grimaced, banishing the thought with a wave. "No, I'm Dressa. I'm currently the only Truthspoken heir on this planet. I am, now and from now on, *the* Truthspoken Heir, confirmed by the Truthspeaker, but that's not been made public yet. I trust you will not do so."

Lesander stiffened. "What happened to Arianna?"

"She's alive."

Lesander narrowed her eyes. "Did you hurt her, then, so you could take her place?"

Dressa narrowed her eyes, too. "I wouldn't do that to my sister." What the hell did Lesander think of her?

Lesander stared, and she stared back.

Had she thought this would be easy, that she'd throw herself at Lesander and proclaim herself to be the Heir, and much more willing to marry her than Arianna, and they'd just fall in love or something? Adeius, she'd watched too many vids.

She was botching this. She was good with simple things, like working a crowd. She didn't know how to navigate things like this, where emotions were high, and the stakes were dire. And her heart, as she watched the sun play on Lesander's gleaming hair, was doing weird things in her chest.

Lesander tilted her head. "My family's not happy that we don't yet have a formal engagement. They want those mining rights to Madad System the Seritarchus promised."

Dressa's mouth drew tight. That broke the spell. Bought for fucking mining rights. And Lesander? Sold for fucking mining rights?

And was Lesander even concerned for Ari's wellbeing?

But then she saw Lesander was watching her just as avidly as she was watching Lesander, watching her body language, every twitch of her face. Ah, that had been a test to gauge her own sincerity.

Ceorre had been right, and her own observations had been right. Lesander absolutely had evaku.

"May I sit?" Dressa asked.

"It's your palace."

"Not yet," Dressa said quietly, and sat very deliberately on a low teal couch.

# 32

# A PROPOSAL

> *Truthspoken are betrothed—they never propose.*
>
> — ARIANNA RHIALDEN, MELESORIE X IN *THE CHANGE DIALOGUES*

Lesander dragged a chair over from the desk to sit across from Dressa.

"I tried to see Arianna this morning, but I don't think my message was delivered. The guards outside the residence said she was recovering and not receiving visitors. Is she really not on the planet?"

"No." Dressa would have to choose her next words carefully, and she might as well start getting used to that. She'd be doing much, much more of that in the days to come.

But Lesander needed to know what was going on. She was absolutely not going to marry the prince without knowing Lesander had made her own informed decision. She wasn't her father. And she didn't care how much her father would berate her for this later.

Mostly didn't care.

"The curse was more substantial than we've led the public to believe," she said.

Lesander huffed softly. "It wasn't a curse, and it wasn't just Green Magics. I was there, Dressa—I caught her. Adeius, I saw you claw the face off that magicker. And I saw you stay glued to her side earlier when you both came down the stairs, and before you handed her off to me. She was already not well then." Lesander regarded her. "Am I that repulsive to her that she'd go through all of this not to marry me?"

"It's not that," Dressa said sharply.

She bit her lip and sighed, rubbing her hands together slowly, one of her own gestures, not Arianna's. "Listen. Do not, absolutely do not, breathe a word of this to anyone—not your family, not the servants, not anyone at court. No one. I'm not going to make that a command, but—"

"Yes. Agreed."

Dressa searched Lesander's face and body language for sincerity. She found it, but she also didn't know Lesander well enough to know how deeply her own evaku went.

"Good," she said, sealing that agreement. "Arianna has the Bruising Sleep. My father sent her away for treatment. It will be weeks or months before she's well enough to return, and we don't know if she'll be well enough to fully resume her place as the Heir."

Lesander sat back in her borrowed desk chair, rocking it slightly. "The Bruising Sleep? Is it contagious?"

"I was touching her, too," Dressa snapped. "And no, it's not. It's contagious *somehow*, or else it wouldn't be a problem, but I know it doesn't spread through touch or fluids. So you're safe."

Lesander spread her hands. "Of course I want to know if I'm safe. Forgive me. Go on."

Dressa squeezed her hands together. "My father ordered me

to be Arianna for the time that Ari is gone. That order still stands."

"So I'm supposed to get engaged to you, as Arianna, and then, what, when the real Arianna comes back, she'll just take over?"

Dressa didn't like her acerbic tone. "You're not in this for a love match."

She bit back on more. No, this wasn't an ideal situation, but why did Lesander have to be so confrontational? Notions of her crush, painfully hot though Lesander was, were ebbing out through her rising hackles.

"And listen—will you just listen? I'm not doing what my father ordered me to do. I have the backing of the Truthspeaker. I'm going to stay Arianna just long enough to abdicate as Arianna. Which is a formality, and a public show—I am already confirmed as the Heir by the Truthspeaker and witnessed by another speaker. And then, as Dressa, I will publicly assume my role as the Heir."

Lesander stilled the rocking chair. Her voice was softer, huskier. Her eyes intent on Dressa, something turbulent and unreadable lurking within them. "You're going against the Seritarchus."

Dressa swallowed. "Yes. Yes, I am. I—the Truthspeaker and I agreed it was not in the best interest of the kingdom for me to follow my father's orders in this. Ari might not come back in good timing or good health. And I'm—I've never been good at long-term immersion. I've been struggling in the short-term, to be honest. I know you don't have siblings, else—"

"But if I did, I'm sure I wouldn't want to have to live their lives at the expense of my own." Lesander studied her, playing with a loose end of her hair. Dressa watched her wind the strand around her finger, slowly.

"So," Dressa said, trying to regain the upper hand, "so, I'm here because I, as the Heir, would like to sign this engagement contract with you, and I would like to marry shortly, legally. I want to be absolutely sure my father will not have a chance to gainsay what I've decided to do. The public part can come later. The private marriage is to assure your family that I'm serious about this alliance. Very serious. The terms of the contract will not change—you're still marrying the Heir. You're still gaining whatever was promised."

"And you're gaining a shield against your father," Lesander said. Though she didn't sound particularly upset by the idea. She knew politics as well as Dressa, being the heir to a high house princedom. "I'm assuming I can't contact my family to consult with them about this."

"No, any communication like that would get back to my father. And we have to move quickly, if you're willing. My father will catch on that there's something amiss soon."

Lesander nodded. Turned to look out the window, as if gauging the mood of the palace from the sunlight. "Well, you at least seem to want to marry me. Or aren't as against the match as Arianna. I'm not happy about the turbulence. But that seems unavoidable." She shrugged, but Dressa marked the tension in the gesture. "My family won't be happy I didn't consult them. But they also won't be able to drag out the process with concessions over you not being the Heir originally promised."

"Right," Dressa said. "My father will kick up a fuss in private, but he won't do anything to destabilize the kingdom in public. And again, I already have the support of the Truthspeaker. If you are willing, we'll go to the Adeium now, and she'll marry us."

Lesander kneaded her hands together, her knuckles quietly cracking. Her lips were too pale around the edges.

"I wish I could give you more time to think it over," Dressa said, feeling the awkwardness of the moment. She swallowed on a suddenly dry throat. This wasn't how she'd ever thought she'd propose to her future wife.

"You're hardly giving me a choice. Marry you, or go back to my family in shame for failing to marry Arianna Rhialden."

"But you have a choice," Dressa said. "And if you don't want to go back to your family, I'll set you up as best I can in court."

"So then I'd live my life as the prince who spurned the Truthspoken's hand?" Lesander's smile held bitter irony. "I don't think so. I don't know you, Ondressarie. But then, I hardly know Arianna beyond one night where she was trying her hardest not to fall over. And I knew what I was getting into, marrying into the Rhialden Truthspoken. I knew my life would be complicated. I still judge it worth the cost, for my family and for the kingdom."

So she hadn't just been sold into this by her family. That was encouraging. And she knew what this alliance meant to the Rhialdens as well. She knew her family was angling toward the rulership and that this marriage would, at least in part, hold that in check for now.

If she knew all that, then she'd be aware of politics in the palace and willing to play them. She was absolutely playing them now, Dressa realized. Every single movement a calculation, just like her own right now.

Adeius, could Dressa possibly hope to gain a partner in all of this mess and not just a wife? Lesander was meant to be a match for Arianna. She'd known her father wouldn't choose someone who would drag Arianna down, but challenge her. Ari met social challenges with the same stubborn doggedness she gave to everything in her way.

Dressa might have to strain to keep up.

"You'll be my consort," she said slowly, "as Truthspoken Heir, and eventually, when I become the ruler."

Those words, spoken out loud, sent a chill down Dressa's spine. Yes, she'd talked about this with the Truthspeaker. But it felt more real spoken to Lesander. Who would, in fact, soon be her wife.

Adeius, her *wife*.

"And truly, Lesander, I would choose you on my own. If you're willing." Her voice cracked, and that was not something she'd meant to happen.

Lesander stopped breathing for the space of several heartbeats. Her cheeks reddened with a flush, and she didn't look away.

"I'm not likely to get a better offer than that," she said quietly. "All right. There is not much more to think about, is there?"

Dressa rose. "There will be fallout with my father. I'll protect you as best I can, and we have the support of the Truthspeaker." She paused. "I certainly won't require anything more than an official marriage, but . . . if there does grow to be more, I'd welcome it. Or at least, the chance. If you want."

Lesander stood, too, turning as she nudged the chair back toward the desk. "We'll see."

Dressa's heart fell, even though she knew this was hardly a good situation, and hardly romantic. Lesander truly didn't have a good choice here—even as beautiful as she was, and as powerful as her family was, her family would have little chance of making another good alliance if she backed out of a Truthspoken marriage.

But Lesander glanced back through red lashes, the smallest smile tugging at her lips.

Oh, shit. That sent a thrill running through Dressa's core, and she couldn't afford that right now. Not when, Adeius, she was still Arianna.

She smoothed her hair back under her knit cap. She was a servant here. She'd walk with Lesander to the Adeium as a servant, leading the prince through the palace.

Lesander paused in her placement of the chair and watched her, gaze sharp and avid.

"I'm a servant until we reach the Adeium," Dressa said. "Until we reach Ceorre's office. You have guards?"

"Of course."

Dressa nodded. "All right, let's go then."

# 33

# HOLDING HANDS

> *This contract you have signed is in effect and binding.*
>
> — FROM *THE BOOK OF CEREMONIES*, THE LEGAL CEREMONIAL MANUAL OF THE ADEIUM

Somewhere in the last hour, Ceorre had reprinted the engagement contract with the necessary changes to the named parties. She had it ready in a neat stack on her desk when Dressa and Lesander arrived in her office.

The signing was over quickly, officiated and sealed by the Truthspeaker and witnessed again by Speaker Ien. Speaker Ien would be in the history books, whether they liked it or not.

Then, the wedding.

They held hands because the ceremony required it. They looked into each other's eyes, because they both knew they had seconds to understand more, to try to grasp so much they didn't know before they were bound for life.

Lesander's hands, despite her outward calm, were clammy. Dressa was smoothing away her own cold sweat by pulsing a light healing trance.

It had occurred to her, halfway through the Truthspeaker reading from the Book of Ceremonies and Speaker Ien waiting like a nervous statue by the door, that yes, Lesander would be permanently attached to her life from now on, and no, beyond the crush, she knew little about Lesander beyond the broadest strokes. She knew Lesander had evaku, had an eye for politics, and would have been a match for Arianna. That she knew.

She'd seen Lesander compensating for Ari's weaknesses the night before, and that spoke well of her compassion. But that could also speak of her ambition. Lesander was charismatic and could skillfully navigate society—but that was only the most basic bar to entry the Seritarchus would have considered. Lesander had been wary of Dressa in her suite, and Dressa would have been worried if she hadn't been.

But who was Lesander, really? What did she dream about, what did she want in life? Was she moving with her family's plans, or her own? Was she after power and position, or did she, like Dressa, want something more? Did she have any hobbies, and how was she with children?

Adeius. They would have children. And not long now, either, Dressa was sure of it. Not with the kingdom as unstable as it was. They'd be meeting with the genetic techs as soon as the public wedding was official. Nine months later, their children would be ready from the incubators, and they would both be parents.

Would Dressa have to raise and train their children as the sole parent, as her father had with her and Ari while their mother wanted little to do with them? She didn't want that.

"Ondressarie Rhialden. Do you, in the eyes of Adeius and before those witnesses present, pledge to carry out the full measure of this contract with the whole of your self and the strength of your house, to make one house united with Lesander Javieri?"

"Yes," Dressa whispered. She couldn't say it any louder.

"Lesander Javieri. Do you, in the eyes of Adeius and before those witnesses present, pledge to carry out the full measure of this contract with the whole of your self and the strength of your house, to make one house united with Ondressarie Rhialden?"

"Yes," Lesander said, more strongly. But the tightness with which she gripped Dressa's hands spoke of her own anxieties.

"Then it is so," the Truthspeaker said. "This contract you have signed is in effect and binding."

She turned and removed her pendant of office from around her neck, placing it face down at the top of the signature page of the contract, on a circle meant for the marriage seal. The engagement seal was already glowing softly beside it. Ceorre murmured a few quiet words, and the metal pendant gave a soft pulse of light. White light marked the contract paper again in the knotwork seal of the Adeium. Now both marked seals radiated light out along the words on the legal paper, the document taking on the particular lines and patterns of a complete and binding official Adeium document.

The document would send a copy of itself to the Seritarchus, Dressa knew. That was unavoidable. But it wouldn't go further than that before they could make all of this public, signing an unofficial copy at their public engagement and wedding.

But her father would know. Maybe was already reading this message and understanding its import. Her name was on the contract, not Arianna's.

Her name and her title as the Truthspoken Heir.

Ceorre hung the pendant back around her neck, looked at them both still holding each other's hands for dearest life, and sighed.

"Congratulations," she said quietly, with all the various nuances and edges that word could bring.

Dressa took a shuddering breath and finally let go of Lesander's—her wife's—hands.

Ceorre pulled something from her pocket—a box with two simple platinum rings, the kind you could buy anywhere in the city. Adeius, she had been busy this last hour.

Ceorre's brows rose. "I keep them here—nobles occasionally decide they must be married immediately while they're at the palace. Usually after they've had far too much to drink, or are in the throes of some scandal or other. I keep stacks of annulment documents, too."

She glanced back at the contract, its legal lines faintly pulsing. They'd always pulse from now on, the legal heartbeat of this alliance. "Though there's no annulment possible here."

A fact, or a warning?

She handed a ring to each of them, then produced thin chains. "You'll want to put the rings on these until your public wedding."

Dressa looped her ring through the chain and fastened the catch behind her neck. She felt the cool metal settle against her chest, against her racing heart.

Lesander let her own ring and chain down inside her shirt, out of sight.

For that moment, Lesander wasn't the elegant and composed woman she'd been last night at the ball, or at any moment until now.

Their eyes met—and looked away again.

Married. She was actually, truly, married. She was the Heir. And this was her wife.

Lesander drew back, regaining her alertness. She looked like she was straining to maintain her calm, just waiting for a disaster to happen. Maybe for the Seritarchus to come in and rage about this, or for Dressa to morph into a different person entirely.

None of which was impossible.

A Truthspoken marriage. Yes, this was definitely a Truthspoken marriage, with all its prickly nuances. Lesander had known that going in.

If they did end up sleeping together, if they did find more than a partnership at court and an alliance on paper, what would Lesander do when she was someone else? How would Lesander react to—

But she wasn't herself even now. And she was the Truthspoken Heir now—there would be plenty of times in the future when she wasn't herself. More so when she eventually became the ruler. That was what it meant to be Truthspoken, and Lesander knew that.

She caught and held Lesander's gaze again. "Thank you. For doing this today." And for more that she knew she wouldn't be able to find the words for just then. For helping her have a way to be herself in all of this, for knowing the circumstances and holding strong.

Lesander gave a tight nod. Her throat convulsed with her swallow.

And she was still so beautiful, in whatever light she stood in, in whatever company. No matter if she was plainly terrified, as Dressa was too.

## 34

# PREPARATION

> *For Truthspoken, to be someone 'in truth' means to completely submerge your own personality in favor of the persona you are currently inhabiting. Then, to the eyes of anyone trained to see such things, you are not a persona at all, but simply yourself.*
>
> — ARIANNA RHIALDEN, MELESORIE X IN *THE CHANGE DIALOGUES*

Ceorre, still standing in front of her desk, set down her Book of Ceremonies, picked up her glass of water, and took a quiet sip. Master of evaku that she was, she'd be picking up on every nuance between Dressa and Lesander. She was giving them a moment of space, a moment in which to breathe.

Between breaths, Dressa traced the line of Lesander's jaw with her eyes, the wisps of red hair breaking free around the edges of her face. She wanted to reach out and touch them. Curl them around her fingers. Run her hand across Lesander's cheek to her lips.

Ceorre set down her glass, and Dressa jumped.

"Ondressarie. I believe haste continues to be prudent. How do you best wish to make this statement of abdication? I would suggest doing it now, in the courtyard. Which is irregular, but gives your father less chance of stopping you along the way. I will accompany you. You can clean off your cosmetics in the washroom, and take some of the clothes from the Truthspoken closet—there are a few that would suit in Arianna's size."

The Truthspoken closet, in one of the training rooms behind Ceorre's office, was much like the closets she and Arianna and her father all kept adjoined to their prep rooms. It held an array of clothes in every shape and size and cut and class, to be used for Change and evaku practice, and used by Truthspoken as an alternate Change station.

She nodded.

"Heir Consort Javieri," Ceorre said, turning to Lesander, who drew in a sharp breath at the new title. "I believe it would be best for you to not be seen at the abdication. But you should absolutely be with Dressa when she is confirmed as the Heir. Tomorrow."

Dressa headed for the door to the practice rooms. "Do you know where my father is right now?" Had he seen the contract yet?

Ceorre tilted her head. "He's had a busy night and morning. I don't know if he's yet returned."

There was an acid hint to her tone that Dressa didn't want to parse just then.

She ducked into the back hallway off of Ceorre's office and into the washroom on the right. Grabbing cosmetic cloths from the cabinet, she began scrubbing at her face.

"Dressa?" Lesander stood in the doorway. "I can choose an outfit for you, if you wish. If that will save time."

Dressa looked up, still rubbing at her forehead.

Lesander drew back. “Adeius, without the makeup, you look so much like Arianna. Well—you’d be identical, wouldn’t you?”

Dressa glanced at herself in the mirror, and away again. One more day. One more day, and she’d never have to look like this again.

“I’ll Change tonight.” She hesitated, lowering the cleaning cloth. “I think it’d be best if you stayed with me in the residence tonight, though. We don’t have to—I mean, we can be totally professional, but I want you near me. I’m your protection. Until I’m officially confirmed as the Heir tomorrow, and until we officially sign the engagement contract.”

Lesander leaned against the door frame. “You think your father will murder me in my sleep?”

“I—no! That’s not what I said. No, he—” She didn’t know how to explain that her father could manipulate the outcome in a thousand less drastic ways she couldn’t see. He could be anyone. He could come to Lesander as anyone and set things on his own course from the start, and she didn’t want to give him that chance. She didn’t ever want to give him that chance.

Would she even be able to keep separate quarters from Lesander, as their contract allowed? Not without fear of her father interfering, she was sure of that. Adeius, she would have to see how well Lesander could read people, and she’d have to train Lesander to spot the Serltarchus’s tells. That was a dangerous thing, but then, all of this was over the line of dangerous.

“But he wants this alliance with my family,” Lesander said. “He brokered it.”

“Yes, but for Arianna.” Dressa took a breath, kept scrubbing at her face. Could she explain that she was very much not the favored child without losing ground from the start? Was Lesander already picking that up? She had to be.

Lesander was quiet, and when Dressa looked again, she was

gone. But she came back a few minutes later with an armload of silks and velvet.

"This," Lesander said, not giving room for argument, and it was a good choice. A black silk shirt and dark green blazer and trousers, conservatively cut. That was definitely Arianna's style.

Dressa took the clothes into one of the practice rooms while Lesander waited out in the hallway. Then she opened the door, and Lesander watched silently as Dressa used the robust cosmetics kit at a small vanity table. She pushed Arianna's makeup less conservative than usual, but not quite the bold rock star vibe of the night before.

Dressa cut Lesander a look. "Does this weird you out?" She moved fully into Arianna's posture and gestures.

"Yes." Lesander narrowed her eyes. "But I knew what I was in for. And I know who you are."

Lesander paused, straightening the edges of her blouse. "Whatever your reasons, thank you for not following your father's orders." Her lips drew tight, her voice low. "That would not have been a good start to our marriage."

Dressa looked up at her and—and didn't know what to say. No, courting Lesander as Arianna wouldn't have been a good start to anything. But did Lesander's words have any more meaning than that?

Ceorre came up behind Lesander. "Dressa. I've made arrangements for an announcement in the courtyard in ten minutes. That is the best I could do—I still don't know the whereabouts of your father. But I'll be with you. He won't contradict me publicly without censure."

Dressa nodded, took one last look in the mirror, and closed the various cosmetics cases and jars.

She would have Ceorre, yes, and she would have the curiosity of the courtiers as her shield. There was at least an illusion of safety in a crowd.

Well. But Arianna had found the night before that wasn't

true. Had her father Changed out of the form of the magicker yet?

The magicker who'd attacked Arianna had been caught the night before, or so the Guard reports she'd read that morning said, the magicker handed over to the Green Magickers for judgement. And how had that gone? Had her father actually been handed over, or had all of that been fiction? Did the Green Magickers know the whole of what was going on? And was he Changed to himself again, or had he Changed to another persona for some other use?

Dressa's stomach tightened. She had no idea what her father would do next, how he would react to any of this, but she was sure it wouldn't be good. Ceorre had said it was best for Lesander to remain here, but Dressa didn't even count the Adeium as safe.

Her father could be *anyone*. Or send anyone to do his bidding.

"Lesander comes with us," she said, standing. "I know it might be better for her to stay, but—"

She was Lesander's shield. She would, from now on, always be Lesander's shield. Lesander would be safest, from her father or anyone else, at her side.

Lesander eyed her, likely reading her tension. "I'll go where you think best." Which was hardly a statement of subservience so much as practicality. She was the Heir Consort now, but she wouldn't have the whole political lay of the land yet. Not from the height at which she now stood.

"Very well," Ceorre said. "Follow my lead. Dressa—*Arianna*—you're up."

Right. Ceorre had said she'd have to be Arianna in truth for the Truthspeaker to witness this was Arianna's truth.

Dressa breathed slowly, closed her eyes, and submerged.

## 35

## ARIANNA IN TRUTH

> *Truthspoken never retire. They're either assassinated or they abdicate.*
>
> — HOMAJ RHIALDEN, SERITARCHUS IX IN A PRIVATE LETTER, NEVER SENT; PUBLISHED IN *THE CHANGE DIALOGUES*

The afternoon air was balmy, the gathered crowd eerily quiet as Arianna Rhialden, Truthspoken Heir to the Kingdom of Valoris, walked solemnly out to a hastily erected dais just outside the Adeium gates. The Truthspeaker in her red and violet robes walked behind, and behind her, Prince Lesander Javieri, which sent a murmur through the crowd. There had been rumors, of course, that the whole business the night before had been a Javieri plot to get out of the engagement, or a Rhialden plot to screw the Javieris over, or a plot from another high house angling for power who did not want to see that alliance happen, or—

Arianna took the center of the dais, Ceorre stepping up to her left. Lesander took her place at her right, and Arianna turned to her, clasping her hand formally, her smile warm, a smile between colleagues.

Another murmur ran through the crowd, quickly dying as Arianna raised both hands. She touched the amplifier on her throat that Ceorre had given her.

A pigeon landed nearby, cooing in the silence.

"People of Valoris! I, Arianna Rhialden, am your Truthspoken Heir. I have been honored and pleased to serve you as such."

Keep it short. Ceorre had said to keep it short. Less to pick apart later. Less to tangle herself in.

"I'm here to inform you that I am stepping down as Truthspoken Heir. I failed you last night. I failed to repel an attack to my kingdom and my person."

Take the fall, Lesander had whispered to her, as they'd walked out through Ceorre's office into the Adeium. And she'd wanted to argue, of course. It made her stomach burn to think of taking the blame for this, for something out of her control. But that was the point, wasn't it? She was Truthspoken. She had been conditioned only and ever for strength. And she'd been conditioned, too, to put the strength of the kingdom above all. Lesander had said to take the fall, and it wasn't as if she hadn't been thinking it, too. It was the best positioning at that moment to preserve the strength of the kingdom.

The crowd did rustle now, a sway with gasps and rising voices.

Arianna held up her hands again.

"I do this with much sadness, but also knowing that my best position is to support the Truthspoken Heir, who will be my sister, Ondressarie Rhialden. I formally abdicate now to second Truthspoken, witnessed by you, by the Truthspeaker, and by Prince Lesander Javieri, who will sign the engagement contract with Ondressarie as the Truthspoken Heir."

A movement farther up the courtyard caught her eye. A

lone figure, with far too many heads turning to follow his approach.

Arianna's throat tightened. Her sense of herself wobbled, and she strained to pull it back tightly around her.

She met the eyes of the Seritarchus, and—and he nodded. He stood a pace back from the back of the crowd, his hands behind him, nothing in his expression or posture conveying anything but that this was supposed to happen.

Slowly, she eased the unconscious tightening of her shoulders.

Ceorre touched her amplifier. "I, Ceorre Gatri, Truthspeaker to the Adeium of Valoris, witness Arianna Rhialden's sincerity and truth. I confirm her abdication as Truthspoken Heir, witnessed by you, by Truthspoken Arianna Rhialden, and by Prince Lesander Javieri. And by Seritarchus Homaj Rhialden." She nodded to the Seritarchus, and he nodded back. "I confirm Arianna Rhialden as second Truthspoken to the Kingdom of Valoris. I will also confirm Ondressarie Rhialden as the Truthspoken Heir when she returns tomorrow."

She turned to Lesander.

"Prince Lesander Javieri. Do you agree to sign the engagement contract with the Truthspoken Heir Ondressarie Rhialden, with no terms but her name changed?"

Lesander touched her own amplifier. "I agree, Truthspeaker. Javieri agrees."

"Then it will be so," Ceorre said. She clapped her hands once, the sound echoing off the walls of the courtyard. "We are finished. Thank you all, who have gathered to witness."

She nodded again to the Seritarchus, and then turned and stepped down from the dais.

Arianna gave the barest glance to her father, who still stood solemn and unmoved. The storm would come, though. She had no doubt it would come.

They crossed the threshold of the Adeium, crossed into the sanctum. Passed gawking penitents for the second time that day, passed the office suite and its workers busily trying not to look interested, shut the door to Ceorre's office.

Lesander eyed her, then slipped her hand into hers. Warm fingers sending frissons up her arm.

Dressa gasped, feeling the weight of Arianna's personality slip away from her. Not just playing the role of Arianna, but being Arianna in truth.

Ceorre watched her, uncharacteristically subdued.

"My father," Dressa said. She shook her head, still shaking off Arianna. She'd been trained, if a mission required, to bury herself so deeply that she could pass almost any close examination by someone trained in evaku. She'd always hated that technique. She found the sensation of floating apart from herself while almost all of her was someone else nauseating. But here, it had been necessary.

"I will handle your father," Ceorre said, settling into her chair with a sigh.

Dressa wanted to say, with equal and rising horror, "My sister." She'd taken the fall. No, she as *Arianna* had taken the fall, and she hoped to everything Ari would understand why she'd had to do that. Pin it not on the magicker specifically, but on her inability to stop them. Of anything she'd done as Arianna, that had been stretching the bounds of probability, but—Arianna knew her duty. She had always done her duty. And her father had seemed to agree in that moment.

"Dressa—do you want to Change here? I suspect, after that, you will want to Change as soon as possible. Lesander is safe here—Lesander, you can stay in the other practice room. If the Seritarchus comes, I will not let him enter the Change areas while Dressa is Changing. I have the right to invoke that privacy."

Lesander, with what Dressa was coming to recognize as her I-don't-like-this-but-I'm-going-to-do-it-anyway face, nodded.

"Dressa, I'll send one of the Speakers for our dinner. How long will you be?"

Dressa did rapid calculations. She could push a Change faster, but not be ready to deal with much on the other side. "An hour."

Ceorre nodded. "Go, then."

Dressa headed for the back rooms, into the practice room she'd used earlier that day. Lesander followed, looking around at the space.

There was the vanity to one side, near the double doors leading into closet space. Two wingback chairs against the wall beside the entrance. A double bed with a generic-looking but finely made quilt.

Dressa opened the closet and took off one of the generic, shapeless robes hanging on the back. She couldn't wear what she was wearing now to Change back to herself—the clothes would be too small and too tight.

Lesander turned around without her asking, and Dressa quickly stripped out of Arianna's clothes and into the robe, belting it loosely.

She strode to the bed and pulled back the covers, took off her shoes. Her heart was pounding. Too many nerves from the day? Her head felt tight and stuffed with wool.

"I can stay," Lesander said. "Don't you usually have someone guard you?"

"Not always. Rarely, actually. It's not needed in the residence, all the entrances to our apartments are guarded and we have no windows in our bedrooms."

There were no windows in this room, either.

Dressa paused. There was worry etched between Lesander's

brows—for her, or for Lesander's own concerns? Either way, it made her breath catch.

Could she let Lesander stay? But Change was such an intimate thing, a vulnerable thing. She didn't have that trust yet. And her nerves were feeling very raw.

"I won't be long," she said. "Ceorre is good for her word. Of anyone in the capital—trust Ceorre."

Lesander inclined her head, her face closing. "Yes. Of course. I'll wait in the other room, as she said."

Dressa grimaced. Adeius, no, she couldn't start this off with mistrust. Absolutely couldn't. Not when her own position was so unstable.

She scooted to the far side of the bed. There would be just enough room for the two of them.

She patted the empty side of the bed. "Okay, come. Those chairs are hardly comfortable."

Lesander hesitated, her mask fading again, then slipped off her own shoes. The bed creaked as Lesander climbed in beside her, not graceful now that her place, the situation, was uncertain.

Dressa half turned to look at her—and she was so close. Her perfume a palpable aura around her.

And Dressa was supposed to put herself in a Change trance now, with her—

With her wife beside her.

In name only. She had to tell herself it was in name only, they had nothing more between them than that.

But Dressa reached for Lesander's hand, held it loosely but securely. She might have needed Lesander's help earlier, to marry her and seal that part of her plans, but now that they were well and truly in this, it was Lesander who needed her help now. To navigate, to know what to do next.

"I know you haven't seen a Truthspoken Change," she said. "It will be—it's odd to watch. It doesn't look like anything's happening, but if you look away, the next time you look, it might be a little different. And then next time again. That's what will happen—all that will happen. I'll Change back to myself. And then I'll wake up, and we'll return to the residence." Her bloodservant, Pria, should be done with her own Change by then—and Adeius, she'd have to Change right back.

Another mess to untangle.

Lesander shifted, her palm damp in Dressa's. "You're sure you're okay that I'm here? The chairs are fine, truly."

Dressa bit her lip. She had never liked people around her when she Changed. Not even Pria. "I'd rather have you beside me, and turned away from me, than watching me from across the room."

Lesander let go of her hand and shifted to lie down, not quite fully turning away.

Dressa lay back, too.

Their eyes locked, and they both stilled. Dressa felt her heart start to pound.

The slightest crease formed between Lesander's brows.

"I'm not what you expected, am I?" Dressa asked, her stomach tightening.

Lesander rolled back over to face her, emotions flickering across her face until she finally said, "No."

She leaned forward and carefully pressed her lips to Dressa's forehead.

Dressa suppressed a shudder, heat shooting through her.

Lesander was so close. Her lips so close, and she didn't want to put herself into a trance for the next hour, she wanted to kiss Lesander, kiss her thoroughly. She wanted to do more in this bed than just Change while Lesander kept watch.

But her lips were not yet her own.

Had she just misread the guarded hunger in Lesander's eyes? No, it was still there, simmering just beneath the surface. But that hunger had to be for Dressa as herself. It had to be.

And she'd have to make sure before she crossed that particular line. It would only entangle them further.

"I'll keep watch," Lesander said, and turned back on her other side to face the door.

Dressa watched the soft movements of Lesander breathing for several of her own long breaths. Then she closed her eyes and slipped into Change.

# 36

# LANDING

> *The Xelenia Sky deluxe model convertible car with dual hover engines is guaranteed to be good as new for ten Valon Standard years after purchase!*
>
> — ADVERTISEMENT FOR XELENIA HOVERCAR

Ari stepped off the *Jade Crescent*'s ramp to the gray pavement of the landing pad. The air was hot and metallic so near the engines. The engines pinged as they shed heat from the landing, though the hull itself would be relatively cool, the worst of the atmospheric entry having been deflected by the ship's shields.

There was a breeze in the sunlight, the smell of grass and flowers.

Bettea shouldered both of their duffels, nudging another hard case with clothes and cosmetics with faer toes. "The estate said their car will be by soon to pick us up."

Fae leaned forward to peer around the ship to better look at the other pads near them. Theirs was on an edge facing the forest, and of the twenty or so landing pads Ari could see, most were occupied by small crafts of varying designs and builds. Most would have been classified as shuttles or small trade craft like theirs, but she saw a few that looked like racing craft and one at the far end, taking up two pads, might have been a pocket freighter.

Ari brushed her short hair out of her eyes, adjusted her sunglasses. Ever so casually, she rested a hand on Bettea's shoulder, steadying her unsteady legs.

Bettea shot her a look, but faer only comment was to smile tightly.

"There," Ari said, pointing to where the sun was glinting on moving metal across the field. "Is that the direction of the house?"

Bettea squinted. "Maybe. I think so."

The car shot straight toward them, hover engines blowing the grass around it like the wake of a boat. Then it banked, slowed, and stopped a few meters away from them.

The car was open-topped, the dark red hull pocked and bug-streaked.

A person jumped out over the side, neglecting the door, holding onto a large-brimmed hat. They straightened, looked toward Ari and Bettea, and for a moment, froze.

Ari watched the tension of their muscles, the way they seemed to hunch in on themself. What had they seen? Had they recognized Ari? Were they attracted to her, intimidated by her? She hadn't thought she was that intimidating as Imorie, not as much as Arianna, anyway. What did this response mean?

But the person took a breath and started forward. As if bracing themself. Eyes on the ground.

"I can get your bags," they said, and reached for the case next to Bettea.

Ari's hand twitched toward it—there was nothing incriminating in there, nothing at all in her possessions here that one

Imorie Rhialden méron Quevedo, contract member of a minor branch of a major house, shouldn't have.

"You're from the estate house?" Ari asked. "Windvale Estate?"

The person nodded. Looked up, and closer now, Ari saw they were young, maybe around her own age. Pale skin, short scraggly dark hair, scruff of dark beard.

The person hesitated, looking at her, their head tilted. That weird tension was back.

Well, and if they were about her age, maybe it was an attraction thing. She was an attractive person—whatever else she and Bettea had done to her appearance, that certainly had not changed.

She offered a smile. "I'm Imorie Quevedo." She'd been about to say Rhialden, to lean into that as she'd planned, but at the last moment gave her other name. It seemed weird and pretentious, in front of this person who was obviously intimidated by something about her, to proclaim herself a Rhialden here. "She and her."

They ducked their head again, eyes disappearing behind the brim of the hat. "Etienne—Eti. He and him."

Ari nodded. "Nice to meet you, Eti. Are you from Windvale Estate?"

"Yes. Here to pick you up—I'm usually a gardener. But everyone's at the party, and everyone else was needed, so . . ." He trailed off. Reached for the heavy case by Bettea and, without another word, hauled it toward the waiting car.

Ari exchanged a look with Bettea.

"Party?" Ari mouthed. Bettea shrugged, adjusted the duffels fae was still holding, and headed after Eti. After the barest moment, Ari followed, stepping carefully to hide her sway. Well, disguise it as much as possible, it wasn't possible to hide it all.

But Eti didn't seem to notice. He wasn't looking at either of them as he secured their luggage in the trunk.

Ari and Bettea settled into the back seat, Ari brushing what looked like crumbs off her side of the seat. None of this was giving her confidence that Hestia was the fabulous resort world it promised. And if this estate couldn't even send out a decent car and a regular driver, what did that say about her future treatments for the Bruising Sleep? Would her father truly send her to a backwater for treatment?

Bettea made an annoyed sound, and fae got out faer comm, pressing the screen as fae looked back toward the *Jade Crescent*.

Ari turned, watching the ramp retract back into the ship's hull. Adeius, they both would have forgotten that. Ari was barely stringing coherent thoughts together, but was Bettea so nervous as to forget that faerself?

Eti climbed back into the car by vaulting over the driver's side door like he had when he'd gotten out.

"Sorry. Door stuck earlier today, I can't get it open." He punched the engines on, and the car vibrated as the engines spun up. When they started moving, at least the vibrations eased.

Would they even get to the estate house in one piece?

## 37

# PARTY ON HESTIA

*I lost my heart on a broken moon*
*Sun only shines for an hour at noon*
*We made our bed to an ancient tune*
*I found my heart on that broken moon.*

— THE RINGS OF VIETOR, IN THEIR POPULAR SONG "BROKEN MOON"

The wind whipping around them made it hard to talk, so Ari just watched the grassy field give way to the forest—which was less a forest, she saw as they passed it in a few seconds, and more a glorified tree line. Past the trees, another rolling field led to a large estate house, with geometric granite framed with black and gold trim.

A large number of cars were parked in a line outside the front entrance. That must include everything the grounds had, because the car Eti was driving sounded in drastic need of a tune-up.

Eti slowed as they pulled into the half circle leading to the entrance, and the wind that had made questions impossible while travelling stopped.

"So what's the occasion?" Ari asked.

"What?"

"The party. What's the party for?"

"Oh. Uh—it's to celebrate—" Eti looked back at her, froze long enough for Bettea to tap his shoulder.

"Brake!" fae said, and Eti did, jolting the car.

They'd stopped bare centimeters from hitting another car.

Ari raked her hair back from her eyes, trying to settle it back into place after being thoroughly blown by the ride.

"Turn to me," Bettea said, and she did, holding still as Bettea made better work of the mess.

She did her best with Bettea's tousled hair in return.

Eti got out of the car, looked toward the entrance where there was only just now a porter coming out to them.

The porter, looking distractedly over their shoulder to the front door, from which the muffled sounds of loud music were coming, said, "Are you Imorie Rhialden méron Quevedo and personal servant Jis Ameer?"

"Yes—thanks." Ari nodded as the porter opened her door. At least her door actually opened.

"I'll take you up to your rooms," the porter said. They snapped at Eti, "You, grab some of the bags. Uh, Evorin? Etan?"

"Etienne," Eti said, taking a duffel over one shoulder. The porter shoved the heavy case at him, too, and took the other duffel themself.

"Sorry," the porter said, walking quickly back toward the entrance. "There's a party happening just now—you'll probably want to drop your luggage and come down. Count Badem and the rest of the guests are all there, as well as some from the neighboring estates. It'll be loud once we get inside, though they'll probably carry the party out to the patio in an hour or so when the sun isn't as high."

The porter opened the front door, and Ari was blasted with a wall of sound. An ear-splitting wail about lost love on a broken moon—Adeius, was that a Rings of Vietor song?

Ari's head throbbed into an instant headache. And this was a place where sick people went to get well? Did they have any actual sick people here just now? Besides her?

Bettea read her mood and hustled them along, following the porter up a flight of stairs to a closet-sized lift and up to the third floor.

The sound wasn't nearly as loud up here, but it was still working on her nerves.

"Do the rooms have any sound-dampening systems?" she grated out.

"Of course," the porter said. "And as I said, they'll be moving outside in an hour or so."

They paused at a door halfway down the corridor and waved their key at the lock pad. "Here—press your hand here to add your biometrics, please."

Ari did so, and then stepped aside to let Bettea press faers, too.

Another grating few seconds of the porter fiddling with the pad controls, then the door clicked open.

The apartment itself was spacious enough, the ceiling vaulting up from the windows to a half peak at the corridor wall. A sitting room was the main room, and Ari saw a short hallway leading to more rooms with open doors and sunlight showing.

Eti set down the bags he carried, glanced around, and then waited awkwardly.

Ari wondered if Imorie should thank someone like Eti, who was obviously out of his comfort zone even as hired help, but she shrugged inwardly and said, "Thanks." For however long she'd be here, it would do her well to at least be friendly to the staff.

The porter took it as their own thanks, nodded, and conducted them on a short tour of the apartment. A small kitchen and dining area, two bedrooms. A small bathroom.

"I'd best get back to the party," the porter said, though they weren't clear on if they were working at the party or planning to join it.

"What are you celebrating?" Ari asked, not liking how Eti had evaded her question before. That was odd. Why keep the subject of a party secret? It certainly wasn't a secret party with how loud it was.

"Oh," the porter said, heading for the door. "We're celebrating the engagement of the Truthspoken Heir."

Ari missed a step, and Bettea steadied her. Well. Well, and she'd known that would happen. She'd known Dressa, as herself, would have to continue the engagement with Lesander.

Her throat tightened. What would she come back to, and how well would Dressa get to know Lesander? Just how much of a gap would she have to bridge as herself—she couldn't pretend to be attracted to Lesander, as she knew Dressa was. She was so seldom attracted to anyone.

The porter was still talking, and the next words caught Ari's attention like a knife to the gut.

"We were all a little worried about how that would work out after the abdication, but I've been watching the vids and there actually seems to be a genuine spark between Ondressarie and Lesander—"

Bettea had stopped too, now, and faer grip was painfully tight on Ari's arm.

"What?" fae breathed. "You said Ondressarie? Dressa is engaged to Lesander?"

The porter's brows knit. "You got the news, right? About Arianna's abdication?"

Ari made a sound that she couldn't help, not at all, somewhere between a protest and a growl.

The porter stepped back.

"Sorry," Bettea said. "Sorry—we, uh—she's a contract member of High House Rhialden, a minor one, we know Arianna, from a distance—at—at least we've met her once, Imorie did—"

Ari clamped her fingers on Bettea's wrist, dug in. Bettea shut faer mouth. And how much work would Ari have to do to divert suspicions from herself after that little confession?

Ari felt something touch her other arm and jumped. Etienne, laying a tentative hand on her arm.

She felt—she felt warmth in that touch, reassurance. She felt, strangely, better able to think through this new disaster.

No, this catastrophe. Dressa, as Arianna, had abdicated? Had that been her father's wish all along? Had he shown up at the ball as a magicker to get her out of the way?

Had she disappointed him so badly?

Eti's grip was firm but not tight on her arm. She felt ire draining away into a turbulent sort of weight on her soul.

The porter was looking at her strangely. "You really didn't know? It's been all over the feeds, absolutely everywhere. Everyone's talking about the gown Ondressarie wore to her confirmation as the Truthspoken Heir—it had holographic butterflies all over it! Not a control freak, this one."

Ari closed her eyes, breathed in once, and recentered. Because she had to. Because she was here, and she was not Arianna. She was worlds away from Valon, and her sister, and her father. She didn't know what had happened. She didn't know what decisions they'd had to make. She just didn't know.

"Here," the porter said, digging a comm out of their pocket and pressing the screen before handing it to her. The picture they'd wanted to show her was their menu background. Dressa, in a frilly, gauzy gown that Ari would never wear, Lesander in flowing silver. Dressa was smiling, looking somewhere to her left. Lesander looked at the camera, as if challenging whoever had taken the image.

Ari tried to read Dressa's body language, read if her expression was genuine or how far from true if not. Dressa didn't seem as open as she normally was, there was more stiffness to her spine. But she projected happiness, if with reserve—and that would likely fit whatever scenario she or their father had concocted to have Arianna abdicate.

Bile rose up Ari's throat. She handed back the comm.

"Thank you. I—I'm tired from travel. I think I'll stay in my rooms, at least for now. Please tell Count Badem I will be down for dinner—when is dinner served?"

"Uh, we're not doing a formal dinner tonight, but I can have food sent up to you, if you'd like."

"Yes. Please do that. You have my menu preferences?"

"If you filled them out with the welcome packet, yes."

Bettea must have done that while she'd been napping on the way in. She hoped Bettea hadn't diverged her preferences as Imorie too far from her preferences as Arianna. She needed something familiar right now.

Ari felt another wave of overwhelm threaten to carry her away.

It was Bettea, this time, who reclaimed her arm and squeezed it gently, moving her toward the bedrooms. Etienne let go and stepped back, looking chagrined.

Ari stumbled on the lip where the living room floor met the hallway floor. Adeius, this estate was a shambles.

When she looked up again, the door was closing, and both Etienne and the porter were gone.

She was too tired to stop the tears, but she bared her teeth against them.

And they couldn't talk here. Couldn't break character. She had no idea of the security in this place, and she had a direct order from her father not to do so. She wanted to run to the nearest comm and fire off a message to him, ask him what the hell was going on, but he'd said not to break cover for any reason. And did this situation merit whatever dire measures were in place as a last-ditch contact? Would she burn up her last credit with him to do so, and so show him just how unworthy she really was?

In the bedroom she assumed was hers, she gripped the nearest metal bed post, forcing her breathing to slow. Closing her eyes against the slow spin of the room.

She wanted to scream. Trembled with the need to vent her tension.

She opened her eyes and met Bettea's, her bloodservant's eyes echoing her conflict, her panic.

What had happened at the capital to so drastically change plans? Was her father well, was her sister well? Had anyone found out about the Bruising Sleep and was the kingdom safe?

Adeius, she didn't know, and she couldn't ask. She couldn't ask for—well, however long it took her to get well enough to go back. She could only watch the news and pray it wasn't as bad as she feared. For the kingdom, or for herself.

But Dressa was the Heir. And Dressa was with Lesander. If Dressa married Lesander—that was it, wasn't it? The Javieris were powerful enough that they wouldn't let their daughter get bumped down again to second-tier consort.

How long did it take to plan a wedding?

She banged the side of her fist against the bedpost, one short, quick vent of tension. And another vent as she cursed from the pain.

Then she sat on the bed, pulling back her calm.

"I'll rest now, Jis."

No, that was still too Arianna. She slackened her posture, scowled up at Bettea. "Why the hell are you still standing here?"

Bettea flinched. Faer gaze narrowed, faer shoulders going stiff. But then fae relaxed as well.

"Yes, ser. On my way out, ser."

And oh, you could cut the air with the edge on those words.

Ari sat on her bed and stared at the faded blue and white wallpaper on her bedroom wall.

Then she pulled her comm out of her jacket pocket, hooked to the estate's network, and started pulling up the news. It wouldn't be the complete picture, but it was something.

This was not the end. She decided it was absolutely not the end.

38

# THE VISITOR

> *Many academic studies—based purely on observation from public records—have been conducted on the long-term psychological effects of being Truthspoken while actively governing the kingdom. Results so far have been inconclusive. The only way to get comprehensive results would be to study the Truthspoken directly, and that will never happen.*
>
> — DR. IGNI CHANG IN "DISCOURSE ON THE HUMANITY OF OUR RULERS"

Ceorre Gatri carefully set down two teacups on the low table in her living room. She set down the teapot and two jars of tea, with her favorite and Homaj's. Then she settled on the couch and waited.

The teapot steamed into the still air. Her apartment behind the Adeium was silent, sound proofed. She was too important for it to be otherwise.

And there was a dizzying thought, in the quiet of the night. It had always terrified her, in the moments when she paused to think about it, which weren't many, how little there was between her and the fate of the kingdom. How actively she could shape it.

And she had that day. She had. She knew it was for the better. Would Homaj see it that way?

The entry door gave a low chime.

"Come in."

It opened, and a moment later one of her guards came in, followed by Homaj.

"Thank you, Lin, you may go," she said to the guard. "I verify."

Lin bowed and quietly shut the front door on their way out.

Truthspoken being Truthspoken, and she being who she was, she verified any visitor she had as safe to enter. No matter if the person was visibly the Seritarchus—she was all too aware that anyone with Truthspoken training could also be the Seritarchus.

Homaj took the overstuffed chair across from her, and without looking at her, began pouring tea. He poured for both of them.

She unscrewed the lid of her jar, using the infuser scoop inside to take a fair amount before she set it in her mug.

He did the same with his.

And when the tea was steeping, they both sat back and regarded each other.

Homaj had Changed back to himself as the Seritarchus. His fine black hair was in a messy bun, his clothes more casual than he wore for court—a loose indigo shirt with embroidered red vines up one sleeve, and a split-paneled red skirt that was a few years out of fashion. She recognized his comfort clothes. Knew the signal they gave—that this meeting wasn't to be formal. That he wanted to talk to his friend, not the Truth-speaker.

And thank Adeius for that. It was what they usually did

after a day that would have been particularly hard for both of them. A mutual debrief, or mutual way to vent. But she'd been worried this time. It had gnawed at her gut that he'd think she'd gone too far.

"I am furious with you," he said calmly, holding his steaming mug to his chin. She let her own steam on the table.

"I expected as much."

He regarded her, and she saw the exhaustion around his eyes. Had he slept at all since the night before, or had he just Changed, which gave a dubious sort of rest?

He set his mug back on the table. "I found I've gained a different Heir. Without my knowledge or permission."

She arched a brow. "Have you talked to Dressa?"

She knew he hadn't. He'd never found it easy to talk to Dressa.

"And I've gained another daughter as well." He narrowed his eyes, stared at her. "I saw the marriage contract. Does Dressa know Lesander is Truthspoken?"

"I've told her enough to keep her wary. I thought it best not to tell all. Dressa can't lie with her soul wide open."

He reached again to remove the infuser from his tea, and she did as well. She pulled her mug to her lips and inhaled. Hibiscus, vanilla, and cardamom.

"Ceorre," he said, and she heard the quaver in his voice. Paused to look up at him.

He met her gaze. "Ceorre, am I truly that off-course? That you'd have to do this? Countermand my orders, and go those steps further?"

She considered. He had been, yes. He'd also still been acting in earnest—he'd truly believed that ordering Dressa to be Arianna had been the best course to go. But then, he'd always favored Arianna because she was more like himself, and she'd always been eager to please. She worshipped him in a way Ceorre didn't think was healthy, especially knowing all of

Homaj's flaws, which Arianna couldn't or refused to see. Dressa had no illusions of her father's grandeur. And Homaj had always struggled to understand Dressa's very different personality, but Ceorre wondered sometimes if he'd also attached to Arianna because she took him at face value when Dressa didn't and never would. He could be challenged by Ceorre, and sometimes by Iata. But being challenged by both of his children might topple the facade he'd given everything to maintain.

"You don't see Dressa," she said. "If you did, you wouldn't have set her an impossible task which would have harmed the kingdom in so many ways."

He spread his hands, wincing as hot tea splashed on his sleeve. "She's Truthspoken trained. She can play the role of anyone I ask her to. She has her duty."

Ceorre pressed her lips tight. "Dressa knows her duty. She knows it so well she just took up a position she never wanted and married a prince who she knows might turn out to be her enemy."

"Of course she was jealous of Arianna," Homaj scoffed. "I'm surprised you can't see that, Ceorre. And she has a crush on Lesander—that will turn into a love match, which we don't want."

"Don't try to antagonize me, Homaj," she said softly. "I'm not going to fight tonight."

He clamped his teeth shut, his jaw working. He looked away. Had another sip of tea.

She took her first.

"Maja," she said, using his private name, not the name of the Seritarchus and his public persona. She knew better. He might have grown far closer to his public persona in this last decade than when he'd started, but he wasn't, at heart, the controlling bastard he made himself out to be.

He closed his eyes at the name and the tone, as if he was bracing himself.

"Maja," she continued, "you started your journey all those years ago bending yourself into a shape that didn't come easily. Do you truly want Dressa to do the same?"

His personality had been much more suited to an Ialorius style of rule than Seritarchus, ruling with fluidity and the ability to assess and adapt instead of with the rigid grip of control. He'd assessed the state of the kingdom at that time and decided that the kingdom would best be served by a Seritarchus—which was ironically a very Ialorius thing to do. She hadn't liked that decision. Rulers who bent themselves against the grains of their personalities weren't always successful. But he had been, for the most part. And, she thought, with much of Iata's help. Iata more solidly fit the mold of a Seritarchus.

"I've done my duty," Homaj said. "I expect no less of my children."

"And they've given you no less." She kept her voice soft, though she felt a surge of anger at his stubborn refusal to see.

Then he drew in a ragged breath, and she saw all the little signs he'd been so carefully hiding. The faint tremor to his hand. The pinched lines around his mouth. The rigid posture, and holding his limbs closer to his body than he normally did.

She sat forward. "Maja."

He waved the name away, and she held up her palm in apology.

"Homaj. Are you still injured?"

"I've healed myself." He stared down at his mug, swirling it slowly.

But he couldn't heal the mental injuries, could he? She'd been appalled at his state in the jail cell, but he'd been lively enough in Jalava's office that she hadn't thought the wounds sustained that night ran as deep as they had. There were many layers at work here, and she thought now too many had culminated in that night in the Palace Guard jail. He'd already been running scared, and the guards' beating had driven it all deep.

His hand was shaking again, more noticeably now, and he scowled at it with a dark fury.

"I've healed myself," he said again, as if the words themselves could make it true. And as the Seritarchus, his words often could make things true.

And then, on top of the injuries he'd sustained in the jail, and whatever had happened with the Green Magickers, and she couldn't imagine that had been pretty, he had somewhere in there realized his daughter and the Truthspeaker had staged a mild coup.

She didn't regret it. It had absolutely been the right choice, and how he was acting now solidified that choice. If Dressa had remained Arianna, Homaj wouldn't have made anything easy for her, because she could never live up to his picture of who Arianna should be. Ari herself could hardly do that. And if Dressa had remained preoccupied with achieving the impossible, and him preoccupied with wishing for Ari, where would the kingdom be then?

But she watched the grimace on his face, knowing he was trying to heal his nervous system, to calm his body's responses, and his body was resisting him. She could stand by her decision and still regret that it had caused further pain

Ceorre set down her mug and reached to take his as well. Then she stood and moved behind him, placing her hands on his shoulders, pressing down firmly. A pressure to calm the storm.

## 39

# PRESSURE

> *A Truthspoken ruler doesn't just bear the burden of the kingdom; they bear the burden of the many versions of themself who rule that kingdom, all the good and all the bad.*
>
> — HOMAJ RHIALDEN, SERITARCHUS IX IN A PRIVATE LETTER, NEVER SENT; PUBLISHED IN *THE CHANGE DIALOGUES*

Ceorre pressed down on Homaj's shoulders, a steady, constant pressure.

Homaj had been in his early twenties when he'd ascended to the Seritarcracy, not much older than Dressa was now. Ceorre had been young for a Truthspeaker, too—they'd both come into far too much responsibility before they were ready for it. There'd been a few times in those early years when he'd trip over into panic attacks, and this had helped. The pressure, the sense of stability, had helped.

His breathing, which had grown more erratic, started to

calm. He was trembling, though. His whole body was trembling, and she knew if he could stop it, he would have.

The Truthspoken had the finest team of loyal physicians in the kingdom, a few trained as well in psychology, but the Truthspoken were Truthspoken. They couldn't afford weakness, even the ordinary, so very Human things that weren't weakness to anyone else. Like recovering from a trauma.

He needed help, and while she had psychological training, it wasn't of the sort that could easily help him now.

Ceorre gently let go of his shoulders, came around again. "Go and Change, Maja. Go be someone else for a few days. Take your guard captain, Zhang. Go into the city. Or the countryside—doesn't matter. Go and be someone other than the Seritarchus for a few days. Iata will manage while you're gone."

It wasn't ideal, especially with everything in flux from Dressa's announcement as Arianna, but Iata was excellent at being the Seritarchus. He was steady and firm. If he didn't quite have the same strategic mind as Homaj, he also wasn't as volatile. And maybe, just now, the kingdom needed that steady and firm hand.

Homaj was quiet for a long, long moment. And she thought, with a wonder, that he might actually take her suggestion.

"I need to train Dressa."

"You don't have to be gone that long. She's already highly trained—a week won't make the difference there."

He rubbed his face in his hands. "And this situation with the Kidaa on the border worlds—potentially with the Kidaa—if they're possibly attacking worlds, if it's possibly not a ploy from warring houses, if they've decided they're not, in fact, culturally impervious to violence . . . then we have a problem."

That was the sharpest understatement. If the only non-Humans they'd met, whose technology was so advanced that no Human had yet been able to explain any of it in two hundred years, decided to go to war with Valoris, or with any of the Human nations, the results could be catastrophic.

"And another noble left court this morning," he went on. "Iata said in his notes—all the signs are pointing to another case of the Bruising Sleep. It's becoming an epidemic, Ceorre. No, it already is. How do we fight against that when no one can come up with a reason for the illness to begin with? Ceorre, it took down my Heir. How long before it claims me, or you, or one of the high house princes or lords—how long until it runs among us unchecked, because the cases have been accelerating this last year. And yes, we can treat it, but we don't know why it's happening, and we don't have a cure."

She felt his shoulders bow under her hands, collapsing under so much weight.

"Maja. You are one person. You can't hold it all together. You have Iata—and that's a blessing most rulers never have, someone capable whom they trust who can spell them for a time so you can rest. You have Dressa, who is also highly capable, if in a different way than you're used to. And you have me."

He reached up, placing a hand over one of hers. "I promised Ari I would keep her life safe for her to return to. I've failed that promise."

Ceorre's lips tightened. He'd otherwise failed Dressa by promising that in the first place, but she wasn't going to say that again now.

He sighed, and as the air left him, it seemed as if his spirit left him, too. The tension left his shoulders, but so did the fight.

"All right," he said. "All right, a week."

She let go of his shoulders, coming back around to sit, to face him. She hadn't expected him to say yes.

Her senses sharpened, evaku-trained instincts gauging every nuance of his posture, his expression, his voice. From the start of his rule twenty-three years ago, he'd been in constant motion, always steps ahead of whatever was happening at court, or at least, reacting with a speed she found dizzying. All while giving the illusion that he was a steady pillar of control, not a kaleidoscope of complexities and movements.

What he really needed was to publicly change his style of rule to Ialorius. He needed space to unbend and embrace his strengths, not repress them. But she wasn't sure, with all she could see of him and all she knew, that he'd even be able to unbend at this point. Not without disaster to himself and the kingdom.

He should have made stronger protests to her suggestion that he take a break. His protests were almost rote, a fulfillment of an obligation.

And maybe, truly, he'd come tonight for permission. Maybe he'd known he couldn't safely run the kingdom in this state, and not just because of the night in the Guard's jail. He'd been working so hard from so many angles this last year, managing and averting disasters before they could fully take hold. Arianna's collapse was just another in a string of crises that were chipping away at the kingdom and its ruler, and those crises were looking to ramp up, not calm down.

Maybe he'd known he needed a break, but needed someone else to tell him to take it. He couldn't stop on his own.

"I'll talk to Iata," she said. "And we'll both work with Dressa. Everything is well in hand. We will weather these next days, and so will you. But not here, not as Homaj."

He nodded, and his quiet capitulation continued to trouble her.

She had no illusions that he wouldn't turn wherever he went into some sort of work trip, but at least he'd be away from the palace. And Zhang, the captain of his personal guard, was well adept at calling him on his bullshit.

He rose, then hesitated. "I will Change here."

Beyond the practice rooms in the Adeium proper—which were occupied by Dressa and Lesander at the moment and guarded by her own personal guards—she had a small spare room with a bed and a semi-stocked closet in her apartment itself. An extra measure for Truthspoken who needed the utmost discretion. And the Adeium had its own underground tunnel connecting it to the network of secure tunnels leading into the palace and out to the city.

It was a measure of his distress that he didn't want to go back to the palace but would rather Change here, even though she knew he was still upset with her.

"I'll call Zhang," she said. She didn't know if Homaj had taken the tunnels from the palace to the Adeium or not—likely not, if he'd come as himself. But Zhang would certainly take them. This had now become a Truthspoken mission—albeit one to stay sane.

And she'd call Iata, too. Had Iata yet Changed back to himself? She hoped not, though by now he could accomplish the Change back to Homaj quickly enough.

"Yes, fine. Tell her to bring city clothes—hers and mine. And my travel cosmetics."

Zhang knew the drill, but Ceorre would relay it all the same.

Homaj strode for the short hallway which led to the bedrooms. He paused, though, before he went out of sight.

"Ceorre. Take care of the kingdom. Whatever else, take care of the kingdom."

She nodded. "I will."

And that, in the end, was why she so often overlooked his abrasive persona, his decisions which she didn't outright contradict but didn't always like. He'd given everything, absolutely everything, to his kingdom. He continued to do so. It wasn't healthy, and she didn't like that either, but she couldn't judge his actions as merely exercising his own power. He was far too aware of how fragile that power really was. She wouldn't give up on him, as long as he remained aware and willing to course-correct if needed. And as long as his decisions didn't move too far into catastrophic harm, as lately they'd started to.

She heard the door to the extra bedroom click shut.

Alone in her living room, she turned away from the hallway and took a long, slow breath.

"Adeius. Strength."

She hoped, she prayed, that his time away from the palace would help him reset. Get him help, get him some perspective. Get him—Adeius, or at least temper—this course of self-destruction. An image flashed in her mind again of him covered in bruises and blood from a beating that hadn't at all been necessary to endure, though he'd seemed to think it had been.

Adeius, as she'd grown older, she'd also grown to hate the Truthspoken system even more. And here she was, the buffer, the one giving her permission for it to continue. She'd helped Dressa out of a bad situation today, yes, but then put her right into another one.

She feared for the kingdom, but she also feared for those who ruled it. She was the Truthspeaker—it was her job to decide if the Truthspoken were steering the kingdom true.

And what if she decided that the only way forward was a kingdom without Truthspoken? What if she wanted to dismantle this broken system! What then?

She closed her eyes against that dangerous, absolutely impossible thought. The Rhialdens would never stop being Truthspoken. She, herself, would never stop seeing everything through the lens of evaku. Even if one of the high houses finally succeeded in overthrowing the Rhialdens, which was looking frighteningly more likely as the months went on, they would only install one of their own illicitly trained members as Truthspoken, and the whole destructive cycle would continue.

She opened her eyes.

Lesander. Lesander Javieri was fully Truthspoken trained,

she was sure of it, and she had to talk to Iata about what to do about that in the next few days, if anything.

And Dressa? She had to pray Dressa would see.

And that Homaj would come back, more fully himself. The kingdom needed his strategist's mind. The kingdom desperately needed his ability to spot his enemies and steer them clear without conflict. Yes, the kingdom could do without him for a few days or a week. But he wasn't wrong that he was badly needed, too.

And if Homaj couldn't resume his duties? If he kept making decisions that drove the kingdom downwards?

Then she'd pray that Iata or Dressa could step up to rule the kingdom and rule it well.

She'd do whatever it took to keep her kingdom safe, but she'd also do whatever it took to save those she loved.

Thanks so much for reading! I hope you enjoyed *The Truthspoken Heir*, and if you did, please consider leaving a review! The story continues in *The Shadow Rule.*

Want to stay up to date on the latest books? Sign up for Novae Caelum's newsletter!
https://novaecaelum.com/pages/newsletter

# THE CAST

*Note: Because this future universe has full gender equality, binary gender characters (male, female) may be cis or may be trans. I've only stated if they're trans if it comes up within the story itself.*

**Arianna Rhialden (Ari):** The Truthspoken Heir of the Kingdom of Valoris. Loves to control things. Agender, ace. she/her

**Ondressarie Rhialden (Dressa):** The second Truthspoken and would like to stay that way, thank you very much. Likes balls and parties. Female, lesbian. she/her

**Rhys Petrava méron Delor:** Lieutenant in the Valoran Navy. Half-sibling to Arianna and Dressa. Has phosphorescent hair. Likes to research the alien Kidaa. Nonbinary, pan. they/them

**Homaj Rhialden (Maja):** The Seritarchus, aka the Truthspoken Ruler of the Kingdom of Valoris. Loves to control things even more. Might be coming unglued. Genderfluid, pan (mostly gay). he/him (usually)

**Lesander Javieri:** High house prince, soon to be Heir Consort. Tall and gorgeous. Might be devious, who knows? Female, bi. she/her

**Ceorre Gatri:** The Truthspeaker, aka the only person who can boss the Seritarchus around. Religious leader of Valoris. Takes no prisoners. Female, bi. she/her

**Etienne Tanaka (Eti):** Gardener on the resort world of Hestia. Loves plants, has lots of secrets. Trans male, pan. he/him

**Iata byr Rhialden:** Bloodservant to Homaj. Acerbic, sharp, more than he seems. Male, hetero. he/him

**Bettea byr Rhialden (Jis):** Bloodservant to Arianna. Takes no BS. Genderfluid, aego. fae/faer

**Haneri ne Delor Rhialden:** Seritarchus Consort, aka Arianna's, Dressa's, and Rhys's mother. Has seen some things, will see some more. Demigirl, pan. she/her

**Vi Zhang:** Captain of the Seritarchus's personal guard. One of the only people who can call him on his BS. Female, gray ace. she/her

**Jalava:** Commander of the Palace Guard. Harried, loyal, usually right. Genderqueer, pan. they/them

# THE FACTIONS

**Kingdom of Valoris:** 187 worlds of theocratic goodness. Ruled by the Seritarchus. Bickered over by the high houses. Shares a border with Kidaa space.

**The Kidaa:** A species of quadruped sentients. Organized into clans, occupy a large portion of space. Far more technologically advanced than Humans. Hard to talk to. Pacifists (theoretically).

**The Onabrii-Kast Dynasty:** Former territory of Valoris, now their own empire. Also share the border with the Kidaa. Not super interested in sharing anything else.

**Green Magickers:** Organized sub-culture of people who manifest the ability to use Green Magics. Marginalized. Can't do violence.

**The Adeium:** Religion at the heart of Valoris. Genderfluid god. Oversees the Truthspeaker and the Truthspoken.

# ACKNOWLEDGMENTS

There are so many people who've helped make this book the book it is, who've shared the journey with me, who've helped fund its creation.

First and foremost: the biggest thank you to Laterpress! Laterpress is a new serial fiction platform that came on my radar early this year, and I was absolutely blown away when they selected *The Stars and Green Magics* as a winner of the 2022 Laterpress Genre Fiction Contest Fellowship. This was truly life-changing in so many ways, and has done more than help give me the confidence and social proof to pursue this writing career thing full-force, it has helped me go so much farther toward my dreams than anything before. Sincerely, deeply, thank you.

This book in its current form, and the ongoing serial it's a part of, would not exist without the advent and launch of Vella in July of 2021. Vella's been a wild rollercoaster of a ride that's launched a whole lot of writers in its wake and helped me go from hoping to someday help support myself with my serials, which have always been my favorite thing to write, to actually starting to make it happen. I've made so many friends through this experience, and to everyone who's come to be a part of my daily life through this wild ride, you rock!

To my subscribers on Laterpress and patrons on Patreon, thank you for being a part of the journey with me through this last year of serials! Your support helps me make fiction happen.

To all the excellent and awesome folx at Robot Dinosaur

Press and Chipped Cup Collective, which this book was published under—you've all become my publishing family! May we all make lots more excellent things together.

To the folx at Codex writing group, who've listened to all my writer angst, ramblings, and triumphs this last year, you all know you mean the world to me!

And to you, dear reader, whether you're reading this serial for the first time here or discovered it first in its serial form, thank you. You are most certainly the best.

# ABOUT THE AUTHOR

**Novae Caelum** is an author, illustrator, and designer with a love of spaceships and a tendency to quote Monty Python. Star is the author of *The Stars and Green Magics*, a winner of the 2022 Laterpress Genre Fiction Contest Fellowship, *The Emperor of Time*, a Wattpad Featured novel, and *[illegible]*. [illegible] short fiction has appeared in *Intergalactic Medicine Show*, *Escape Pod*, *Clockwork Phoenix 5*, and Lambda Award winning *Transcendent 2: The Year's Best Transgender Speculative Fiction*. Novae is nonbinary, starfluid, and uses star/stars/starself or they/them/their pronouns. Most days you can find Novae typing furiously away at stars queer serials, with which star hopes to take over the world. At least, that's the plan. You can find star online at novaecaelum.com

## ALSO BY NOVAE CAELUM

**The Stars and Green Magics**

*The Truthspoken Heir*

*The Shadow Rule*

*A Bid to Rule (early access, prequel)*

*Court of Magickers*

*The Nameless Storm (early access)*

**Lyr and Cavere**

*Good King Lyr: A Genderfluid Romance*

*Borrowed Wings (early access)*

*Shattered Self (early access)*

**The Space Roads**

*The Space Roads: Volume One*

**The Watered Worlds**

*The Watered Worlds (early access)*

**Standalone**

*Magnificent: A Nonbinary Superhero Novella*

*The Throne of Eleven*

*Lives on Other Worlds*

*Grim Birds: Five Tales of Cosmic Horror and Wonder (early access)*

*Sky and Dew*

*Visit Novae Caelum's website to find out where to read these titles on your favorite retailers or direct from the author!*

*https://novaecaelum.com*

## ALSO FROM ROBOT DINOSAUR PRESS

TERRA INCOGNITA BY MATI OCHA
Hiking in the Peak District at the moment Earth is—accidentally—infused with magic and thrown into an indifferent and muddled system, Will returns to his Derbyshire village to find a ghost town.

HOLLOW KING BY DANTE O. GREENE
Barridur finds himself in Hell where he meets the fabled Hollow King. A cruel and capricious god, the Hollow King offers Barridur a chance to return alive to the living world. All Barridur has to do is defeat the Nine Champions of Hell. No pressure.

YOU FED US TO THE ROSES: SHORT STORIES BY CARLIE ST. GEORGE
Final girls who team up. Dead boys still breathing. Ghosts who whisper secrets. Angels beyond the grave, yet not of heaven. Wolves who wear human skins. Ten disturbing, visceral, stories no horror fan will want to miss.

A WRECK OF WITCHES BY NIA QUINN
When you're a witch juggling a sentient house and a

magical plant nursery, you already think life is about as crazy as it can get. But scary things start happening in my mundane neighborhood when my friend goes missing. It's up to me and my ragtag group of witches—oh, and the ghost dogs—to get things under control before the Unawares figure out magic's real.

These Imperfect Reflections: Short Stories by Merc Fenn Wolfmoor
From living trains to space stations populated with monsters, these eleven fantasy and science fiction stories from Merc Fenn Wolfmoor will take you on otherworldly adventures that are tethered to the heart.

Flotsam by R J Theodore
A scrappy group of outsiders take a job to salvage some old ring from Peridot's gravity-caught garbage layer, and land squarely in the middle of a plot to take over (and possibly destroy) what's left of the already tormented planet.

The Midnight Games: Six Stories About Games You Play Once ed. by Rhiannon Rasmussen
An anthology featuring six frightening tales illustrated by Andrey Garin await you inside, with step by step instructions for those brave—or desperate—enough to play.

Sanctuary by Andi C. Buchanan
Morgan's home is a sanctuary for ghosts. When it is threatened they must fight for the queer, neurodivergent found-family they love and the home they've created.

A Starbound Solstice by Juliet Kemp

Celebrations, aliens, mistletoe, and a dangerous incident in the depths of mid-space. A sweet festive season space story with a touch of (queer) romance.

Printed in Great Britain
by Amazon